# WHEN THEY COME ALIVE

# WHEN THEY COME ALIVE

SARAH FLEMING MOUNTFORD

Atthis Arts

# WHEN THEY COME ALIVE

Text copyright ©2019 by Sarah Fleming Mountford

This is a work of fiction. Any names, characters, places, events, or incidents are either the product of the author's imagination or are used fictitiously. Any similarities or resemblance to actual persons, living or dead, events, or places, is entirely coincidental.

Cover design copyright ©2019 Jennifer Zemanek, Seedlings Design Studio
Editorial services by Abigail Hodges
Editorial services by Christabel Barry



Published by Atthis Arts, LLC
Detroit, Michigan
www.atthisarts.com


ISBN 978-1-945009-36-5

Library of Congress Control Number: 2019935920

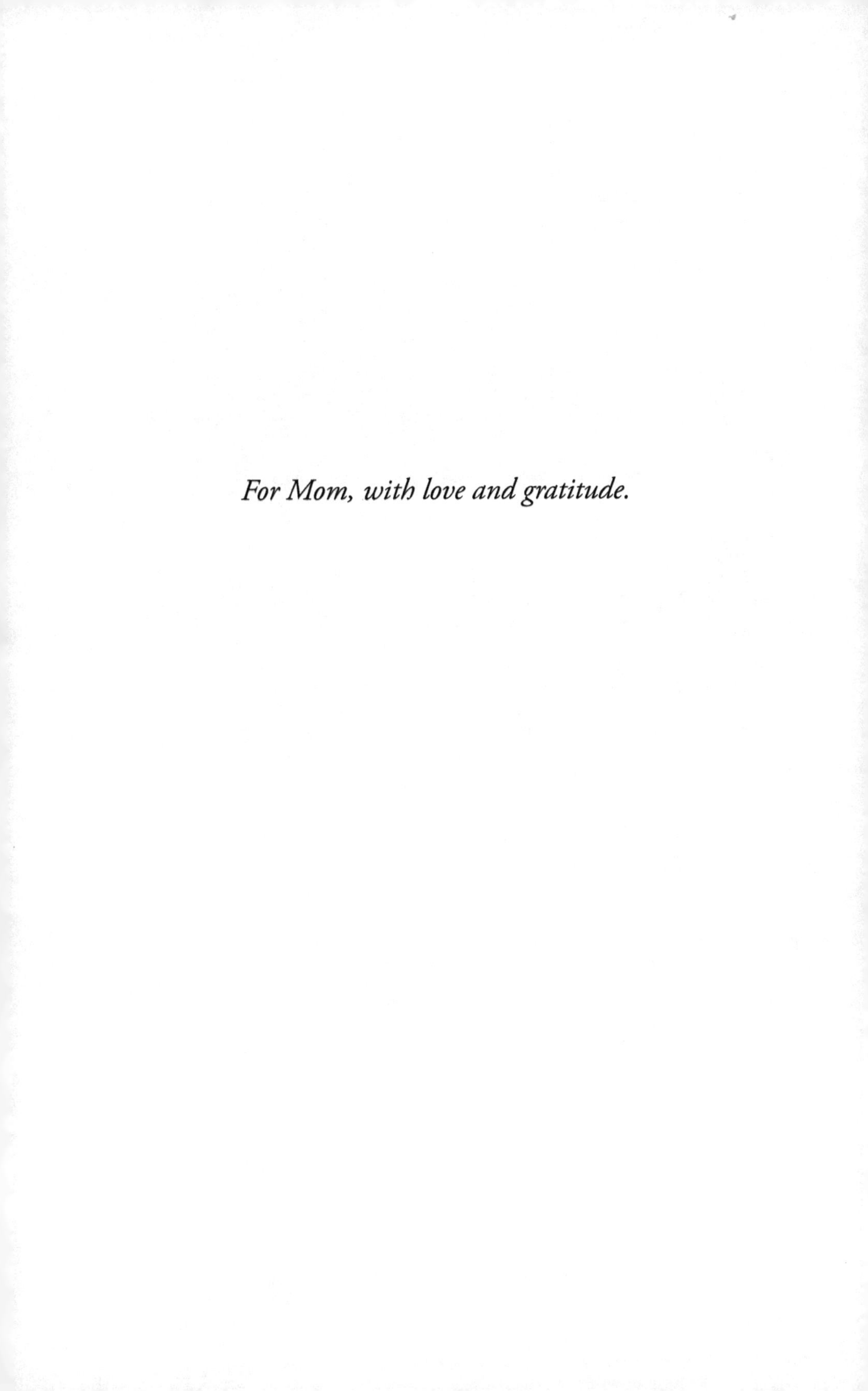

*For Mom, with love and gratitude.*

# CHAPTER ONE

**M**Y HAND TIGHTENED on the car door handle and I clenched my jaw. The tail lights of the trucks in front of us fused together in red streaks against the night.

"Can you drive any faster?"

"Do you want to spend more time with the police, Anna?" Chaz shot me a look, his eyes nearly indiscernible in the darkness.

"I don't." I couldn't fault the police for the hours of interviews after I'd been the primary witness to a hostage situation and then kidnapped. Rehashing the details of how I'd come to murder someone wasn't necessary—they wouldn't believe me if I told them the truth anyway. Shying away from the memory, I focused on Chaz. The light from the dashboard shone on the whites of his eyes and the sharp lines of his face. His hair was a thatch of black which he kept in a crew cut, though longer now than the military style he'd worn in the Marines. Fit arms and a well-muscled torso made up for the fact that he wasn't as tall as he would have liked. He cleared his throat and I realized I was staring at him.

"Are you okay?" He kept his eyes on the road, and I thought he might be afraid of the answer. I knew I was.

I forced myself to laugh in an effort to break the tension, but it was a strange sound, like a duck choking. "I don't know." I swallowed the lump in my throat and tried to channel my medical school training on how to stay calm under extreme stress. They hadn't given lessons on how to behave after you'd committed murder.

Chaz ran a hand through the thick spikes on top of his head, the sole sign of stress he'd displayed since we started driving an hour ago. "You look like hell, and I'm more than a little worried about you."

"I've been up for about twenty-four hours now, banished fifty-some ghosts in that time, and I've got my lover's soul inside me." Or had I been up for two days? The hours were blurring together, but

I was pretty sure it was just yesterday that the most important men in my life had been arrested after I'd killed a living man. I closed my eyes, but the images rushed in. The force of my power had thrown Marcus' body into the air before it dropped to the ground, lifeless. He'd been holding a gun to my head, but knowing that my action was justified didn't dampen the sense of guilt. It wasn't his fault he was possessed.

"Is Jed hurting you?" Chaz guided his Audi into the left lane to pass a semi, his fingers were curled around the black leather steering wheel, knuckles white. The road was wet, but the night air was warm enough that for the first time in months, we didn't have to worry about the water turning to ice.

"No. He's being very well behaved." Jed *was* trying to be a polite guest; curled inside me with as much substance as a ball of smoke. Even with his silence, his presence was a disconcerting itch I couldn't reach, a muscle ache in a spot I couldn't figure out how to stretch. Was he quiet because he was taking care of me, or was it a sign of how weak he was? Despite the brief amount of time we'd known each other, he'd become as entwined in my life as he was now in my soul.

"He better be." Chaz's tone said there'd be hell to pay if Jed hurt me, that it didn't matter how much bigger Jed was than him. Assuming I could get his soul reunited with his physical body, that was.

"What if we don't make it in time?" *If I've failed him now . . .* I didn't let myself finish the thought.

"We'll make it." Chaz took his right hand off the wheel and reached towards me. I flinched at the sudden motion and his hand fell into his lap.

"Sorry." Was I apologizing for flinching? For not wanting to be touched after everything I'd been through?

"Don't be." His hand regained its grip on the leather covered wheel.

I took in the dark interior of the SUV. It still smelled of new leather and polished wood accents. Chaz had bought it while he was possessed by a ghost, and then kept it. I wondered if ghosts left a piece of themselves after they possessed someone—if there was a piece of the possessor's personality that stayed behind. Had Chaz kept the car because of that? What would Jed leave with me?

"They meant to kill me last night."

"You were too strong for them." Chaz's eyes never left the road as he spoke.

"I guess." It hadn't been me alone that defeated the Council, but I didn't point that out.

"Tell me what happened out there."

"Christiana was there, along with the rest of the Council."

"I thought the Council was supposed to be good, maintaining the balance of power between the living and the dead. Isn't that what Jed said?"

"Some of them believe that. Blaise did."

"I'll crush his throat if I ever see him again." Chaz's voice was full of dark intent and I didn't have any doubt he would kill the man who had abducted me, probably with his bare hands. If Jed didn't get there first. When had I started surrounding myself with dangerous men?

"Don't forget that Blaise was possessing a living man. It wasn't Father Lombardi's fault.

"Is Blaise dead?"

He had been to begin with, but I didn't point that out. "There was a ghost there, from the Council. She looked like a dragon and thought she was a god." That wasn't relevant, but I couldn't think of her without seeing the midnight blue skin and fearsome visage. "Blaise attacked her, to buy me some time. I don't think he made it." He had known he wasn't strong enough to kill her. Even though Blaise had been the one to take me into danger, he'd redeemed himself some when he'd tried to save me. Only some, though. It was still Blaise's fault Jed was inside me instead of the body he belonged in.

"Is the Council working with Adoni?"

Jed's brother, Adonijah, had possessed Chaz for even longer than he had me and Chaz didn't like to talk about it any more than I did. Jed had killed Adoni when they were both alive, and in the three thousand intervening years, Adoni hadn't forgiven him. "Christiana was working with him, but I don't know if any of the rest of them were."

"You're saying they may not all be bad."

"Several of them tried to protect me. But keep in mind the dead have a different moral code than we do. They say there's no honor among thieves, but I think the same is true of ghosts." Chaz let out a deep-throated chuckle, but I wasn't trying to be funny. "I don't think they recognize their actions as evil, but I don't know how many of them are truly good."

"What about the ghost they call Master? Was he there?"

"I don't think so." If he was as strong as they said, I wouldn't have survived an encounter with him—unless he'd wanted me to.

"They're trying to kill you because you can stop them."

"That's pretty much it. I don't think I'm the first person with my gift that the Council has attacked. They knew how to hurt me."

"I can tell." Chaz's voice had a brittle edge.

My fingers went to the gash on my forehead, held together with strips of surgical tape. I wasn't sure how long Jed would last inside me, so I hadn't taken time at the hospital for stitches. At least it had stopped oozing, so I looked a little less like the star of a bad horror film.

My hand started to tremble, and I cradled it in my lap. I closed my eyes for a moment against a wave of exhaustion-fueled nausea, leaning my bruised cheek against the cold window.

"If you need to throw up, warn me so I can pull over."

I didn't blame Chaz for not wanting me to ruin the inside of his car, but nothing would prompt me to delay our trip to the city. Jed's body was waiting at a hospital there and we didn't have time to waste.

Jed couldn't help the fact that he was absorbing my body's energy. I knew he needed it to recharge his soul. He'd nearly destroyed himself fighting to save me. Without my energy restoring him, he would have either moved on to wherever the dead were supposed to go, or faded into a wisp of a soul in the land of the living—a shade of a ghost.

I'd used enough of my power that I was at risk. I needed to nurture the small sun of energy inside me, but Jed was putting a drain on my ability to regenerate my own power. Without it, I couldn't protect us from the ghosts. Around six hours had passed since I'd invited him to join me.

"What happened back there, before Jed followed me?" My voice shook with the remnants of the distress I'd felt when I saw Jed collapse in the street. I'd been afraid he'd killed himself, had some sort of terminal event related to chasing the car I was in down the street.

"When those priests abducted you he told me he had to follow the car so he could protect you." They hadn't actually been priests; one was a possessed vagrant playing dress up, and Blaise, a dead saint possessing the body of a priest. I didn't correct Chaz. Without his sword, Jed had a harder time killing another ghost, but he had helped save me from the dragon and distracted Christiana enough that I was able to release her. "I told him to go get you," Chaz continued, "and he asked me to take care of his body. Said he intended to come back for it."

"Which you did."

"That's why I had Ty follow Jed's body to Kansas City when the hospital decided to transfer him there. We had a deal."

Ty was Chaz's life partner and my best friend, along with being a world-class nurse. "I'm impressed that you were able to convince him to leave."

Chaz's voice spoke volumes about how much conflict it had caused. "Ty wouldn't leave until he knew you were safe again. He wanted to stay with you when you arrived at the hospital, but Jed was being transported by that point. He's not happy with me for insisting he leave. I convinced him that you needed an attorney more than a nurse at that particular moment and that your boyfriend needed a nurse more. He left about an hour after Jed did."

There weren't words that expressed how grateful I was. "Thank you, for taking care of Jed. And of me."

"I hope you don't mind that I gave Ty your car."

"It's fine. You know whatever's mine is yours." I'd loan either of them my car anytime, without hesitation. Besides which, they were using it to make sure my boyfriend's body was safe.

"Can you . . . hear him?" Chaz gestured to my midriff as though I were expecting a baby. This couldn't be what that felt like—to nurture another life inside you. Besides, Jed wasn't hanging out in my pelvis. It felt like he was lurking in my ribcage, tucked behind my liver.

"I can't. I've tried to talk to him, but I don't know if he can hear me or not." I hoped he could, because the time was coming when I'd tell him to get out and I needed him to understand me, and leave without a fight.

Being inside me was dangerous for him too. If I had to use my power to banish another ghost—if we got attacked again—I feared that burst of energy would destroy him. I didn't know for sure, and we didn't have the luxury of experimenting to find out.

"We should get you something else to eat," Chaz suggested. I knew he was right, with another soul inside me I needed salt and lots of liquids. There was something about the extra energy that caused an adrenergic reaction, similar to what happened to lightning strike victims. Electrolyte imbalance, hypotension, and tachycardia were common reactions to being possessed by a ghost.

"Next time we stop, we can grab something to drink and get some chips." Jed wasn't trying to control me, but having him there at all might cause disparity in my electrolyte balance. I hoped that my body wouldn't react as poorly to my current guest as it had to Adonijah possessing me by force, but it might. There weren't any clinical trials to rely on. I was a living experiment. Staying hydrated was my best defense. A good dose of steroids would help too.

"We're almost to Kearney. There's a gas station there, and fast food if you want more than that."

I didn't feel like we had time for another delay, but if I didn't take care of myself we'd have bigger problems. "All right."

We were back on the interstate twenty minutes later. I relaxed back in the smooth leather seat for a moment, focused on a bag of trail mix, a side of cheese-coated chips, and a sports drink that was an unnatural shade of blue. I couldn't help but chuckle at the look of dismay Ned's wife, Carrie, would be sporting if she saw me chowing down on the bounty of processed foods in front of me.

"What's so funny?" Chaz glanced at me, perhaps concerned that I was going insane.

"Carrie. She'd be horrified to see me eating like this."

Chaz raised one eyebrow. "Yeah, she takes the Mother Earth thing to the extreme."

"We all have our quirks."

"Speak for yourself. You're like the crazy cat lady except with ghosts."

"This was not my plan. Besides, there's nothing wrong with having cats." I wanted to go back to my old life, the one I'd had before my world was hijacked by the spirits of the dead. Now that ghosts were actively possessing the living, I doubted if life would ever return to normal. In my old life, I hadn't had Jed, either. Maybe the ghosts were worth it.

"Plans change and we have to deal with it."

"I'm dealing." I hoped I sounded half as capable as the words suggested.

"I think you're doing as well as anyone could." Chaz looked over at me, his solemn expression lit by the faint glow from the instrument panel.

I wasn't sure that was true, but I appreciated him saying so. "I'm sorry you got swept up in all this, but thank you for helping us out of that legal mess yesterday."

"You guys aren't free and clear yet."

"I know." I swallowed the bitter taste in my mouth, suppressing the urge to whine about how unfair it all was. I'd long since learned fairness wasn't a God-given right like it's made out to be in kindergarten. "They won't charge Ned with anything, will they? If they do, I'll have to confess." My hands trembled again with the strength of the memory. Power had erupted out of my body with such force it had thrown Marcus Wilson off his feet, killing him instantly. Ned's gunshots followed, striking Marcus with perfect precision in the chest before he even hit the ground. The image of his body, devoid of a soul, was burned into my mind. His eyes had been empty, except for that final shock of death. The police thought it was Ned who'd killed him, but there was no doubt the fault was mine. I'd sent plenty of ghosts into the next world, but Marcus was the first living person I'd murdered. I'd blasted his soul out of his body along with the ghost that was possessing him.

"I saw the security tape from the hallway, Anna. You did the right thing. He'd have killed you."

"If I'd been calmer, waited for the right moment, I could have gotten the ghost out of him. Marcus didn't have to die."

"This is a war, Anna. Civilian casualties are an unfortunate reality." Deep down I knew that Chaz was right, but I didn't want to accept it. My first identity was as a healer, not some modern-day warrior. Chaz kept talking, maybe to keep me focused on the sound of his voice, like he knew I needed something to hold onto. "To answer your question, I don't think they'll charge Ned, and you're sure as hell not confessing to anything." Chaz's hands tightened again on the steering wheel. "They wouldn't believe you even if you did."

"I won't let Ned take the fall for what I've done."

He sighed and I thought it was a sign that I was frustrating him.

"He neutralized a gunman at a hospital—one who had already shot one person and was in the midst of abducting you. In the police's eyes, he did them a favor by taking this guy out before anyone else got hurt." Chaz's voice was strong, confident. He'd slipped into the tone I could imagine him using with a jury. "Ned also has a valid conceal and carry license. He maintains his safety training with more diligence than he's required to. He's a small business owner and he's never been in trouble with the law." Chaz tapped the steering wheel with his index finger. "The most he'll get is a slap on the wrist for disobeying the posted 'No Concealed Weapons' sign. Maybe lose his conceal and carry license for a couple of years."

"I hope you're right." I stared back out the window and tried to ignore the sensation of creeping nausea. The human body didn't like having more than one soul in residence at a time. "What about Jed's sword? How do we get that back?"

"Shit, Anna. I don't know. Why do all the men you hang out with have to get caught with concealed weapons?"

I refrained from pointing out the obvious. That sword was the only weapon we had—other than myself—against ghosts. Chaz drew in a sharp breath as if he'd heard my thoughts and was reacting to them.

"I'm not an expert in that area of law. I'll have to do some research." He had done some prosecutorial work in his early law career, but now he was in the corporate field, working for a pharmaceutical company. We were pushing our luck having him act as our defense attorney. If we needed to hire someone else, we could, but we hadn't had time to look into it yet. We also couldn't tell another lawyer the truth, which complicated that kind of relationship.

We passed another semi as we entered the northern suburbs of the city, another mile closer to getting Jed out of me. His brain dead body had been ventilated at Unionville Regional and then airlifted to a Kansas City hospital. The medical team at Unionville hoped the resources of a major medical center would be able to help Jed.

The body wasn't even Jed's, but had a morbid penchant for surviving death. Jed had come across Tobias Peters' body in a long-term care facility in Switzerland, brain-dead and without a soul in residence. Jed had taken it as his host, which was the first time Tobias had an unexplainable medical recovery. Maybe he could star in the next zombie apocalypse movie. If we survived the ghost apocalypse that we were already in.

Ty had been in the awkward position of calling Tobias' mother and letting her know that her son was unconscious again, and on the way to a hospital. Ty couldn't tell her that I was on my way, carrying the ghost that had been living in her son's body. I did not envy him that conversation.

My biggest concern was getting Jed integrated back into his body before the hospital started to think about other options. The protocol for organ transplantation was for the patient to have two EEGs demonstrating no brain activity twenty-four hours apart, so I had a little bit of time before I had to worry about them harvesting Tobias' organs, but not enough to make me comfortable. How long would it take Jed to take control of Tobias' body again?

If something went wrong and Jed lost that body, I didn't know what we'd do. He couldn't stay in me, and finding another empty body to take over in the same condition that Tobias' body was in would be difficult.

*It's bad enough that I'm in a relationship with a man who's been dead for thousands of years. It somehow seems worse if he doesn't have a body.*

When Chaz pulled into the hospital parking garage, the sky was starting to hint that dawn was coming. The oppressive darkness we'd been driving through was tinged with gray in the east.

My skin was itching with restlessness, and when I got out of the car my head swam. I leaned back against the icy metal and waited for help. Chaz wrapped one strong arm around my waist and braced me against him while he dialed his cell phone with his other hand. Ty wasn't answering his phone so Chaz asked for directions at the front desk and guided me through a maze of hallways to the intensive care unit where they were caring for Jed's body.

A middle-aged attendant sat at the waiting room reception desk, sipping a cup of coffee and perusing an entertainment magazine. I leaned against the counter in front of her, but she didn't look up until I spoke.

"I'd like to see Tobias Peters, please. He was brought in earlier tonight and I understand he's here in the ICU." Lines framed her forehead in a look of chronic consternation. Clearly I wasn't the only one who'd had a long night.

"Are you part of his immediate family?"

"Not immediate family." I tried a hopeful smile but it didn't work.

"I'm sorry, ma'am." She didn't sound it. "Visiting hours are from nine to two."

"I have to see him," I insisted. The thought of keeping Jed inside me for any longer made me tremble in a sudden panic. My body was reacting to his presence, evidenced by my dizziness and the way I could feel my heartbeat thumping fast in the base of my throat. *Low blood pressure, Anna. Tachycardia. You need fluids and steroids.*

The attendant peered at me over blue plastic eyeglass frames. If the sight of my battered face surprised her, she didn't show it. "The ICU is closed to visitors right now."

"I'm Dr. Anna Roberts. I run a clinic over on Main Street." Maybe my status as a physician would gain me some professional courtesy.

"You don't work here." She turned back to her magazine. "Family only until nine a.m."

"His family isn't here. I'm his girlfriend."

"Are you his legal guardian or medical representative?"

I considered lying but someone would have asked for proof. "No."

"And you're a doctor, so you know I can't let you in. I'm sorry," she reiterated. She flipped through her magazine, her eyes glued to pictures of women in skimpy evening gowns.

"What now?" Chaz muttered, eyeing the woman like he was coming up with a plan to overpower her.

"We wait." I was not happy about it, but was hoping to avoid adding more felonies to the list of crimes I'd committed in the last few hours.

We retreated, Chaz escorting me into a waiting room that looked like it hadn't been updated in several decades. Scuffed beige walls were accented by cracked green and white plastic chairs placed in an alternating pattern that made me dizzy. The fluorescent lighting was too bright for the early hour and the room smelled of disinfectant and despair. I didn't relish waiting there but didn't have a choice. I let Chaz escort me to an aged plastic chair away from the other cluster of people waiting, after making sure none of them had ghosts in them.

*Three more hours.* Would I still be conscious by then? I didn't know how my symptoms would progress but it didn't look good. *Jed,* I tried to project my thoughts throughout my body and hoped he could hear me. *We're here. Your body—Tobias—is just down the hall. Go to him.*

Jed didn't stir. Was he too weak to move? Was my body giving him enough energy? I hoped he wasn't getting too comfortable where he was because it was not a permanent resting spot for him.

If the attendant went on break I might be able to slip past her, but the keypad against the wall indicated that it was a locked unit and I didn't have a badge that would unlock the door. I drummed my fingers on my thigh to keep myself awake while my mind wandered through the list of who I might know that worked there. There wasn't anyone on the list who I would feel comfortable asking to break the rules and risk getting fired. I didn't like to think of Jed's body in there, alone, and I didn't want his soul inside of me any longer than was necessary.

A familiar face breezed into the waiting room cradling a cardboard beverage carrier filled with cups. He paused mid-stride when he saw my face.

"You look like shit," Ty announced. "Lucky for you, I brought coffee." The cup he handed me was dark and bitter, but it was scalding hot and smelled like heaven. Ty gave me a gentle hug around the cup, careful not to spill it. "I'm glad you guys made it."

"Me too. Thanks for the coffee."

"The old bat won't let you in, will she?" Ty nodded towards the woman at the reception desk, who in my opinion didn't quite qualify for "old bat" status even if she hadn't been particularly helpful.

"She has rules to follow." I found myself defending her, and Ty snorted, taking the seat to my right. Chaz was on my left, and I wondered if they were intentionally surrounding me, worried that I might pass out.

Both of them leaned in across me, talking in whispers so we couldn't be overheard. Claustrophobia set in with them hovering over me and the extra soul crowding inside me. I needed more space, not less. I kept the panic at bay by focusing on Ty. His skin was the color of dark velvet, the product of African-American and German heritage. His eyes were mahogany, flecked with gold. His engaging personality combined with fine facial structure meant he got hit on by women as often as he did men. Chaz was the only one for Ty, though.

"What happened after I left?" Ty demanded. "You sent me down here after Jed like a damn ambulance chaser."

"Anna filled me in on the drive, but I'll let her tell you."

"You missed a lot." I leaned my head back against the white-washed wall and tried to figure out where to start.

"You said the Council was there, and I know that priest took you, which was when Jed . . . left his body," Ty prompted.

"His name was Blaise, the priest that abducted me." Saint Blaise, the patron saint of sore throats from someplace in Turkey. "When it came down to it, he wound up being one of the few allies I had there. He died trying to protect me. I found the body he stole lying unconscious in the snow and was able to get him away from the house. His body only had one soul in it when I found it." I took a breath to calm my emotions. There wouldn't be any more dubious miracles for St. Blaise.

"What happened to him?" Ty nudged me and I realized I'd quit talking.

"He attacked Christiana and he lost. She was stronger. She killed both Scipio and Blaise. Jed couldn't beat her either." Using the term "killed" while talking about people who were already dead didn't make sense, but Ty and Chaz knew what I meant. The ghosts had crossed over to wherever they should have gone when their bodies died the first time. Ty let out a low whistle and the group sharing the waiting room with us looked over at us. Ty gave them an apologetic nod. "There were a bunch of them that were on Christiana's side," I continued. "They were . . . hurting me."

"Is that where these came from?" Ty gestured to my face. My hand went to the tender bruise on my cheek and then the taped up gash on my forehead.

"They were throwing things at me. Wood and pieces of metal. I let her think I was too weak, and when she got close to me, I released her."

"She's gone, then." He breathed out in a rush of relief and then leaned closer to me. "But that won't stop what's happening, will it?"

"I don't know." I took a deep breath and admitted the truth. "I don't think so."

"I hesitate to ask this, but where is Jed?" Ty looked around, like he thought the man in question could materialize on demand. "I know where his body is, but where is *he*?"

I touched a hand to the base of my sternum because the pressure in my chest made me think he was centered between my lungs.

"That is fucked up." Ty leaned back in his seat and crossed his arms, rigid with tension. A woman across the room stared at us, eyes sparkling with curiosity. "He shouldn't be inside you. When he gets out we're going to have a chat about this."

"I don't like having him in me either," I assured him. I had to control the laughter that wanted to bubble out of me at the idea of Ty, who was as petite as I was, taking on a man like Jed, who was built like a lumberjack. "It was the only way to save him. I daresay you'd have done the same for Chaz. I need to get to Jed's body so I can convince him to move back into it."

"You know how to get him out of you." Ty phrased it like a sentence, but it was part question, and I answered with a careful nod, one that wouldn't make my head spin.

His fingers closed around my wrist. "Your heart rate is fast. What if Jed doesn't want to leave?"

"He'll go," I promised, hoping Jed was listening. "When it's time."

"How'd he find you?"

"I don't know, but he helped me kill Christiana," I spoke a little too loudly and eyed the woman across the room who was leaning in our direction in her ongoing effort to figure out what we were talking about. I didn't make eye contact and lowered my voice again. "I don't know if I could have done it without him. Thank you, for coming here with him."

"Anytime. If he saved you, then I guess he's worth it." Ty folded his fingers around my hand and gave a gentle squeeze.

"What happens now?"

"After we get my boyfriend back?"

"Yeah, sunshine. Your lover boy comes first, we got it." I tried to find the energy to elbow Ty but didn't have it so I settled for a brief smile instead.

"They keep bringing the fight to me and I'd like to change that. Adonijah is still out there. So is the Master." I didn't know who the Master was, but Christiana and Adonijah had worked for him, and

Jed got worried every time his name came up. The Master seemed to be behind the possession event, and every attack against me in the last three months.

"What the *hell* do they want?" Chaz asked with a hiss that earned us another appraisal from across the waiting room.

"Adoni wants to get back at Jed for murdering him in their first life, that much is clear."

"And the Master?"

"World domination?" I suggested, but in reality, I didn't know.

Ty leaned back in his chair, giving me some much-needed breathing room. "How many people out there are possessed?"

"There are a few dozen that we know of up in Unionville. I don't think that's all of them, though."

"Why not?" I thought Chaz knew the answer and wasn't sure why he wanted me to say it out loud.

"I don't have any way of knowing, but I think we're seeing the possession cases that weren't successful. There will be more out there, like Blaise, that took a host and kept it."

"What if Jed decides to take control of you?"

"He won't," I said with more confidence than I felt.

"What if he tried?" Ty persisted, like a three-year-old.

"I have enough power to destroy him, but he would never make me do that." My tone of voice said I'd do it if I had to, and that it wasn't a topic I felt the need to continue.

*How much longer can I keep him inside me? How much more time does Tobias have?*

Losing his host body wouldn't be that damaging to Jed. I was the one who cared about the body a few rooms away from us. Jed might not need it for his soul to survive, but to me, he and Tobias Peters were one and the same. Being involved with a ghost wasn't as difficult to rationalize when he had a living body. How could I be in a relationship with someone who had as much presence as a puff of wind? Jed's soul shifted inside me like a contented cat in a sunbeam and I squirmed at the sensation of pressure against my chest wall. *Don't get too comfortable in there.*

"You got ahold of Tobias' mother?" I asked, closing my eyes against the glare of the fluorescent lights.

"Yeah. That was a shitty conversation to have." I couldn't blame him for being upset. I added it to the lengthy list of reasons I owed him. I reached my hand out and he took it again, twining his fingers with mine. How had Tobias' mother handled the knowledge that her son was in a vegetative state again, ventilator dependent?

"Were you the first to reach her?"

"No, a doctor in Unionville got ahold of her before I did. I assume they found her phone number in his cell phone."

"I'm sorry, but thank you for doing it."

"You're lucky he's a foreigner. It will take them longer to get all the necessary approval to start harvesting his organs."

"I'm worried about that, too, but they still have to wait twenty-four hours to confirm brain death." The woman across from us was straining so hard to hear us that I was concerned she might fall out of her chair.

"Don't worry, Anna." Ty gave my hand a tighter squeeze. "She's not going to let them take him off life support. At least not until you've seen him."

She'd kept her son Tobias on life support for a long time after he'd died in a skiing accident, which was how Jed had found the soulless body and took possession of it. I didn't think she'd give up on him this time, but it wasn't worth risking. Jed needed Tobias' body and I needed Jed.

My cell phone rang, a local area code but a number I didn't know, and I silenced it.

"Who was that?" Ty was quick to ask.

"Probably a reporter," Chaz answered. "After the news reports of her helping those possessed people in Unionville, someone got her phone number. She's gotten a few calls." I appreciated him not using the word "miracle," which was the inaccurate term the media had thrown out. Jed's form inside me shifted, coiling against my lung and making me cough, which brought my attention to a different problem.

"I have to pee." I stood and then wavered a moment before Ty had his arm around me. I leaned on him as he escorted me to the restroom, every step draining me. I hoped that when this was done, I'd have time to sleep.

While I emptied my bladder I contemplated the cause of my weakness and exhaustion. Was it the presence of a second soul that exhausted women who were pregnant? Maybe Carrie would know. Like her, my body had two energy sources to feed. I was both comforted and disconcerted by Jed's constant presence and wondered if it was the same for Carrie.

I washed my hands and dried them on a rough white paper towel, and looked at myself in the mirror. The bruising was shocking against the backdrop of my pale skin. My dark eyes registered exhaustion and my usually wavy, nut-brown hair was limp around my thin face. Beyond the hematomas, I was still there. I found some strength in that and stood a little straighter.

Ty walked me back and settled me into my seat between him and Chaz. I focused on a yellowed print of downtown Kansas City hanging on the wall and listened for the being inside me. *Jed, can you hear me?* Silence was my answer.

"Anna." Chaz roused me and I was surprised to realize that at some point I'd closed my eyes. Had I been sleeping? "Karin Peters is on the phone." He handed me my cell and I blinked at it in confusion for a moment before I took it.

"Mrs. Peters, how are you?"

She ignored my pleasantry and spoke with impeccable, accented English. "Have you made it to the hospital?" It was a good connection, for an international call. Her voice was clear, practical, and to the point.

"We just got here a few minutes ago," I told her, and then wondered if that was right. Somehow it felt like I'd been in the waiting room for hours.

"Have you seen him?"

"They won't let me in until visiting hours since I'm not family." I looked at the clock on the wall. "We have to wait for three more hours."

"I will see if I can do anything about that," the voice on the other end informed me with crisp determination. I thought I'd like Karin Peters very much, though I pitied her for this situation. "They have called me again, Anna. They tell me that there is no hope that Tobias will come back to me."

They wouldn't have hope, not with a medically brain dead patient hooked to a ventilator. "I think there's always hope," I told her, "don't you?"

"You are kind."

"He came back to you before," I encouraged, and she sighed.

"I am afraid he used up his miracle."

"I hope not."

"I hope not, too."

"I need to see him, Mrs. Peters," I reminded her.

"He tells me of you, when he calls." She paused and I wondered what scene she was looking at as I stared at the tired beige walls and waiting room furniture. "Do you love my son, Anna?"

My eyes filled with tears as I nodded. "I do."

"Then you are part of his family. I will call the doctor back. Let me see what I can do." The connection ended without so much as a goodbye.

I leaned back and closed my eyes again, aware of the sudden stillness inside me. Was he all right? Was I losing him? *Stay with me, Jed. I didn't get the chance to tell you that I love you.* He didn't move and I hoped he could hear me.

"Dr. Roberts?" The voice startled me and I opened my eyes in confusion at finding myself in the same waiting room. I'd fallen asleep again. The attendant from the ICU was standing in the doorway.

"Yes?" Chaz answered for me while I tried to rouse myself.

"You can see him now. If you'll come this way." She nodded towards the closed door that led into the intensive care unit and walked back towards her station.

"Karin Peters must have convinced them to let me in," I murmured. *Jed? Can you hear me? It's show time. You've got to get moving.* He was unresponsive, as quiet as he'd been for the last hour.

The same attendant buzzed us through the frosted glass door. "Three doors down on the left. Dr. Chan will be with you shortly." I pushed through the opaque door, afraid she would change her mind.

The hallway was wide with a series of rooms either side. Each room had a clear glass window with the privacy curtain drawn from the inside. A nurse's station and lab were on the left side of the hall and a series of closed doors that likely held cleaning supplies and linens for the critically ill were on the right.

I approached the third doorway with trepidation, as if it was my first time in a critical care unit. Chaz pulled me forward, guiding me to the door.

*Get your shit together,* I lectured myself, *not your first rodeo. You're a doctor so act like it.* It was different, though, when it was someone you loved lying there.

# CHAPTER TWO

H E DIDN'T LOOK THE SAME, bereft of Jed's soul and hooked to the machines. I didn't know if it was brain death or the fluorescent lighting, but his skin was gray. He hadn't shaved in several days, making him look disheveled and unhealthy. I recalled a few days prior the scruff had seemed sexy.

Jed had chosen well when he picked Tobias. He was the size of a muscular grizzly bear, with thick black hair that Jed kept shoulder length. He wasn't handsome in the classical sense, but his dark eyes were magnetic and I'd noticed that I wasn't the only woman who was drawn to him. The cut on his forehead where I'd stitched him up the night we met had turned into a scar that made his face more interesting.

There was little sign of that man here. The pads from the EEG were scattered over his scalp, tucked into his thick dark hair, with wires leading to one of the machines behind him. There was a tube tucked into the side of his mouth, taped into place and connected to the large machine that forced air into his lungs and then let it out again.

I lingered in the doorway, coming to terms with how he looked while my mind started cataloging the information on the monitors around him. Other than the bed and monitoring equipment, the room held a lone burgundy colored chair next to a large window that looked towards downtown.

"He'll be okay, Anna." Chaz nudged me closer, through the doorway and towards the bedside. I reached out to touch the still arm closest to me and then stopped myself, not wanting to know how lifeless he would feel. It was a memory I didn't need.

"Dr. Roberts?" A woman walked in, her dark skin contrasting with the white jacket that denoted her status as a physician. Her voice was brisk and confident, but with her black hair pulled back in a neat ponytail she looked like she was ten years younger than I was. I wondered if I had ever been that young. "I'm Amal Chan. I'm Tobias' neurologist."

"It's nice to meet you." I shook her hand and introduced Ty and Chaz. They hung back while I leaned against the bedside and forced myself to take the still hand in mine. I swallowed, blinking back tears as I watched the level flutter of his EEG line, showing a complete lack of brain activity. It looked more like an EKG tracing than the spiky saw-teeth of normal brain activity. I couldn't imagine how life could come back to this man. It was inconceivable, medically impossible.

I tried to reach inside myself. *We're here, Jed, anytime.* He didn't respond. If he couldn't hear me, then I was just talking to myself.

"I'm afraid there's no brain function at all." Dr. Chan began in a kind, but matter-of-fact, tone. I didn't point out that I could read the EEG. "I know this is very difficult but you know that in these cases there's nothing to be done." Normally, I'd have agreed with her on the prognosis.

*Jed!* There was no answer from inside me, no feel of him rasping against my chest wall. This wasn't the best time for him to be taking a nap.

"As difficult as I know this is, your friend is a fit man with a healthy body. If the family was willing to donate, he could help so many people. I've talked to his mother but thus far she isn't willing to discuss it." I touched Tobias' face and ran my hand down his arm, alarmed at the lack of activity inside me. What the hell was he waiting for?

"It hasn't been twenty-four hours yet," I reminded her.

"It hasn't, but in these cases, it's best if everyone starts preparing themselves. He could help so many people."

"I'd like to be alone with him for a while," I told her, stalling for time. What was Jed doing? We were here—this was his body.

"Of course." Dr. Chan's face was suffused with polite sympathy and she turned towards the door. "I'll check back in a little while, or if you need anything, you can have the nursing staff call me." She indicated the nurse call button which they'd left close to Tobias' right hand, as if there was any chance of him using it.

"Thank you." I dismissed her, turning back to the still form next to me.

"Well?" Ty prompted, hovering over my shoulder.

"I don't know. He's not moving." Somehow I'd thought it would be easier once we got to his body. I wasn't sure if crying or screaming was the appropriate response. I felt like doing both.

"He's not moving?" Chaz growled at the same time Ty protested. "What does that mean?"

I perched on the edge of the bed to keep myself from falling down. "I've never done this before, not this way." I ground my teeth and ignored the tremor of anxiety that vibrated through me. I needed time, and having the two of them hovering over me wasn't going to help. "Why don't you two go get some coffee and give me a few minutes with him to figure this out?" I hoped that was all it took but what did I know? This wasn't an area that anyone I knew had expertise in.

Ty looked like he wanted to argue with me but Chaz took his hand and drew him out of the room without another word. The door closed behind them and I was left alone with Jed's still body, and the discordant wheezing of the ventilator.

"It's time, Jed," I urged aloud to the being inside me. I wanted to scream at the answering silence but didn't think that giving voice to my impatience would help. "You can't stay in there. You're hurting me." I spoke to the deepness inside of me, the still spot of his soul, though if anyone had been watching they would have thought I was talking to Tobias' body.

Another shiver ran through me, laced with panic-induced nausea, and my power flared in response, ready to protect me if I needed it. I tamped it down and then stilled as I realized the flare of energy had roused Jed. I felt him stir inside me, tickling the edges of my pleural cavity.

He quieted, as if he wasn't ready to be born again. *What if he isn't strong enough yet? What if this doesn't work?* It had to work, though. He couldn't stay inside me. *I need you, remember?* I urged him and he shifted like a dog turning in a circle before it lies down again.

"You have to go," I demanded, anger spiking my power again in a flare of heat. He retreated from it and then settled, using my sternum as an uncomfortable shield.

"I don't want to do it this way but you leave me no choice." I gathered a string of my energy, channeling it to find him. He felt me coming for him and moved to avoid it, sinking deeper into my pelvis. Fire burned through my veins as I chased him, corralling him like a wild horse. He fled from my power, sliding through my sinews like water flowing through a sieve. I lowered my chest over Tobias like a lover ready to grant a kiss and drove Jed towards my heart.

The strangeness of it made me queasy, and when he dropped from me into Tobias, I felt lightheaded and shaky. I pulled back from his form, collapsing in the faux leather recliner next to his bed, and waited while the glow of his spirit settled into Tobias Peters' still body.

Pressing my fingertips to my jugular vein, I felt the rapid throb of my pulse. My heart was fluttering in my ribcage like a hummingbird's wings, the rate too fast. I knew from experience that my blood pressure was dropping again. It was a sign that my body wasn't reacting well to the imbalance caused by the addition of another soul, and then the sudden departure of it. I felt strange without him, like a hole had opened in my chest.

I had hoped that my reaction wouldn't be as severe as the time that Jed's brother had possessed me, since Jed's soul had been invited in and hadn't caused any trouble while he was there, but it was clear the response I was having was similar. I needed fluids and steroids, and with a little luck, I'd avoid getting a spot next to Jed in the hospital. Dragging the chair close enough to Jed's bed to hold his hand, I settled in and watched him.

I waited longer than I expected to, listening to the wheezing of the ventilator. Watching the monitors, I followed the rhythmic spikes of his heartbeat and the minor tenor of the EEG line. Memorizing every change in his systolic pressure kept me from passing out. *How long does it take for a soul to repossess a body?*

It felt like hours had passed when the EEG line suddenly registered a spike, and then another, before the constant line of saw-teeth flowed in a steady pattern, indicating brain activity. A few minutes after that, the fingers I was holding twitched. I let out a deep breath, tears of relief clouding my vision. I'd expected him to wake up, but had no way of knowing for sure that he'd be able to recover his hold on Tobias' body. I slid out of the recliner, holding on to the metal rail of the bed until the floor stopped tilting under me. I crawled onto the mattress so I was sitting next to him, so he could feel the pressure of my hip against his. It was important that he knew I was here, that he heard me. I didn't know how much he had grasped from his time inside me.

"Jed, you're hooked to a ventilator. You need to not move until they unhook it or you might hurt yourself." His eyelids fluttered, suggesting that he'd heard me. I'd never been on a ventilator, but I understood they could be unpleasant. I didn't need the big man panicking because he had a tube down his throat.

With a shudder, his face went from slack to aware, transforming him from a near-corpse to a living human being again. I clasped his arm, forcing myself to choke back sobs that wouldn't help him. He'd made the shift. His eyelids opened wide and one hand clenched the sheets as he started fighting the ventilator. It was an automatic response, one he'd have to struggle to control.

I squeezed his arm and spoke close to his ear, hoping my presence would help him stay calm. "Jed, it's me. The tube down your throat is what's been helping you breathe." I grasped his fingers, put my other hand on his shoulder, and shifted until we were face to face. I hoped the physical connection between us would help keep him calm. I waited while his pupils focused on my face. He stilled for a moment, his expression softening with a tenderness that made tears well in my eyes again.

I touched my fingers to his face and blinked them back. Getting emotional wouldn't help him. "If you can stay calm, I'll get the doctor. I don't know how quickly we can get them to remove the ventilator, but it shouldn't be too long." He'd have to prove he could breathe on his own, but now that he was, they shouldn't make him stay on it.

Jed's eyes narrowed at that as the machine forced air into his lungs and he tried to expel it. His body shuddered with the effort. He opened his mouth, trying to talk, but he couldn't with the tube interfering with his vocal cords.

"You can't talk, Jed. Don't fight the ventilator," I reiterated, knowing it would take an incredible amount of self-control not to. "Try to time your breath so that it coincides with the pace of the machine."

His hand gripped my upper arm with bruising strength, eyes wild with panic as the machine forced air into his lungs as he was trying to exhale. "You've done this before, Jed. Remember what it was like when you woke Tobias up the first time. Don't fight it."

Jed gave me an awkward wave of understanding and I grinned at him like an idiot.

"You don't know how happy I am to have you back." I reached across him and hit the nurse call button as the machine took another breath for him and he panicked again. He grabbed the bed rail and shook it hard enough that the whole bed rattled. "They will be surprised to find you awake," I warned him, hoping the constant string of my conversation would help distract him from the automatic terror that he was feeling.

He gripped my arm tighter in response and fought the ventilator again, his big body shifting in distress. I forced myself to stay clinical. I couldn't afford to get caught up in his anxiety. If I could stay calm, it would help him stay calm.

A middle-aged nurse with graying hair and the physique of a runner entered with clinical efficiency and a clear, "Can I help you?" that was directed at me. She automatically checked the monitors and her eyes widened in disbelief before she looked down at her patient. His teeth were gritted around the tube, his dark eyes fixed on her.

"Oh my," she murmured, frozen where she stood. Jed lashed out in another fit of ventilator-related panic, knocking the metal bed rail. The nurse forced herself to recover, the needs of her patient taking precedence over her immediate surprise. She closed the distance to the bed with alacrity. "Mr. Peters, my name is Emma and I'm your nurse." She spoke in slow, clear tones. "Can you blink to let me know you understand me?"

His eyes squeezed shut and then opened in a narrow glare. Even with the tube, his expression let her know he thought it was an insulting question.

"That's good. You need to calm down, or I'll be forced to sedate you." She looked up, her eyes meeting mine. "What happened?"

I hadn't prepared a plausible story, but the relief I felt, combined with the intensity of the last day took over. The tears I'd been fighting spilled over, cascading down my cheeks. My words came out in between hiccups and sobs.

"I was talking to him and he started responding."

The machine pushed air back into Jed's lungs and he shuddered beneath my fingers. Emma spoke to him, her training taking over. "Tobias, don't fight the ventilator. Time your breathing with the machine so it's easier for you."

"He goes by Jed," I told her and she nodded to let me know she'd heard me. "He's not doing well with the vent." I kept my fingers entwined with his in reassurance.

"I imagine not." She stepped into the hallway and returned with a rolling cart that had a laptop and monitor built into it. The fingers of one hand fluttered over the computer keyboard, bringing it to life while the other grabbed the phone on Jed's bedside table and dialed a series of numbers. "Bridgette, would you please page Dr. Chan and let her know that Mr. Peters is awake?"

Bridgette issued a startled squawk on the other end of the line and then disconnected with an audible thud that made Emma wince.

"Mrs . . ." She made eye contact with me and I realized I hadn't introduced myself.

"I'm Dr. Anna Roberts."

"You're a physician?"

"Primary care." I didn't always introduce myself with my credentials, but it would help us both if Emma knew that I was in the medical field too.

"You've had a quite a day, haven't you?" Her face relaxed into a smile and she tucked a loose strand of hair behind her ear. "I've got to get some vitals on Jed and check the equipment. Can I get you to sit back for a minute?" She nodded at the recliner to indicate that she'd prefer I be out of the way. I was glad to see she was recovering and able to focus on her job.

"Of course." I pulled away from Jed with reluctance as he shuddered again. He drew his knees up and planted his feet on the bed and I hoped he wasn't going to buck the next time the tube forced him to breathe. "You're doing great. Keep timing your breath to the machine," I reminded him. "Just a few more minutes."

Emma retook Jed's blood pressure and pulse, checked his temperature, and made notes on the computer. She also kept up a constant litany of questions about how he was feeling, all of which were able to be answered with a yes or no, indicated by the number of times he blinked. I could tell that this wasn't the first time she'd communicated with someone who had a tube down their throat.

A much younger nurse, who I assumed was Bridgette, opened the door and popped her head in. She caught sight of Jed answering one of Emma's questions by waving his hand towards the tube that he so clearly wanted out. The woman let out a squeak and the door slammed shut again as she withdrew. I imagined Dr. Chan had called in and told her to go check on Emma, because she had to have misunderstood. Brain-dead patients, after all, didn't wake up.

Dr. Chan entered a minute later, breathing as if she'd run there. She kept the expression on her face professional but I could see the alarmed glaze to her eyes. If this man was awake it meant that she'd either missed something critical during her examination of him, or that something inexplicable had occurred. Having things happen that don't fit the order of the known universe is very unsettling, as I well knew. I felt sorry for her, wished there was some way I could tell her she hadn't made a mistake. But there was no way to explain that.

Retreating as far into the recliner as I could, I texted Ty to let him know that Jed had made the jump, and asked for another sports drink. If I didn't get busy replenishing my body's electrolytes, I'd earn myself a hospital bed for the rest of the week.

Emma bent over Jed, talking into his ear and holding on to him, trying to keep him calm while Amal Chan ticked through Jed's computerized medical records and looked over the numbers aggregating on the monitors behind his bed. She listened to his chest, looked in his eyes, and asked him yes and no questions as she performed a mini mental state exam.

Tucking my legs up into the recliner to stay out of their way, I forced myself back into clinical detachment. If I absorbed Jed's panic, I'd drive myself crazy. He was safe. He was scared—an instinctive response his body controlled, but this wasn't going to hurt him. He was going to be okay. I focused on the healthy spikes of the EEG and metronomic hum of the ventilator while I watched Dr. Chan and Emma do their work.

Ty walked in and stopped at the sight of the big man in the bed gripping the handrails so tight they looked like they might snap off. Ty took a wide berth around the clinical activity in the center of the room to reach me.

"Here you go." He offered me a chicken salad sandwich wrapped in plastic and a bright red beverage with loads of sugar that claimed to be healthy.

"Thank you." I gripped his hand and saw my exhaustion mirrored in his eyes. "You guys should go home."

"I'm relieved he's out of you." He said it loud enough that I worried the others had heard us, but the flurry of activity never stopped.

"I'm glad, too. I never want to do that again."

"Are you feeling all right?"

"I'm tired, but not too bad." I was lying but Ty nodded like he believed me. Maybe he knew I needed to keep up the pretense. "Where's Chaz?"

"He's out in the hallway. It seemed like there were too many people in here already."

"You guys should get some rest," I reminded him.

"You should too."

"I will, but I'm going to stay here with Jed until he's settled down. Then I'll go home."

Ty glanced over at Jed who was now lying rigid in the hospital bed and I shrugged. They weren't likely to release him too soon after his inexplicable recovery, but I wasn't going to leave him until after the ventilator was out.

"Call us if anything changes, or if you need anything at all," he insisted, and wouldn't give me my car keys until I'd promised.

Dr. Chan summoned the pulmonologist to evaluate Jed's breathing status and then gave Jed a mild sedative to take the edge off his panic, which allowed me to relax more too. While they alternated between celebrating his recovery and trying to figure out how it had happened, I drank two more colored beverages from the waiting room vending machine and polished off the mayonnaise dominant sandwich that Ty brought me.

It didn't take long for Jed to demonstrate he met the pulmonologists criteria for extubation, so they disconnected the ventilator and pulled the tube from his throat. He gagged and choked, and then, unfazed by his hoarse voice, cursed them all with a creative string of words that weren't often used together in the English language. I stepped between Jed and the clinical staff and sat on his bedside again, stilling him with my touch.

"Thank you, all. I think he needs to rest now."

They left us alone, though I heard the group of them in the hall-way, arguing over how Tobias Peters had spontaneously recovered. I couldn't help them explain it because they'd never believe me, but I knew the mystery of it would haunt them and make them question every similar patient for years to come.

Exhausted from his body's effort in fighting the ventilator, and the amount of energy his soul had used reclaiming Tobias' body, Jed slept.

Watching over the man I loved, I called Tobias' mother.

"Anna? Have they let you see him?" Someone else might have thought she was curt, but I thought her manner of speech was prob-ably a reflection of her personality. I envisioned a determined woman in her early sixties, both neat and efficient.

"Karin, they were wrong about him." It was easier for me to explain that than to say he'd had another miraculous recovery. "Jed woke up and I think he's going to be fine."

Silence echoed through the connection as she absorbed my words. "This is wonderful news." When she spoke her voice had a slight quiver to it, the only emotional reaction she gave. "He has not been the same, though, since last time."

I chose my words with care. "He told me that he is different, since the first accident."

"And now?"

"He seems the same as he has been, since I've known him," I clarified for her. The noise I heard might have been a sigh of disap-pointment, or relief. I wasn't sure which, but it wouldn't have been unreasonable for her to hope her son's original personality was back.

"May I speak with him?" The formality she spoke with made me smile.

"He's sleeping right now, but I'll have him call you when he wakes up again."

"Very well. I'd like to hear more, Anna, if you can take the time to speak further with me."

I filled Karin in on her son's recovery in as much detail as I could, and when we hung up, I sat staring at Jed until my eyelids started closing of their own accord.

I jolted awake from a dream filled with violence and death in a hospital hallway that looked like the one outside Jed's door. With my heart racing, I gave up on sleep. Instead, I paced the confines of the small room, chasing the happenings of the last two days and trying to figure out what came next.

As the sun lifted over the city that I used to live in, I stared out the window and realized it wasn't my home anymore.

# CHAPTER THREE

"**W**HAT IS IT that troubles you?" Jed asked, and I started at the raspy texture to his voice. It had been several hours since they'd pulled the ventilator tube out and he still sounded like he was recovering from a bad cold. He was sitting half upright in bed, the pallor of his skin healthy and pink under the dark scruff growing on his cheeks and neck.

"I was thinking about how I can't go back."

"Go back where?"

I suppressed a smile. Jed wouldn't appreciate my amusement over his tendency to literal interpretations. "I can't go back to my old life, the one I had before all of this started. Everything's changed too much."

"That may be," he agreed. He looked better than he had, but dark shadows under his eyes betrayed his exhaustion. Based on the numbers on his EKG and blood pressure monitor, his body was adapting well to being repossessed, but that made sense. Bodies were meant to have one soul in residence. It was when there were two that it seemed to cause problems.

"How are you feeling?" I crossed to his bed and attempted to perch on the edge of it. I gave up on subtlety, and settled in deeper next to his legs.

"Better. Are you well?" He surveyed the damage to my face, and his fist clenched the sheets. "They hurt you more than I realized."

I snorted. It was so like him to worry about me when he was the one in a hospital bed. "I'm well enough." I didn't need to tell him about the rapid heart rate and the fact that every time I stood up I felt faint. I felt better than I had, so I didn't think I would wind up in the emergency room, but I needed to sleep.

"That was a foolish risk for you to take. Did I cause you harm when I was inside you?"

"You didn't hurt me, and I don't think you had any other options."

He paused before he answered, as though reluctant to share what was on his mind. "I was weak." The admission was rare for Jed. A heartbeats worth of vulnerability he didn't want to admit to. I took his hand, drew it into my chest and held the warmth of him close to me.

"It's okay. I took care of you but I'm happy you're back in your own body. I don't like having an extra soul inside me."

The deep sound in his throat was meant to be one of amusement but came out more like a cough. "I'd imagine not. Thank you, for taking me in."

"I couldn't bear the alternative."

His hand curved around the back of my head, his thumb searing a brief stroke across my cheek before he dropped it again. "You are fierce enough to bear that and more, my warrior." Calling me his warrior was as close to a declaration of love as Jed was going to get, and I was surprised he'd said it. Maybe he was right, but I didn't want to find out how much more I could take. I changed the subject to one that was a bit more pressing.

"Do you feel well enough to talk to Karin? It's all I could do to keep her from getting on an airplane."

"Yes, I can call her. Thank you, for talking to her." Jed shifted up in his bed, his expression a mixture of regret and guilt.

I nodded, wanting him to know that we were in this together. "I'll give you some privacy to call her. I need to get something else to eat."

Jed gestured at his picked-over tray of food. A selection of the hospital's "soft diet," as if they were worried that a man who'd just come back from the dead was going to choke to death on a cracker. "This is not food."

"Well, your highness, I'm afraid when you've been recently intubated and declared brain-dead, that's what you get." I attempted a bow and earned another choke of a laugh.

I dug around in the cabinets and found the bag of personal belongings Unionville had gathered up and sent with him. His cell phone was mixed in with the clothes he'd been wearing when he collapsed. I made sure it had enough battery left and handed it to him.

"I'll be back in a few."

When I came back from the cafeteria with a granola bar and cup of well-sugared coffee, Jed had finished his call. His eyes were misty like he'd been crying and I assumed Karin was in a similar state. I didn't remark on it.

"You should sleep, and I need to, too. If you're okay for a while, I'm going to go to my condo and get some rest."

Jed pushed himself up on one elbow, his phone falling forgotten to the sheets. "You shouldn't be alone. Stay here with me."

"I tried sleeping in that chair already, and I can't. I'm exhausted."

Jed nodded. "Then I will come with you. I don't need to be here."

"I know you think you're fine, but you need to stay." I pointed to the IV in his arm. "It's important that you get rehydrated and make sure you aren't going to suffer any of the negative reactions the rest of us had."

"I will not."

I sat on the edge of the bed again and took his hand in mine. "We need to know the results of your blood panels before you do anything else. You were just on a ventilator. We need to make sure your body is healthy."

"I'm worried about you."

"I know you are. I'm worried about you, too, but I will take good care of myself. Part of doing that is going home for a while. I just want to sleep for a few hours and then I'll come back. By then, we should know how you're doing and maybe we can convince them to discharge you."

He pushed himself into a sitting position with the level of defiance I'd come to expect from him. His legs swung over the edge of the bed and he pushed himself upright for a moment, swaying like a tree branch in the breeze. I was about to move to catch him when he had the sense to sit down again.

"See?" I glared at him.

"I will recover momentarily." Weakness of any kind was foreign to Jed, but he was going to need a few days before he was up to his usual strength. Some part of him must have known that, because he slumped back into bed and drew his legs back into the mess of covers.

"Where's my kilij?" he grumbled, groping around the blankets as if he expected to find the magical blade in bed with him.

"The police in Unionville confiscated it, remember?"

"We need it." His voice was a fierce growl at odds with his reclining body and the blankets half pulled over his legs.

"I'm aware of that but there's nothing I can do about it right this minute. Chaz is looking into how to get it back."

"Where are Ty and Chaz? They could stay with you."

"They went home, and they can't do much against ghosts anyway." His continual insistence that I had to be watched every minute was exasperating. It was everyone else who needed *my* protection.

He struggled to rise again and failed, looking down at his recovering body with a combination of disgust and contempt.

"Jed, you are no good to me dead." He gave me an odd look. Jed's first body had died thousands of years ago, but there wasn't an easy way to say that. "Fine. Look, you need Tobias' body, and it needs to heal. I'll be careful." I stressed the last word and crossed my arms against further discussion. "Will you please get some rest? I'll be back in a few hours, after I've slept."

I didn't point out how much having him inside me had drained me, not to mention how many ghosts I'd banished in the last day. Being in a hospital again at all was stressful, given what I'd been through. He ought to know.

"It's not safe to be out walking." He didn't like to be defeated, but seemed to be accepting the fact that his body wasn't going anywhere yet.

"I'll drive." I held up my car keys. "Ty brought my car down yesterday."

He glared at me but fished his cell phone out of the sheets and laid it on his chest in a gesture of defeat. "You will call me if anything happens."

"Of course," I agreed to forestall any additional conversation. It wasn't worth arguing that he wouldn't be in any shape to help me if anything did happen. I gathered my bag, walked over to him, and intertwined my fingers with his. He gave them a reluctant squeeze.

"Get some rest." I walked out, letting the door click shut behind me.

I found my car in the parking garage by pressing the lock button on my key and following the beep. Ty wasn't much taller than I was, but I still needed to adjust the seat a few inches when I got in. Pulling out of the parking garage into the incessant afternoon sunshine was a shock, blinding after so many weeks of gray skies.

The hospital was so close to my condo that I could have walked there, but as tired as I was, I was grateful to have transportation. Squinting to protect my eyes from the sunshine I coasted past a string of trendy restaurants and wondered how anyone's life could be continuing on as normal.

Midtown was an eclectic blend of the economic spectrum; halfway between the upscale Plaza shopping district and the Art Deco downtown skyscrapers. Restored craftsman-style two-story homes sat side by side those still in disrepair. Former commercial buildings had been renovated into lofts, and charming brick apartment buildings with gracious front porches housed students from the two nearby colleges. As always, the least fortunate wandered the streets.

After a stint of being considered an affluent part of town that lasted until the 1960s, the area had fallen into serious disrepair until the last decade. Same-sex couples moved back in first, buying decrepit three-story Victorians and painstakingly renewing them to their former glory. They'd been followed by young people who didn't want to live in the suburbs, and then the older affluent crowd had started to pay attention to the area.

The economic divide was extreme. There were still plenty of neighborhoods that were poor, where residents lived in neglected  homes a stone's throw from the shining restored Victorians. Desperation and foreign sports cars blended in equal measure.

Maybe it was because I'd been gone, but the area seemed more disheveled than I remembered it. Trash bags were piled on sidewalks in haphazard heaps, and the people who were out appeared to have taken less care than normal when dressing for the day. One man wore a flapping trench coat over his bare chest and I saw another wearing a fur coat paired with tennis shoes and jogging pants.

When I stopped at a red light, several people darted into the street, picking their way between cars in their rush to jaywalk. A man in a shabby sweatshirt and scuffed jeans stopped in front of my car in an abrupt move and peered through the windshield like he thought he knew me.

I identified the hazy sheen of a second soul in him as his eyes widened and he ran into oncoming traffic. Most of the ghosts seemed to know who I was now. I didn't know if my face was on some poster in hell or if they shared a communal mind, but this one didn't want to be anywhere near me. I held my breath as he ran, horns blaring around us. A sedan screeched to a halt inches from the man's thighs but he ran on, oblivious, disappearing around the corner of a bar.

I hesitated as the cars in front of me surged forward now that the street was clear. A horn honked behind me and I added enough pressure to the gas pedal to guide my car towards the next corner and then took the next left, the same direction he'd gone.

The street between the low rise commercial buildings was empty save for a few parked cars. The man could have gone anywhere. He might have stepped inside one of the buildings, run farther down the street, or hidden behind a car. With my sixth sense, I could see the bright lights of the living souls all around. Whether one of them was him, or someone else, I didn't know for sure. Ghosts alone looked different than people, but when they were together in the same body, I had to be closer to be able to tell if the person was possessed. I made another left down a short block towards the street he'd cut down and coasted past a row of apartments on my right. Faded green paint peeled off the facades in strips that flapped in the wind, but the only sign of life outside was a skinny orange cat huddled under an eave.

To my left the brick wall ended, opening up to a parking lot behind the bar. My victim was there, arms crossed and legs planted. He had reinforcements. Three other men were with him. I was close enough to see the shimmering overlay of the ghosts' souls on top of the living. It would have looked like a group of friends meeting up for an afternoon drink if they weren't all possessed and tracking the slow movement of my car like a pack of hungry coyotes.

Four sets of eyes bored into mine, and as one they started moving forward. My heartbeat skittered, raising the alarm to flee. Calculating the chances of success didn't take long. I had to get close enough to touch them to release them without harming their true souls. There wasn't any way to release their ghosts from inside my car without killing the hosts or risking myself. I planted my foot on the gas and pulled away as the men gave chase, running after me down the street. Drifting around the corner at the next stop sign, I sped down the road for a block, taking another turn, and another until I was nearly downtown and sure I was well away from them.

I wanted to stop, pull over and wait until my hands stopped shaking, but I didn't dare stay out in the open. If four possessed men were running through the streets of midtown then there were more. The only true safety was to get far away, but I wouldn't leave without Jed. I kept driving, making my way back towards my place in the city as I kept a wary eye on my surroundings and made sure I wasn't being followed.

I drove past it once, checking for nefarious activity. I searched with my sixth sense and found my condo devoid of life, and nothing nearby but what appeared to be the souls of the living in their own homes. My street was quiet, too. It looked like a movie set before the scene started. Bereft of leaves, old growth oak trees towered overhead, and cars lined the curbs on both sides. Because I'd always been able to see ghosts, I preferred to not live in old houses, which were more likely to have unwanted residents. My condo was part of a newer project to replace dilapidated buildings with higher density housing. The units were all attached, more like modern town-homes than apartments. Instead of having multiple stories, they attached at the back, with the other set of units facing out on the next street. Unlike most of the houses on the block, each of these also had the convenience of an attached garage, which I appreciated given the tendency for snow, ice, and hail.

I paused in front of my drive, stretching my senses into the building, rechecking every nook and cranny. The condo was still empty and I exhaled a breath I hadn't realized I'd been holding. I'd downplayed it for Jed, but there was some risk to going home. The ghosts had found me here before, but it felt safer than being out on the streets.

I didn't want to bother Chaz and Ty, and going to their place brought more danger to them than if I stayed away. Adonijah had found them there once already, though, and used them to get close to me. There weren't any good answers. I backed into the garage and sat in the car until the garage door closed in front of me, afraid that something or someone would jump in after me.

*You've been watching too many horror movies. Stop being ridiculous,* I told myself.

I entered the stillness of my condo, realizing that the modern design gave it a sterile atmosphere I hadn't noticed before. The wall of windows and white paint contrasted with the dark granite counters with as much warmth as a hotel room. The décor was minimalist, reflective of my lack of a life. It was worlds away from the farmhouse, which was always filled with people and the knick-knacks from my childhood. No photos of loved ones or fun days were on display in my condo. They would have just been collecting dust anyway. The flat could have been a high-end rental unit for all that it looked like someone's home.

It was a different woman who had lived here: a doctor with a quiet, dull life. She had few friends, a career that consumed her, a nice car, and a bank account with a comfortable balance in it. Sheltered in these solitary walls, she'd let the years pass by. That woman didn't exist anymore. She'd transformed into a fighter in a war the rest of the world didn't yet know was happening.

My shoes thudded on the glossy concrete floor as I crossed to the counter and dropped my keys on it with a clatter that echoed across the vaulted ceiling. I felt like a stranger and a rush of homesickness for the familiarity of my farmhouse swept through me. Jed and I had been staying in my childhood home since I'd met him three months before, when the ghosts started attacking us.

An enterprising spirit had dropped through my oven vent to get to me, and then attacked me with my own butcher's knife. Maybe that was the memory that had me feeling so unsettled. After all, I hadn't been back since then. *Get a grip. You live here and there aren't any ghosts around.* I pushed away the desire to call Ty and ask if I could come over.

I usually waited to arm the alarm system until before I went to bed, but I pushed the buttons on the control panel to set it and then turned the bolt on the door to the garage. A glance at the front door reassured me it was also locked. Too much of what was after me didn't need a door to come in, but it made me feel safer. Leaving my jacket on, I wrapped my arms around myself in a futile attempt to get warm. Given the ghost-killing fire that burned inside me, I felt cold a surprising amount of the time. I increased the heat a few digits and turned my attention back to my house, checking to see if everything was as I'd left it.

The countertops were covered with a fine layer of dust, though not as much as they should have been given that I'd been gone for more than two months. My friend and clinic manager, Rita, had been by a few times since I'd been gone to check on the place for me. She must have been cleaning up while she was here.

I ran my hand along the cold stone, stopping to touch the shiny black handles of my Japanese kitchen knives. The last time I'd seen them, the ghost from the oven vent had been trying to carve me up with the largest one. A shiver of fear ran through me. *Jed's right. I shouldn't have come home alone.* I could protect myself from ghosts, but my collection of awful memories was growing at a frightening pace.

My sixth sense didn't detect any unusual activity, but I switched off the kitchen light in hopes that the house would look as empty as it had been in recent months. There was enough light filtering through the edges of the blinds for me to navigate through my small condo.

I recalled leaving my bedroom in disarray after the ghosts attacked us that night. I'd packed in a frenzy, dropping unneeded clothing and toiletries on the bed and floor. Everything was clean now, showing Rita's touch. There wasn't even any dirty laundry in the hamper. My bed was made, and from how neat it looked, I guessed the sheets were clean too. I felt a rush of gratitude to Rita because it was easier that no evidence remained of the night when everything started to go wrong.

I paced around the bedroom. Exhaustion radiated through my body, but without even my cat, Luna, to keep me company, I couldn't face the stark solitude of my bed. Being alone at all felt strange after two months of near constant companionship. This house didn't feel like my home anymore, but for now, it would have to do.

The muscles in my legs ached with restless tension, as if the stress from the last few days had settled into the long fibers. Stretching, I tried to ease the uncomfortable sensation and wondered if I could fall asleep at all. I found a votive candle tucked behind the flour on a pantry shelf and lit it, certain that it wasn't enough light to alert anyone outside to my presence, even as the late afternoon sunshine gave way to dusk. I took refuge on the couch, tugging a warm afghan blanket over my legs and tucking it up under my neck to stay warm.

Watching the shadows thrown on my coffee table by the flickering candle flame, I listened to the foreign sounds of the city. Cars drove by on the street outside, doors opened and closed. A lone dog barked in the distance. I watched the undulating flame until it sputtered and darkness closed around me in a soft embrace.

"Finally, we meet." The voice was insistent, pulling me from the shadows of a sleep I hadn't realized I'd fallen into. I wasn't alone. I bolted up and grasped for my power. It wasn't there.

I strained my eyes in the dissipating dark at the being standing in front of me. It was a ghost, wasn't it? The soul was bright like the light of a living person. If this wasn't a ghost, it meant that someone had broken into my house. For some reason, I didn't feel as alarmed about that as I should.

She had cropped dark hair and strong features set in a youthful face. She wore black jeans and a fitted black leather jacket over what might be a trendy concert T-shirt.

I tried to shake off the disorientation from emerging suddenly from a deep slumber. This stranger shouldn't be in my living room and I needed to wake up so I could protect myself. Ghosts almost always brought danger with them, even the friendly ones.

"Who are you?" I tried for an authoritative tone of voice but what came out was more akin to bewilderment.

"You may call me Eli." The woman settled into a red chair across from me and that struck me as odd. I didn't own a red chair. The details in the rest of the room weren't quite right either; the blanket on the sofa was a shade brighter than the one I'd gone to sleep with, and this space was smaller than my actual living room. She'd fished in my head for the details of where I was, but the proportions were off. The fact that she'd somehow seen my thoughts enough to know what my living room looked like filled me with righteous indignation.

"This isn't my house and you're a ghost."

Even though I was mad, that knowledge confirmed that she wasn't from the land of the living, because I'd never seen another real person in the space in-between. Just me and the dead. If we were in that realm, it looked different than it had before. I felt like that detail was significant, but I couldn't figure out why.

Jed had described it to me as the space between the world of the living and the dead. I'd been here a few times before—often enough that I knew I was defenseless and that I couldn't leave at will. It was too bad I couldn't use my power in this strange plane of existence to banish ghosts, because I was tired of being brought here against my will.

"In a manner of speaking." She gave me an indulgent smile that forgave my ignorance. "It was easier to bring you to me than for me to come to you."

"You guys usually take me to the cave. Are we in the same place?" It had been a large cave until I'd figured out how to alter the scenery. I'd removed the rock roof, opening it to the sky. That reminded me that I wasn't completely without power here, as long as all I wanted to do was change the drapery. I at least had the advantage of knowing that. The other ghosts had been frightened when I'd changed it before—like that was something I shouldn't have been able to do.

Eli laughed, a strange, entrancing sound. "Christiana lacked imagination. This plane can become what we choose it to be, with a little effort." If she was aware of that, my ability to change the scenery likely wouldn't impress her much.

"Why did you pick my living room?" Had she chosen the place, or had I?

She flipped her hand palm side up like the funerary images of Egyptian queens, her fingers pointing at the sofa. "This is where I found you."

I shuddered and forced myself to refocus. "You were in my house?"

"Not quite."

"How do you know Christiana?"

"She was with the Council."

"Are you Council?"

She paused before answering, like she was searching for words that wouldn't qualify as a lie. "I'm not an official member." That was what Jed had said about it, too, and it sounded like, "close enough" to me.

"Are you going to try to kill me, too? It didn't work for Christiana," I reminded her, stiffening my spine and hoping my demeanor showed more bravado than I felt.

"I hoped we could assist each other." She lifted a scant eyebrow and settled farther into her chair, like she was trying to offer physical proof that she was just there to talk. Then again, she hadn't answered with a definitive no, so attacking me was on the table, just something she was hoping she didn't need to do. Maybe she didn't care for the mess.

"I don't want your help," I said. She waited in silence. "I'm done working with the dead. Go away and let me get some sleep."

She laughed. "You don't get to choose."

"I don't know where you're from, but in my country, in this era, free will is an actual thing." I was willing to provide a lecture on the Constitution and the inalienable rights it upheld but I wasn't sure she would comprehend it. Depending on when she was from, it might not be a concept that she could easily grasp. Her head tilted at a calculating angle like she was picking fruit at the market and couldn't figure out which peach looked best.

"You truly believe that. How quaint."

*Why were the dead so damned condescending?* "Why come here to ask me if you don't believe I have a choice in the matter?"

"It is possible that I know where Adonijah is."

My spine stiffened. "Where can I find him?"

"I said that we could work together. I wouldn't have said that if I had nothing to offer you."

"What is it you want from me?" I didn't try to keep the acrimonious edge from my voice. She smiled.

"I may need your help one day."

"What kind of help?" I wanted to find Adoni, but I needed to know what the price would be. How did one go about finding a ghost that wasn't bound to the same physical restraints as the living? I didn't know how fast they could travel, or how much energy it would take him to move from one place to another. He'd been at my farm the last time I'd seen him, but he could be anywhere in the world by now.

"Blaise must have thought highly of you, to be willing to sacrifice his life to protect you." I thought she sounded bitter about it and wondered if she'd been close to him. She glanced around the artificial space as if she could glean some insight into my character from her recreation of my living room.

"Blaise and I had a brief and difficult acquaintance. I don't know what he thought of me." Blaise had abducted me and taken me to the Council like a sacrificial offering. His change of heart when he realized the Council meant to kill me didn't mean we'd liked each other, though. I didn't think he'd sacrificed himself for me. He'd fought for what he believed was right. I was a disposable pawn in his moral code, one he'd been willing to risk to serve his own needs. "Do you know if he's really dead?" I asked.

"There are not stages of death. One is or isn't. He has been." She maintained a placid smile.

I realized I hadn't asked the right question. "I know his first life is over. Is his spirit still on Earth?"

She stared at me instead of answering, I couldn't tell if it was because she didn't know, or didn't want to tell me. I chose a different tactic. "How many of you are left?"

"There has only ever been one of me."

"I meant the Council."

"The Council was facing a crisis before they came for you. Divisions have bred among them for as many centuries as they have been aligned."

"That didn't answer my question. How many of them are left?"

"Not as many as there once were."

Her cryptic answer was less than helpful since I didn't know how many there were to begin with. "Whose side were you on? Christiana's or Scipio's?"

"I do not take sides."

If she was telling the truth, it worried me. "Does that mean there's a third faction in the Council? What do they want?"

"If there are a hundred spirits of the dead, then there will be a hundred different agendas, Anna. The dead are not so unlike the living. They each serve their own needs and care not about the others. Some seek redemption, others depravity. That may be why they have not succeeded."

"What is it that you want, then?"

She shifted in the chair and tucked a wisp of hair off her forehead. "I need to know if I can trust you, or if you'll try to destroy me, too."

I held back a snort of laughter. "That's funny."

Something flashed across her face, but I couldn't tell if she was disconcerted or annoyed. "I wasn't attempting to amuse you."

"I don't trust the dead."

"Even Jedediah?"

"He's different."

"Is he?" The look she gave me said she was older than the twenty years her form suggested. "He has charmed you too, then."

"Did you really come here to talk about Jedediah?"

"No," she admitted. I was used to ghosts attempting to erode my confidence in Jed, at this point. Christiana had done her very best to breed a wariness between us. The only way I'd been able to combat that was to never appear to waiver in my confidence in Jed.

"I'm not interested in playing these games. If that's all you came for then you can send me home."

"I did not come to spar with you, Anna. I came to see if I could trust you. If we do not share trust, then we cannot work together."

"Your Council," I controlled my tone so she wouldn't know how upset the topic made me, "has done nothing but work against me, abduct me, and try to kill me." I inhaled in a long slow wave to keep myself calm. "I don't trust any of you and if I could destroy you right now, I would," I spoke without emotion.

She tilted her head. "There can be a certain trust in that, too, Magos."

"How's that?" Magos was the ghost word for people with my power. I thought it translated into English as "witch."

"Indeed." She looked satisfied, as if she'd drawn the winning hand. "I understand you now."

I felt like I'd given something vital away, but I wasn't sure what. "How so?"

"Adonijah was a part of you, wasn't he?"

"That's a random question."

"I can tell, you know. I can sense him inside you."

A shudder of revulsion swept across my torso. I felt suddenly dirty, like I should take a shower. Did I carry a visible taint from him? Like red wine spilled on a white carpet, a stain that I'd never be able to get out?

"When the stronger soul takes over a body, they can leave a piece of themselves imprinted forever on the host soul."

"Is there a point you're trying to make?"

"You are more like him than you want to admit."

"I am nothing like Adonijah." I couldn't help but rise to her taunt.

"Maybe there's a ruthless edge to you that you didn't have before." She had the calm tone of a college professor delivering a well-practiced lecture.

I itched to destroy her, but there was little I could do in this place. My nuclear core that banished ghosts was back in my physical body, in my real living room.

"You would banish me for telling you a distasteful truth, wouldn't you? Perhaps we could be great friends if I told you a more agreeable lie." She purred and I flinched. Was she right?

"What were you doing a few nights ago while I was fighting for my life?" I countered, trying to gain some measure of control again. "Throwing chunks of wood at me?"

"I did not take part in that attack against you." She said it as though she had no stake in lying. I believed her.

"There were several ghosts there that helped me," I admitted. "Were you one of them?" Her head inclined in a slight nod.

"Thank you, for that." I wouldn't have survived without their help. I adjusted my tone, hoping to come across as less combative. "Why did you help me?"

"Why?" I had finally caught her off guard.

"Why did you help me, if you weren't on Scipio's side?"

"It was not your time to die. Your death would have upset the order of events to come."

I swallowed against the sudden lump in my throat. "How do you know? What events?"

"Some of us have the ability to foresee." It wasn't lost on me that she only answered one of my questions. Jed had told me once that the Council could see the future and had known how to find me based on when I was supposed to die, but I hadn't died that day because they'd sent Jed to save me. Was it this spirit that told them?

"You know when I'm going to die?"

"I do." There was a strange glint in her eye. "Do you want to know?"

"I'm not sure." My palms were sweating and I rubbed them against my jeans. "Would you tell me if I did?"

"The knowledge of it could drive you mad." My own mortality hung over me like a full moon with a suddenness that took my breath away. The desire to *know* blossomed in my chest as I breathed in again.

"Tell me."

"I'm not quite ready to lose you to madness, Magos. You will have to wait. I can tell you it won't be today."

There had been so many days in the last three months where I'd feared for my life. It felt like she'd given me a small gift by telling me that today, at least, I didn't have to worry. Then anxiety struck.

"Am I going to die tomorrow?" Would she grant me another day free from worry? Maybe an entire week? There was a pause before she answered that seemed to stretch on for an eternity.

"You see, now, how the knowledge of life and death can drive you to insanity? Already the thought of it distracts you. Even those who know their time is quickly approaching can't bear to know the exact day." That was probably true. I was already spiraling in my mind because she hadn't answered my question about tomorrow. I refrained from asking again. I didn't want her to know how much the reality of my own mortality unsettled me.

"How is it that you can tell when someone will die?"

"Time does not flow the same way for me as it does for you. It is not linear."

"Theoretical physics isn't my forte."

"This isn't a theoretical conversation. I'm telling you what is true. Your inability to comprehend time doesn't change the truth of it."

"Maybe you could explain it to me?"

"That isn't necessary."

"But I'd like to know." I was burning with the desire to know. She had me.

"Soon I will have need of you, and then I will have this to trade." She smirked, the power of knowledge on her side. "It is enough today that we have met one another."

"Don't go." I sounded more alarmed than I meant to. "I need to know what I'm up against." She pursed her lips and assessed me as though debating how big a treat to give the dog under the table. I tossed another question into the silence she'd left, hoping to engage her again. "Are you one of the original Council members?"

"This modern era amuses me." At first I thought that was all she'd say, but then she continued. "Your disbelief is too evident. Ask what you really mean. You want to know if what Jedediah told you was true." She leaned forward. "It's good that you don't trust him too much."

"I do trust him," I protested.

"If you did, you'd believe what he told you. You want me to tell you if the Council are angels that were cast from heaven."

"Yes," I admitted, grudgingly.

"And you want to know if God exists."

"I don't believe in God." My response was automatic.

"There are some that claim your world is flat. Their beliefs don't change reality."

"You're telling me that God is real." My voice dropped in disbelief, and maybe in relief.

"I'm telling you that whether you do or don't believe in a thing has no bearing on the truth of it." She curled back in her chair with smug satisfaction.

"How can I find Adonijah?" At this point I was throwing every question I had at her, hoping for a straight answer.

"You will have the chance to take your revenge on him soon, but act with care. There are forces at work greater than you comprehend. The danger is real."

"Are you saying you don't think I should release him?"

"Your hatred for him will change you. It already has."

"I'll keep that in mind." I repressed a shiver and changed the subject again. "We were talking about the original Council, and you."

"Why do you worry about a council comprised of spirits that were cast from heaven by the wrath of a god you don't believe in." Her eyebrow quirked up, a sardonic glimpse into how ignorant she thought me.

"Maybe because they keep possessing people and trying to kill me. Are you one of the . . . angels?"

"Not exactly. I am something older, even, than they are." I had noticed that the dead rarely chose to appear as they must have looked when they died. Apparently even ghosts maintained some level of vanity.

"You're a ghost, then?"

"I have never lived a human life." Eli smiled, letting the statement stand alone.

"What are you?"

"There are many things you cannot understand."

"It's difficult to understand when no one will explain anything." I bit each word off and tried to control my frustration.

"I play my own role in the Council's fight to keep balance between the living and the dead. That is all you need to know right now."

"I don't need all the answers. I just need to know how to find Adonijah." I didn't really expect an answer at this point, and I wasn't disappointed.

"You need not concern yourself with him. I can protect you, if you will let me."

"I don't need protection and I don't want yours. I just need to find him so I can destroy him."

"Let me help you, Anna."

"I don't think so."

She shrugged. "When you are ready, then. If it is not already too late."

"That's a bit melodramatic."

"Making light of this does not make it go away," she scolded.

"Why is all of this happening now?"

"The fight between the living and the dead is not new."

"Maybe not, but something has changed."

"The world of the living has become narcissistic." She waved at the recreation of my condo and I saw the gleaming silver appliances and dark marble in a new light. "It is easy for darker things to take hold. The living are weak and in good supply, enjoying longer lives in more luxury than we have ever seen before. There is much to tempt the dead to try and live again."

"People have always been self-absorbed, and most modern luxuries have been around for the last fifty years," I pointed out.

"The Magos, like you, appear to have been neutralized."

"What happened to the others?" I was sure I knew the answer. The Council members who had attacked me were experienced with killing my kind.

"They were murdered," Eli confirmed my suspicions with a matter of fact dismissal.

"Why is the Council executing people with my abilities?"

"Many were involved, but not all in the Council have been against you." Her reminder was part rebuke.

"Agreed, but that's a bit of a technicality. Let's assume we are talking about the ones that are against me. Why do they want to kill me? Why now?"

"People have always hunted those who can destroy them. Survival is an instinct that stays strong even in death."

"There's more than that, though. What aren't you telling me?"

Her lips curled. "You are perceptive, for a living being." I waited in silence for her to answer my question. "Science has helped them."

"How so?"

"The dead are not incapable of learning. They know now that the gift is passed on through generations."

"My ability is genetic." I'd guessed as much, but hadn't been able to prove it.

"We believe so."

"And by eradicating people like me, they prevent it from being passed on." A rare recessive gene, one that could disappear from the gene pool in a few generations if the dominant carriers were eliminated. "Genocide."

She shrugged, the matter was of little concern to her. "Of a sort."

I thought that the potential eradication of my kind mattered a great deal. "Are there any people left living that are like me?"

"They are not all gone," Eli conceded. "Those that survive are silent, as you were for many years." *Must be the only way to avoid being murdered by a bunch of homicidal ghosts.*

"How do we stop the ghosts who are possessing people?"

Her eyes were unblinking and disconcerting. "I don't know that you can."

"Are they following orders or acting on their own?"

"They were given permission to take over the living, encouraged to do it. No one controls them."

"Who told them to?" I was pretty sure I knew the answer, but wanted confirmation."

"There is only one being I know of with that kind of influence."

"The Master?" Eli's lack of response seemed like confirmation. "Can you help me find him?"

Her body stilled, her eyes were fixed on me. Was that fear I sensed? "You can be sure the Master is close at hand."

I forced the tension from my limbs, unwilling to let her see how much she unnerved me. "Will you help me find him?"

"It depends on our ability to come to an arrangement."

"And what exactly is it you want?"

"Trust, Anna." Her companionable smile conflicted with the challenge in her gaze. "Everything starts with trust."

# CHAPTER FOUR

"**A**NNA." The voice was insistent and I tried to roll over to escape from it. "Anna." A hand gripped my lower leg and gave it a vigorous shake. I moaned in protest. "You have to wake up."

Through the engulfing darkness, I recognized Ty's voice, but Eli was still talking. What was she saying? I thought it was important.

"She's not waking up." Ty's voice was distant.

"Do they have her?" Jed's voice cut through the darkness like a blade and I felt myself slipping from Eli's presence, pulled towards the doorway I'd never been able to find on my own.

"I don't know. Give me a minute." Ty's clipped tone was all business. Jed wasn't supposed to be here, but I couldn't focus on that. I needed to finish my conversation with Eli. She was my best chance to find Adoni and the Master.

I turned back to her, but she was standing farther away from me, as if the room had stretched to separate us. Anger was etched into every feature on her face. What was she mad about? It wasn't my fault I'd been pulled away. She raised her hand and something invisible pushed me backward, like a heavy gust of wind.

I tried to sink back into the darkness in my mind, but Ty shook me again, calling my name. My consciousness extracted itself from the place between with a painful snap.

"Go away," I muttered, trying to bury my face in a cushion.

"We're not going anywhere. Wake up." He was relentless.

Giving up on the fantasy of getting back to Eli, I mumbled a few curses into the back of the couch and then worked my eyes into a slit, squinting as my pupils objected to the bright light. Hadn't it been early evening when I'd sat down on the couch?

"I swear to God I'm taking your key away. You better have coffee."

"Working on it!" Chaz's voice called from the direction of the kitchen.

"She's with us," Ty announced with relief. He moved his hands to my face. When I tried to pull away he held me tighter, peering into my eyes. "Your pupils are different sizes. Are you feeling okay?"

I batted his hands away. "I was just sleeping. I'm fine."

"Did you drink last night, or take something?"

"You make it sound like I'm some sort of lush, and no I didn't." I glared at him, and he glared back. Jed's face appeared in the edge of my vision, his brow furrowed into ridges.

"It has taken too long to wake you."

"It did," Ty confirmed. He squatted back on his heels, staying close as though worried I'd slip away from him again.

"What are you doing here?" I tried to sound authoritarian, but my words came out in a slurred mumble.

"You weren't rousing," Ty repeated. "I'm not sure you're fully awake now."

*How long had I been there, talking with Eli?* I tried to shake myself awake but forcing my mind back to alertness was more difficult than it should have been. I just wanted to sleep.

"Anna." Ty patted my cheek as if he sensed he was losing me again. "Did you take your sleeping medication?"

"I don't take those anymore." They had never left me unable to wake up.

"I didn't think so." Ty looked scared, so I made another effort to clear the last vestiges of the dream world from my head.

"I was in that place, talking to a ghost. Well, maybe not a ghost. I don't know what she was."

"Who?" Jed demanded, grasping for a sword that wasn't there.

"She said her name was Eli, and that she's sort of part of the Council. She said she's not one of the original members—she claimed to be older than they are."

Jed gave a slight shake of his head, which I took to mean that he didn't know of her, which seemed strange. My mind filtered sluggish bits of information as I pushed myself into a sitting position. There was something wrong with Jed being here at all.

"You were in that place in your mind that they take you to? The one you can't get in and out of?" Chaz approached us with two mugs of coffee, handing one to Ty and one to me before turning back to the kitchen to get two more.

I glanced at the blinds, noting the bright rays of sunlight coming through, and hoped I'd managed some real sleep before I spent half the night talking with Eli. The kitchen clock said it was half past eight.

"Eli supposedly knows how to find Adonijah."

"Why would you want to do that?" Ty's voice arched up an octave at the same time Chaz voiced with satisfaction, "It's about time we went on the offensive."

I cradled the hot mug of coffee to my chest, its aroma helping me become more present in the real world. Jed drew a dining room chair over and sat with a groan he couldn't suppress. I realized why Jed shouldn't be here.

"They didn't discharge you this early in the day," I announced, and Ty rolled his eyes. They'd apparently covered this already, while I was in another place. "You can't walk out of the hospital against medical advice, Jed."

Jed shrugged, dismissing the rules of this world in that one slight gesture. "I am well enough."

I could imagine the hospital staff chasing after him while he walked away from the intensive care unit and suppressed a grin. They couldn't force him to stay, but discharging yourself without physician approval was frowned upon. Chaz settled into the chair across from me with a serious expression.

"We found Jed on your front porch, about to break the door down when we got here. I guess he doesn't have a key."

"How long were you out there? It was freezing last night, and it can't be much warmer now. Why didn't you call me or ring the doorbell?"

"I did both. I called you first, and when I didn't reach you, I left the hospital," Jed informed me before taking a sip of his coffee. The slight tremor in his hand belied his casual demeanor.

"How did you get here?" The hospital was within walking distance, but Jed's body had been through some trauma in the last two days and needed time to rest and recover.

"I walked. I have known worse cold." He had, too. He'd spent a few nights on the streets when he first came to Kansas City and was trying to find me. I couldn't fathom what hardships he'd faced in his first life. Being a king, he'd undoubtedly had an easier life than most people in his time, but I didn't relish the thought of living without modern comforts like running water, electricity, and good dental care. "I became concerned when you didn't answer your phone. That's when I called Ty and Chaz, to see if they had heard from you."

"Maybe I have the volume turned off." I was trying to find a normal explanation, one that didn't involve me being hijacked by the spirit world.

"You don't," Chaz answered with pragmatic simplicity. "I tested it when we got here. It rang." I looked around for my phone, blanking on where it was, and Chaz pulled it from his pocket, sliding it across the coffee table towards me.

"It was in your bag. I went looking for it when you weren't waking up and I didn't see it near you."

I flipped it open, digging through a string of missed calls that went back a couple of hours. In addition to Jed and Ty, I had missed calls from Ned and Father Grayson Harwell. Grayson was a Catholic priest I'd met at Unionville Regional while I was trying to help people possessed by ghosts. There were also a few numbers I didn't know, but none of them had left messages. My volume was turned up, and the kitchen counter wasn't far enough away that I wouldn't have heard it. How could I have slept through that?

"When Jed called us, we headed this way since we couldn't reach you, either." Chaz brought me back to why he and Ty were there. I was surprised Jed had been willing to wait if he was that worried about me. "The place was so dark, we weren't sure you were even here."

"I guess I didn't leave the front porch light on, did I?" I shrugged, looking around the sparse room. "I'm not used to being here. It felt strange when I got home last night. And I didn't exactly want to advertise my presence." I took a sip of coffee and breathed in another hot breath of caffeine-tinged steam. "Thank you for letting him in, and for waking me up. How long have you been trying?" I wasn't sure I wanted to know the answer.

"Long enough to start getting worried." Chaz glanced at his partner with a look that said Ty had been the most concerned.

"How are you supposed to get out of that place?" Ty demanded.

"I don't know." I hated that I didn't know. There was supposed to be a way for me to make my way back by myself, some sort of metaphorical door. Since I didn't like being at the mercy of whatever ghost felt like talking to me, I'd spent some time trying to figure out how to find the door in my head. I didn't know where to look for it, and I hadn't been able to find it. "The ghosts send me back when they're done talking to me. I guess you brought me back this time. Eli and I were in the middle of a conversation."

"Sorry if I interrupted." Ty rolled his eyes.

"I didn't mean it like that." I touched his arm, and his hand closed over mine in forgiveness.

"I hesitate to ask, but does anyone know why Ned and Grayson have been trying to find me?"

"Grayson called me when he couldn't reach you. He says you need to go back up there," Chaz explained.

"Why?" Jed demanded

"I didn't ask for details since we were so worried about Anna, but if I had to guess, I'd bet they've still got a problem with spooks." A bunch of them, actually. There had to be at least a dozen people in Unionville that were still possessed, but getting Jed back to his rightful body had been my first priority.

"He didn't specify if it was a new ghost problem or the usual?"

"No."

I kept my expression neutral while I dialed Grayson's number, but I wanted to roll my eyes, annoyed that they hadn't gotten more information. When Grayson picked up, he didn't wait on pleasantries.

"Father Costas is preparing for an exorcism." The familiar gravelly voice came through the phone but the words didn't make sense.

"He's doing what?"

"He will attempt to exorcise a spirit from one of the possessed this afternoon." There was a pause while he considered his words. "We believe she's afflicted."

"You aren't sure?" Grayson had told me that Father Costas was the official diocesan exorcist, but I didn't think that meant he was capable of dealing with ghosts. Jed was in favor of it, though. He thought the rites of exorcism might drive a ghost out of the person they were possessing.

"We can't be certain without you to confirm it, but she has the same symptoms."

"If you want my validation, you may have to wait a bit. I don't know if I can make it back up there today." Another pause, not even the sound of his breathing to confirm he was still on the other end of the line. I thought through the implications of what I'd just said and made another decision. "Tell him not to wait on me. If she's sick, and he thinks he can help her, then he needs to."

"Agreed," Grayson replied. "There are more people here, though, Anna. They heard about the miracles on the news, and they've come seeking help."

"People with ghosts in them? At the hospital?"

"In the parking lot, and around the hospital. I don't think they're from here. I don't know how many of them have ghosts. I suspect many of them have other ailments. I've seen one that looks like a cancer patient and several others that have physical disabilities. They all appear to be quite infirm."

"I see." I didn't think the ghosts would be seeking out a host that was already ill, but I didn't know for sure. Maybe weakness was all they looked for. The media had used the word "miracle," and the power of hope could drive desperate people to take desperate measures.

"Is Jed all right?" Grayson asked and I felt a twinge of guilt. The last time Grayson had seen me, I'd been climbing into Chaz's Audi in a panic to get Jed back to his own body. I hadn't thought to let Grayson know yesterday that we'd made it, and that Jed was going to be okay.

"He's fine. Everything's back to normal." The man in question hadn't taken his eyes off me since I'd roused. He stood back against the kitchen island, legs braced against it and arms crossed, a cold cup of coffee next to him on the counter. Most people relaxed when they leaned against things, but his body was taut with controlled tension and there was something in his gaze I hadn't seen before. Grayson was still talking, and I broke the connection with Jed's eyes so I could concentrate on the conversation.

"Will you come back tomorrow if you can't today? There isn't anyone else who can help us the way you can." Grayson sounded calm, but there was an undertone of desperation. Common sense said I should run. From the Council, from the threat of ghosts, and from the possession epidemic in Unionville.

"I'll come."

"Thank you. How are you feeling?"

"I'm not sure. There are strange things happening."

"There are, indeed. I'm worried about you." I was a little worried about myself, but I didn't want to admit it. "We all need your help, but that's a big burden for you to carry."

"I'll be up there as soon as I can." I flipped the phone shut to end the call, aware of the three men watching me. "I've got to get back up there today or tomorrow. They've got more ghosts and Father Costas is going to attempt an exorcism later today."

Ty rolled his eyes with feigned exasperation. "It's a good thing your boyfriend let himself out of the hospital, it saves us time not having to spring him on the way."

"You guys aren't coming," I protested with alarm. "You've been in enough danger because of me."

Ty and Chaz shared a long look and then spoke at the same time, their decision made. "We're coming with you."

"You need help, Anna." Ty hopped up from the couch and headed for the kitchen. "We may not have any superpowers, but I think it's pretty clear that you need us."

There was no doubt they'd both been invaluable. Ty was a great nurse; one who had single-handedly saved my life a few months ago. The healed fractures in my ribcage still ached when it rained, thanks to his CPR handiwork. Chaz had taken on the role of our pro-bono attorney, and it was clear that our legal woes weren't over yet.

"Don't you guys have to work?"

"Saving the world is what personal days were made for," Chaz informed me with a tilt of his eyebrows.

My eyes teared up. "It's not safe."

"Honestly, I feel safer with you than I do here alone," Ty said as Chaz snorted in protest.

"What am I, chopped liver?"

"You, boyfriend, are more likely to be possessed by a mad ghost with an old grudge against his brother than you are to protect me." Ty folded his arms and nicked his chin towards me. "Anna here can kick their ass six different ways." I stood, using the couch armrest to steady myself when I wobbled. *Some superhero, Anna. If you can't stand upright, how are you going to save the world?*

"I'd better get cleaned up. I feel too gross to get back in a car."

"Do you need help?" Ty offered. It would have been a strange offer from any other man but I didn't keep many secrets from my friend, and he'd seen me naked more than once. It wasn't a big deal since I wasn't exactly Ty's cup of tea.

"I might." I felt weak admitting that and forced my trembling muscles to obey. I knew they were more than capable of holding me upright, and proved it to myself by taking a few steps. "I'd rather manage by myself, though."

"I will assist you," Jed informed me. Again, I declined.

"You should still be in bed. At the hospital." I crossed my arms and tried to look fierce, which was difficult ten minutes after waking up. "Relax. I can handle a shower by myself." Jed's glare said that he had no intention of resting, and he wasn't pleased I'd suggested he was less than fit. I noticed that he sank into my spot on the sofa, though, and that his skin tone was paler than usual. He would deny it, but he had to be feeling the effects of the ordeal he'd been through.

"How about breakfast from The Corner Cafe?" Ty offered. "Chaz can go get carry out while you get ready."

"That would be great." I couldn't keep the enthusiasm out of my voice. We could always count on me being hungry.

As I closed my bedroom door, I heard Ty and Jed murmuring to each other. I waited by the bedroom door, eavesdropping.

"I don't think it's safe to leave her alone," Ty was saying. "They might come for her again. You rest and I'll stay with her." The image of Ty telling Jed what to do made me let out a little laugh. Jed had close to twelve inches on Ty, and was built like a tank.

"I do not intend to leave her alone. I will go to her when you depart." Jed's voice was tinged with an emotion I couldn't identify. Maybe it was exhaustion.

I was already in the shower when I heard the bedroom door open and close, and Jed's heavy footsteps cross the hardwood floor. *I know they're all worried but why can't they just leave me be for a few minutes?* Leaning my forehead against the tile I let hot water cascade over my back and breathed a small sigh of relief when he didn't come into the bathroom. Having someone with me at all times made me feel like a caged animal. Then again, when I'd been alone the previous night was when I'd gotten into trouble. *Could I have gotten back without Ty's help? Would Eli have sent me back or left me there alone?* I had to figure out how to get out of there myself.

After I'd pushed the hot water tank to the edge of its capacity, I turned the taps off and dried myself with a towel as gently as if I had a sunburn. My skin hurt and I avoided looking in the mirror. I didn't want to see how the rainbow of colors was evolving. I wrapped up in my bathrobe to hide some of the bruises before I joined Jed in the bedroom. We'd become lovers, but I didn't feel ready to share the full extent of my physical damage with him. I needed to be strong, and having him know the truth would somehow make my own vulnerability real.

Jed was lying down on the bed, but pushed himself into a sitting position when I walked back in. I thought the fact that he was on the bed at all was an indicator of how rough he was feeling. He should stay here and rest another day or two, but I needed to go back North, and Jed had proven he'd follow me anywhere. I perched next to him on the bed while he evaluated my face with critical concern.

"Your injuries are worse than I realized." He hadn't had time to take stock, unless he'd been trying to tally them up while he'd been inside me. I didn't think he'd been able to, though. He'd kept himself closed off from me so he wouldn't hurt me.

"I'm just a little banged up. It's nothing serious." *Doesn't he know I need to be strong? Reminding me of my human frailty isn't helping.* I moved to get up but froze when he leaned forward and wrapped his arms around my upper torso, pulling me back against him. I pushed away from him but he didn't loosen his grip. Panic flared in a momentary rush and then subsided as he dropped his arms.

"I won't hurt you," he reminded me, leaning in close and pressing his lips against the side of my head. I turned towards him then, and his arms folded around me, offering me refuge from the outside world. He bent down so his chin rested on top of my head and it felt like I'd stepped inside of him. Is this how he'd felt in me? Safe and cared for?

Relaxing in stages, I focused on the deep rush of his breaths and the faster, shallower gulps of air I drank down. His steady heartbeat became the guide to calm my breathing as my cheek pressed against his chest.

"I'm sorry I couldn't get there sooner. I was afraid Christiana had you," he whispered into my hair. "I shouldn't have worried about you. You were fearsome." I'd nearly died, and would have if he and some of the other Council ghosts hadn't come to my rescue, but I didn't point that out.

"I was smarter this time. I saved enough power to take Christiana out."

"You've grown stronger." Jed's voice was filled with admiration and I savored the reality that he'd found me, and wanted me as much as I wanted him. A man who cared more about strength and intelligence than beauty was unusual, in my experience.

"I was afraid I'd lose you when that coward Blaise stole you away." His words were thick with emotion. His hands clenched my robe.

"I'm okay, though." I rubbed my hands up the thick bands of muscles on his upper arms. "Thank you for coming to help me. I know it was a huge risk, but I needed you. I don't know if my power would have worked on that dragon ghost." She hadn't really been a dragon, but it was the shape she'd chosen.

"I think it would have." His hands relaxed their hold, satisfied that I was still there. I wasn't the only one that needed a bit of connection to bring me back to myself. I wasn't used to it being Jed that needed help feeling grounded. I pulled back from our embrace and looked him in the eyes. Were his a little moister than usual?

"How do I stop them from taking me to that place?"

"You have to find the door in your mind, and close it." He'd said that before, but I didn't know what it meant.

"How do I find the door?"

He shook his head slowly. "I'm afraid I don't know."

I shrugged. It was one of many problems that would have to wait until later. "Stay here, and I'll get us another cup of coffee. We can drink them while I get ready."

"I'll make the coffee. We were in such a hurry last time, you didn't take much when we left. Perhaps there is more you'd like to bring?" Jed glanced around the room.

*Being attacked by murderous ghosts did put a damper on one's ability to pack.* "I thought I'd put together a few more things."

I thought about arguing with Jed about the coffee, but when he proved he could stand without assistance I decided to let him make it. He could rest in the car on the way back to the farm while I drove. Since he didn't know how to use my espresso machine, it would probably be the Turkish variety that he'd made the first morning he'd stayed with me.

I listened to the clanging of pans while I dressed in clean jeans and a navy zip front hoodie sweater. Feeling more confident now that I was clothed, I braved an inspection in the mirror, and had to admit I looked pretty rough. The bruises on my face had a bluish hue. The sleeves of my sweater covered the purplish one on my forearm but I wasn't skilled enough with makeup to disguise the discoloration on my cheek and forehead.

If anyone asked I could just tell them I had been in a car accident, but hopefully no one would be rude enough to inquire. Though I'd rather they think that I'd been in a wreck than a bar brawl, which is what it looked like. The reality, as usual, was impossible to explain. I curled up on top of my comforter and called Ned.

"Where the hell have you been?" The abrupt words were cased in decades of complicated friendship, and I knew he spoke from fear, not anger.

"Sleeping. I was tired."

"People who are sleeping tend to wake up when they get a dozen phone calls."

"I didn't hear my phone." That was as close as I could get to not lying. I didn't feel like going into details over the phone.

"With everything that's going on, you should have that thing superglued to you. Everyone was worried." His reprimand was automatic, and he didn't waste any more time on recriminations. I smiled, because what he meant was that he'd been worried about me, which meant that he cared. "When are you coming back?"

"Today, I guess."

"Good." He sounded relieved and I could imagine him standing in his farmhouse living room rubbing his hand across the top of his head like he did when he finished something stressful. "What's the situation there?"

"Jed's out of the hospital and back where he belongs. He's okay. A bit shaky." I left out the part about how Jed had discharged himself without permission.

"What about you? What aren't you telling me?"

I cursed him under my breath for knowing me well enough to pick up on my reticence. "There are ghosts here, too. I came across four men who were possessed yesterday."

"At the hospital?"

"No. Out on the street. They seemed healthy." Which meant the ghost was strong enough to control the host spirit.

"Did you take care of them?"

"I couldn't. It wasn't safe."

"I'm glad you were able to make that decision. You need to get back to the farm. It's safer here." He was correct in that the farm offered physical isolation from other human beings, but we'd been attacked there by thousands of ghosts.

"I don't know that anywhere is safe for me." He didn't respond right away, but the change in his breathing told me that he was focused on our conversation. The intensity of it ricocheted through the airwaves and I sat up in bed.

"You'll get hurt, or worse, if you stay there, Anna. This situation has gotten beyond what you can handle. You need to come back home."

I steadied myself and voiced what I knew in my heart to be true, but hadn't been able to say out loud to anyone else. "I can't win this."

"I know you can't. That's why you need to come back to the farm." Ned's tone softened, taking on the warm timbre he used when talking to spooked horses.

"I may not be able to keep you guys safe."

"Our chances of survival together are higher than if we separate." I could tell he believed that with every fiber of his being. If I couldn't trust Ned, my childhood friend and first love, then there was no one I could rely on.

"We'll head back soon. I've got to get some stuff from the clinic, and I'm going to pack a few things from the condo."

"I need you to do some shopping on the way up. I'll send you a list."

"All right." Picking stuff up in the city for Ned and Carrie was nothing new. It was hard to get everything we wanted, at the price we needed it, in the country.

"Drive safe, Anna."

"Of course. We'll see you later today."

I was used to complicated shopping lists from Carrie, but the list Ned texted me was more extensive than any I'd seen before. I reviewed it, calculating how much space his purchases would take up, and how much room I'd have left for the things I wanted to bring.

Chaz brought back breakfast, still hot and satisfyingly greasy. I polished off a southwestern omelet and hash browns at an embarrassing speed.

"Should we get you another order?" Ty asked and I felt my eyes narrow into slits.

"Watch yourself. I might decide I want the rest of yours."

He curved a protective arm around his potatoes and glared at me. "Keep your distance."

"I didn't eat dinner last night," I offered in explanation as I cleared my place.

"So we all have to suffer?" Ty asked, as the doorbell rang.

We all froze. Then Jed was in motion, grabbing the sleek, forged steel butcher knife from the block and moving towards the curtained windows with a degree of stealth his large body shouldn't have been able to achieve. He leaned against the wall when he got there, the only sign of weakness he allowed himself.

Chaz slid out of his seat and entered my bedroom just as quietly, and I heard the rustle of the blinds as he checked the exterior. I focused my second sense on the glow of the soul outside my front door.

"Living, one person, and I don't think they're possessed," I whispered, loud enough for both Chaz and Jed to hear me. Whoever it was, they weren't a ghost and I didn't want anyone else to get hurt.

"There's a van across the street that wasn't there earlier," Jed informed us.

"Open the door. Let's find out what we're dealing with. But put the knife down before you hurt one of my neighbors," I suggested, and was ignored.

"Get out of sight," he ordered, bracing himself against the wall again.

"Let me get the door," Chaz rounded the corner from my bedroom. "I don't think you're strong enough to handle it if someone tried to attack us right now."

Jed glared down at Chaz for a long moment and then flipped the knife blade over in defeat, handle extended towards Chaz. Jed settled on the armchair closest to the door. If anyone got past Chaz, he'd be the next thing in their line of sight. I pulled Ty away from the kitchen island, behind the wall that led to the guest room.

Chaz braced his foot in front of the door while he unlocked it, and then opened it a crack, the knife hidden behind the door.

Ty and I would only be visible if he opened the door all the way, but we couldn't see anything other than Chaz and Jed either. I'd never been this anxious about what was probably someone trying to sell magazines or find a missing cat.

"She doesn't live here anymore," Chaz growled an answer to an inquiry we couldn't hear.

"Way to be subtle," Ty whispered.

I couldn't suppress a quiet laugh. "Whoever is looking for me definitely knows I live here now."

The door slammed with a definitive thud and Chaz braced it closed with his foot again while he slid the bolt home so that no one could burst through in the second between closing the door and locking it.

"Someone from the media?" Ty asked and Chaz nodded.

"I think so." Chaz looked out again at the road. "He returned to the vehicle but isn't driving away."

"We should go before your current location is shared," Jed suggested. He pushed himself off the armchair and then used the back of it to steady himself.

"I appreciate your desire to leave, but I'm not ready yet. Why don't you stay there while I get some things together?" I wasn't planning to get chased out of my own home again.

"We've got to run home and pack up a few things ourselves. We left in too much of a rush this morning," Chaz stated, "but I'd hoped we could drive up together this time."

"I think it's safer that way," I agreed. "We can meet at the clinic when you're ready." I felt guilty for not answering my phone and inconveniencing everyone. "There's no need for you guys to come back here."

"Wish there was a way to lure your stalker away but I'm not sure I could get him to follow us."

"Don't worry about it. If it is a reporter, maybe when we leave we can give the impression that I'm still here." If not, he'd be following us. I wasn't sure which would be worse, though—having someone watching my house, or trying to follow me.

Chaz and Ty walked out through the front door, bundled up in jackets, hats, and sunglasses so their skin was barely visible. If the person in the van was taking photos, they'd be difficult to identify. Neither of them was feminine or Caucasian enough to be mistaken for me, though, so I didn't have any hope the van would follow them.

Deciding what of my life to take with me was challenging. I threw some comfortable clothing into a small duffel bag and then turned my attention to the kitchen. Dried goods packed up easily and would come in handy. I could restock the condo if I needed to, but I had a feeling we'd be away for a while. Canned beans, applesauce, and jars of marinara went into one canvas bag while I filled a second with packages of dried pasta, a bag of brown rice, and a container of quinoa. I emptied the contents of my freezer into a cooler. Most of it was meat from Carrie and Ned's cows, but it didn't need to stay in the city when we could make good use of it on the farm.

I carried the bags out to the garage and let Jed pack them into the car while I cleaned up from breakfast and hauled the trash out to the garage. Since the house was being watched, Jed took it out to the can at the curb.

My phone vibrated and I flipped it open to read the short text message. "Ty and Chaz are on their way to the clinic."

"Are you ready to go?"

"I think I have everything except the coffee machine. Can you take it to the car?" I didn't like asking a man to carry something heavy for me, but the damn thing weighed about thirty pounds, which to Jed, even when he didn't feel well, was nothing.

I walked through the condo one last time. I didn't want to leave a mess like I had the last time we'd left. Turning off the lights in my bedroom, I glanced at the bed. I hadn't slept in it, so it was still neat, like Rita had left it.

*Am I ever coming back?* I didn't think so. It should have made me sad, leaving a place I'd lived for ten years, but it wasn't my home anymore. I'd never made it mine. After checking to make sure I'd lowered the thermostat, I set the alarm and walked out, closing the door behind me.

"I want you to get in the back and lie down. I don't want them to see that you're in the car," Jed ordered, handing me a blanket. I stopped short.

"What?"

"Get on the floor in the back," he repeated with careful enunciation as if he were speaking to someone who didn't speak much English. "We have to drive by that van. They may follow us. I'd like you out of sight."

"You don't know the city well enough to drive us around and get to the clinic."

"I spent a few weeks here before I found you. I know my way well enough."

I supposed he did, when it came down to it, but I offered my own route suggestion. "Turn left outside the drive. They're facing the other way, so if they want to follow us, they'll have to get turned around first. You can head East on 41st and then hop onto Gillham. The road splits there and with any luck, you'll lose them before they can catch up.

"There are a dozen small side roads we could hop onto from there and then make our way back to the clinic. They won't know which way we've taken if we get to the split before them." There was a fifty-fifty chance they'd choose the right one, but by then we had a chance to be out of sight.

I slid into the back seat and sat on the floorboards like I had when I was a little kid, before we knew as much about car safety. "Don't hit anything, okay? I'm not buckled in."

"Once I get past them you can put your seatbelt on, just keep your head down." Jed tossed the blanket over me and then got into the front seat. I lay down on the floormats with the blanket tucked over me, and hoped that I looked like a lumped up blanket and not a human being.

"Make sure the garage door goes down. I don't want anyone going inside the house."

"I will," Jed answered in the tone of voice that said he already knew what to do, but if it made me feel better to tell him, he'd humor me. I heard the garage door open, and then the vehicle started forward, paused, and then lurched to the left. I braced myself between the back seat and the front passenger seat since I didn't have anything to hold onto. The engine roared, vibrating through my body as Jed accelerated down the street and then slowed before making an abrupt turn. I didn't hear the turn signal.

"Stay down, and hold on," he ordered as the car made another quick turn and accelerated.

"Are they following us?"

"Yes," was the only answer I got. I stayed quiet and held on as best I could. There wasn't enough room for me to move too much, so as long as he didn't hit anything, I'd be fine. I tried to keep track of what road he was on but my mental map got lost after the third turn. Were we on Gillham, or had he gone farther? I couldn't tell, and then he turned again. The seconds felt like they slowed as I listened to the roar of the engine changing gears and the dizzying turns that Jed took at what felt like high speed.

It felt like an eternity before the car slowed and Jed spoke again. "I don't see him anymore. You can get up, but try to keep your head out of sight just in case."

I slid into the backseat and fumbled the seatbelt on while Jed kept to the side streets, leading us back to the clinic. I bent over at an awkward angle that I thought kept my head out of sight but allowed me to see the passing tree limbs through the upper parts of the windows.

He drove past the clinic once, I could tell from the signage on the shop fronts, and then turned around in the blood bank parking lot. "I could see a car parked in back, a green sedan."

I sneaked a glance over his shoulder but couldn't see it from the angle we were at. "Rita drives a green sedan."

Jed made a non-committal noise as Chaz's Audi drove by on Main Street and pulled into the parking lot. I texted Ty for confirmation.

"Rita's the only one there right now. Ty says the clinic's closed for the lunch hour." I never seemed to manage a formal lunch hour when I was working, but the residents who were covering for me had strict standards around how many hours they could work. Jed pulled into the parking lot, choosing a spot next to the building where my car wouldn't be seen from the front.

"I think it's safe. You can come out."

I checked to make sure I didn't sense any other spirits inside and then slid out of the car, jogging the few steps to the back door of the clinic, feeling both ridiculous and exposed.

Rita sprinted down the hallway, her long brown curls bouncing as she ran. She grabbed me in a fierce hug before I made it all the way through the door.

"My God, Anna! Is everything okay? I've been so worried. You're all over the news." She sucked in a breath as Jed followed me through the doorway. "Hello, Jed." Rita drew out the hello so it was more suggestive than a greeting tended to be.

"I'm fine," I drew her attention back to me, "and don't believe everything you see on TV," I cautioned her. She laughed, a tinkling sound that contrasted with the tired building.

"You're an awesome doctor, but don't worry, I'm not following the miracle craze. It has kept us busy here the last two days."

"Sorry. Hey, we don't have lots of time—I have to get back to the farm, but we need some supplies. Mind if I raid the supply closet?"

"Of course not! Everything here is yours, and I can reorder anything we need." She wrapped an arm around my shoulder and drew me towards the room in question, lowering her voice as if that would keep the others in the small hallway from hearing us. "I'm so glad you're still seeing Jed. This is wonderful, tell me everything."

"Soon," I promised, hoping that the day did come when we could share a glass of wine again and enjoy a long chat.

"When are you coming back?" She asked the same question every time I talked to her, and I still didn't have a different answer.

"I don't know."

Ty helped me raid the supply closet while Rita took notes on what we were making off with. Since I owned the clinic, I felt justified in taking any supplies we might need. It was a lot easier to get what we needed from a well-stocked supply room than the local pharmacy, and Rita could reorder what they needed. In order to keep our accountant happy, I always paid the clinic back for anything I took for my personal use. Rita didn't question what we needed the supplies for, and we didn't tell her, though I knew she'd wonder.

Liter bags of lactated ringers and their IV start kits, pre-packaged surgical sets, ligature, and packets of sterile gauze went into boxes that Ty loaded into my backseat. Ty and I each took a supply of latex gloves in our respective sizes, boxes of alcohol pads and single-use packets of antibacterial ointment. Ty grabbed his stethoscope and ransacked the collection of bandages while I picked through the towering stack of mail in my office, relegating much of it to the recycle bin.

With the local teaching hospital covering the clinic in my absence, any mail of importance—labs and reports from other doctors—had all been handled by their residents.

We drove north again in a two-car caravan, my Subaru followed by Chaz's Audi. Both cars stopped on the north side of the city at a members-only bulk food store, and we wasted an hour while I worked my way through Ned's shopping list. Jed refused to stay in the car, so he and Chaz pushed carts while Ty and I loaded them to the brim.

"What the hell are they going to do with sixty pounds of dried beans?" Chaz muttered while I pointed at the twenty-five-pound bags of wheat flour and held up five fingers to Ty.

I didn't answer Chaz, because I didn't know for sure, but Ned had a survivalist streak in him. He was intrigued by the idea of long-term self-sufficiency. I knew he and Carrie had some pretty serious food stores already, but it was clear that they were adding to the warehouse. In case. The reasoning used to be in case of mass computer failure, or nuclear war, but ghosts were as good a reason as any to be prepared.

Chaz raised one eyebrow at the four-figure total while I tried not to flinch and handed over my credit card. We distributed the weight of our purchases between the two vehicles. Massive sacks of grains, brown rice, and dried beans stacked in neat layers that caused my vehicle's frame to lower a few inches over the tires.

"I don't think I've ever had this much weight in it." I handed Ty a five-pound can of diced tomatoes that he set into his backseat before turning around for the next one. Several family-sized packages of mixed pasta followed.

"Who does he think he's going to be feeding?" Ty turned back for another item and I handed him a box filled with large containers of spices. Salt, bay leaves, cinnamon, a variety of chili powders, paprika, and peppercorns. They weren't organic, which Carrie wouldn't like, but in the event of an apocalypse, you couldn't be too picky.

"Us, I guess." He loaded in several boxes filled with grains while I broke open the packages of toilet paper and paper towels and wedged them into open nooks and crannies. Ned was preparing for a nuclear winter. Not one caused by weapons, but Armageddon from the dead.

With the shopping delay, it was late afternoon by the time we neared the farm. I called Grayson but his phone went to voicemail.

"What time are they planning to perform the exorcism?" Jed asked.

"Sometime this afternoon. I'm not sure when." I tapped my fingers on the steering wheel in an impatient staccato while I directed the car off the highway and onto a side road. I should have reached out to Grayson sooner. Was I missing it? Had it gone well? What if the person wasn't possessed by a ghost? What emotional harm might the ceremony cause them?

"Don't fret," Jed offered. "He will return your call as soon as he is able. I failed to stifle a snicker. "What?" He looked offended.

"We don't really use the word 'fret' much these days. It sounded funny." More so when it came from a large, formidable man.

He tilted his head sideways at me. "And it amuses you?"

"It does."

"Then I shall endeavor to use it more frequently. I find that I like the sounds you make when you are happy."

My laughter came out in a snort I couldn't suppress, followed by a series of giggles. Jed stared at me, bemused, as I pulled off the highway.

"I amuse you."

"Sometimes I could forget that you aren't from this century, and then you use words like 'endeavor' and 'fret'." I didn't point out that it made him sound more like someone's sweet granny than an ancient warrior.

I turned onto the private road that led to my farm and pulled over as I realized Ned was on the corner with his chainsaw.

"What the heck?" I mused, killing the engine and getting out. The Audi slid past me and stopped in the middle of the drive, but Ty and Chaz stayed in their car.

"What are you doing?" I yelled over the noise of the chainsaw and zipped my sweater up, hugging my arms to my chest. I felt the winter chill through the thin fabric.

Ned killed the engine on his chainsaw and I repeated my question. "I'm cutting these trees down," he answered as if it were the most rational thing in the world.

"I can see that." I glared up at him, resisting the urge to grab him by the ear like his mother used to do when he sassed her. "Why are you chopping the trees down?"

Ned wasn't in the habit of arbitrarily cutting trees down, and if he needed more firewood, he'd harvest it from a naturally downed tree in the woods, not a green cut along the drive. There were plenty of fallen limbs and trunks to choose from in our woods, all well-cured and most likely to decompose before we could use them.

"I'm clearing space to install the new gate." He lifted his chin in an adamant challenge. He wore heavy canvass coveralls, work boots, and safety goggles. Wisps of brown hair escaped from underneath the orange cap that Carrie had knitted for him. The police had confiscated his Colt handgun after the shooting as part of their investigation, but he had a backup strapped to his waist.

I didn't feel inclined to argue with him about the gate, but we usually made decisions about changes to the property together, since we were equally responsible for the expenses on our shared road and lands. When it came down to it, though, I trusted his judgment. If he thought we needed a gate, then we would have one.

"Of course you are. You can tell me about it later."

"Did you shop?"

"All of your survivalist needs are taken care of."

The goggles came off so he could impress upon me the importance of the situation. "This isn't funny, Anna. What you just bought might last the six of us ninety days."

His words took my flippant mood down a notch. "Right. Well, I brought some stuff from the house too." That sounded pretty lame. I was packing up canned goods from my home pantry while Ned was figuring out how to keep all of us fed long term, if we needed it.

"Where do you want everything?"

"In your cellar, if you can store it there."

"I have some space, but I'll need a bunch of plastic bins or something, in case I get mice."

"You have a cat."

"Luna is not an awesome mouser." She also didn't go outside, but I didn't point that out.

His brow furrowed. "I'll get you a barn cat."

I crossed my arms. "Ned Joules, I am not locking a feral cat in my root cellar."

"Fine." He sighed and rolled his eyes. "I'll bring you some storage bins in a bit."

"Thank you. We'll head on up to the house and get unpacked."

"Your face looks pretty bad," Ned informed me, as polite as ever.

"Thanks. I'd already noticed that."

"Are you okay?"

I shuffled my boots in the slush coating our drive. "I guess. How about you?"

He shrugged and fired up the chainsaw again, turning back to his task. *Great. Ned's mad at me too.* Not that I could blame him.

"Does he need assistance?" Jed asked when I got back in the car.

"I don't know. He says he's clearing space so he can put in a gate."

"Good. We are in need of fortifications."

"We are?" I was confused.

"Indeed. Your home is too accessible."

"I live in the middle of nowhere," I reminded him, glancing at the trees and farmland around us.

"Off a road anyone can access."

"I don't think very many people know where I live," I protested. Jed gave me a level stare that reminded me that a number of ghosts had found their way to me. Adonijah had been able to drive straight to my front door and there wasn't much to stop him, or anyone else from doing it again. Still, a gate seemed like something that pretentious people had, and we were farmers. We used fences to keep livestock safe, not to keep people off our land.

I tried to imagine how a gate would change the look of our landscape and failed. Starting the engine, I flashed my lights at the Audi so they'd know we were ready, and Chaz headed for the long hill that divided the valley that Ned and I lived in.

Coming down the hill into my side of the valley brought a sense of relief. Anxiety that I hadn't realized I was holding on to flowed out of me. I was home. It felt like it had been a long journey over the past two days to get back to where I belonged.

The brick two-story bungalow where I'd grown up was nestled into the snow-covered valley in front of an iced-over pond. It normally looked like something out of a quaint children's movie, but with the cracked helicopter in the field to the south of the house, it was ready for the final scene in a surreal horror film. Adonijah had been responsible for the helicopter crash, I was certain, but the official inquiry blamed it on the weather. I'd been assured that as soon as the weather permitted, they'd remove the shell of the craft from my field, but until then, I was stuck with it.

Some people went on cruises or skiing in the mountains, but I took all of my vacations at the farm. Before the ghosts had come, I'd spent my winters ice skating on the pond. All summer long I rode my horse through the wood-covered hills behind the house. When you had land, there was always something that needed to be taken care of. Tending my aunt's garden and mending the rifts in the fences my uncle built gave me a sense of peace. I'd grown up here doing the same things. Sometimes I wished I had traveled more, seen the world, but this farm was a part of my life. For all I'd tried to escape it with a life in the city, I was tied to the land here as much as Ned was. Every time I drove in, I felt the same blend of longing and love.

"What's wrong?" Jed asked.

"Nothing. I was just being nostalgic." I pulled in next to Chaz's Audi and got out. The woman who spent her holidays here didn't exist anymore. The world had changed and she was changing with it.

Two days had passed since I'd been home, but I felt like a lifetime of changes had occurred since then. I opened the front door to find my black cat blinking with reproach from the fourth stair. She yowled her complaint at having been left alone so long.

"I'm sorry, Luna, but I know Carrie checked in on you." I greeted her with chin scratches. She walked into the parlor to my right and jumped onto the small sofa, her pride appeased. I passed through the wood-lined dining room with its mahogany table for eight and into the small farmhouse kitchen.

The house was warm, and the cat had food and a full bowl of water, further evidence that Carrie had been there to care for her. She hadn't just taken care of the cat, though. She'd left a pile of provisions in the fridge. I lifted the lid on a large cast iron pot to find red beans and ground meat in a tomato broth. Carrie had left us chili, and she'd made enough to feed a small army.

The small house reverberated with the sounds of feet traipsing upstairs as Ty and Chaz moved back into their small guest room.

Jed carried my espresso maker into the kitchen and set it on the counter, sweat beading his brow. He leaned against the counter.

I laid my hand on his cheek. He was clammy, but not feverish. "You need to rest."

"After we get everything in."

"No. Now. You know you're exhausted. You aren't Superman." Jed gave me a blank stare. "You don't know who that is." I shook my head, adding the movie to a list of things we should watch when we had time. "Look, just go upstairs and get into bed for a while so you don't end up back in the hospital."

Jed turned and walked out of the kitchen making it clear he didn't like being bossed around. I waited in the kitchen until I heard his heavy footsteps on the stairs. The fact that he didn't argue with me told me how bad he must be feeling. Deciding I'd force him into a mini-physical after he'd rested, I installed my espresso machine next to the drip coffeemaker with satisfaction. In sharp contrast to my modern dwelling in the city, I'd kept the farmhouse almost as my aunt and uncle had left it when they'd died, and the shiny silver Italian contraption looked ridiculous and out of place. No matter, though. We'd have much better coffee.

Chaz deposited two large sacks of flour on my kitchen table. "Where do you want all of this?"

"The mudroom, I guess."

"What about your root cellar?"

"Not until we get some solid storage bins. There's no way to keep mice out of there."

It took us another half hour to unload all the dry goods from the car and stash them in the mudroom in a way that left space to walk through. I was sweating and cursing my lack of fitness by the end of my eighth trip. By my last load, I'd lost count of the number of times I'd gone up and down the porch stairs. Ty and Chaz, who kept fit with their gym membership, looked like they were enjoying an easy workout, which annoyed me more.

# CHAPTER FIVE

I PULLED MY CELL PHONE out of my pocket, registering the lack of signal with a mental shrug. We were too far out, and too low in the valley for good cell phone reception. I could see a missed call from Grayson, but there was no hope of calling him back on the cell phone. I looked up his number with one hand while I grabbed the landline with the other and dialed.

"This is Father Harwell," he answered with formality.

"Grayson, it's Anna. I tried to call you earlier but I didn't get through." I tucked the handset between my shoulder and my ear and used both hands to start putting away the groceries we'd brought with us from the condo. Ty and Chaz had gone upstairs to shower.

Grayson relaxed into familiarity as if we'd been friends for years instead of a few days. "Where are you?"

"At my house, just outside of Trenton."

"Matthew isn't doing very well."

I paused, one hand outstretched towards the cabinet, holding a can of beans. "Matthew?"

"Father Costas. He performed the rites of exorcism and now he isn't doing well."

"I see." I set the can down and leaned back against the counter so I could give Grayson my full attention. "How is he not doing well? How is the person he performed it on doing?"

"He seems shaky. I think it worked because my congregant seems herself again."

"Maybe I should look him over?" Shaky I might be able to help with.

"I think you should," Grayson answered. "If you are willing."

*Where did the ghost go?* I wasn't sure if exorcism would work in the same way my power did, or just remove the ghost from the body it was possessing. If the ghost hadn't moved on, there might be another reason Father Costas wasn't feeling well.

It was close to dinner time, and thanks to Carrie I had enough chili to feed every Catholic priest in the diocese. These two wouldn't be any trouble.

"Why don't you guys come here? I can check on Father Costas and see if he needs medical help, or just some downtime after his . . . ordeal. We have plenty of supper to share too, so you can stay for dinner and we can talk."

"We don't want to impose. We could meet you—" Grayson began.

"It's not an imposition." My tone said unless he truly had other plans for supper, he didn't have much choice in the matter. *I haven't even been home for an hour, and I don't want to leave again. Ever.*

"Thank you," Grayson spoke in a rush. He was clearly still worried, and I was glad I'd insisted. "I will bring him to you," Grayson promised. "What's your address?"

I gave him directions and then hung up as Jed walked in with another sack of groceries. He didn't look as tired as he had earlier.

"Where did that come from?"

"It was on the dining room table. I thought you'd want it in here, or I can put it in the mudroom if you prefer." Instead of heading outside, he leaned against the counter. "Are you well?" He reached out in a slow motion, like he was approaching a scared deer. He brushed a few stray strands of hair off my cheek and over my shoulder.

"I'm fine. Just trying to get things put away. Did you get some rest?"

"Yes." Smoothing a gentle finger over the bruise on my cheek, he closed the small space between us. When he spoke his voice was low enough that we wouldn't be overheard. "You saved me."

"You saved me too, remember?"

"It was a great risk you took." He bent down, his lips brushing against my ear. Fighting to ignore the sensation, I focused on the conversation. We had houseguests so it wasn't the best time to get frisky in the kitchen. "I could have hurt you."

I shivered at the combination of danger and sensuality in his voice. "I trusted you not to."

"I had no way of knowing what harm I might do. I've never

done that before." He'd never been inside someone without possessing them, and I'd never willingly let a spirit inside me.

"A first time for us both." I held on to his jacket to steady myself as he gave me a slow kiss that was full of promise. He leaned me back against the cabinetry with a satisfied smile, as if he could tell the exact impact he'd had on me.

I took a step back to give myself some space from his intensity and he shook his long curls off his face, helping to break the mood, and exposing the healed scar on his forehead.

"I think I should offer Ned my help. May I borrow your car?"

"Are you sure you feel up to it?" He'd had a tracheal tube down his throat a little over twenty-four hours ago, and had been tired enough to take a nap in the middle of the day. I extracted the keys from my jeans pocket and handed them over when he glared at me.

*Pick your battles, Anna,* I reminded myself. It was a phrase I'd heard my aunt use, and felt like I was starting to understand what she'd meant by it. Jed had to still be feeling like hell, but he wasn't going to let that stop him from doing whatever he felt like he should.

"Fathers Costas and Harwell are coming for supper."

"Very good. We can strategize."

It sounded like Jed had a military discussion in mind, while Grayson and I were more concerned with helping the people who were possessed. Jed and Chaz had told me more than once that I needed to go on the offensive. They weren't wrong about that, but it was a hard leap to make when all I'd ever been was a healer. Jed turned on his heel and strode out of the kitchen as if he'd never been ill.

While Jed headed down the drive, I turned my attention back to unpacking. I'd brought more clothes than I had room for in my small bedroom without reorganizing. I left half of them packed up and shoved the suitcase under my bed, to be dealt with when I had more time. Chaz and Ty made themselves useful by starting fires in the living room fireplace and in the small sunroom off the dining room. They wouldn't warm the whole house, but they helped take off the chill of winter. The house felt cozier with the fireplaces lit.

Jed had chopped enough wood in the last two months to last me a couple of winters. I hoped he did it because he enjoyed it, not because he thought he wouldn't be here at some point in the future to do it. "The future" was a concept I didn't have time to think about.

I heard the cars coming up the driveway and joined Ty and Chaz on the front porch. Jed was leading an aged silver sedan down the drive. He parked and waited at the bottom of the porch stairs. I didn't need to ask why he'd come back, Jed knew what Father Costas' problem was and didn't want to leave me alone with him. The second soul in the backseat occupant stood out like a new color. I took a deep breath, centering my energy and bracing myself for the inevitable pain that came with releasing a ghost.

"Father Costas is possessed. Let's put him in the living room," I ordered from the porch. Jed and Chaz obeyed without hesitation like they were used to being my nursing staff. "Ty, we'll need—"

"I'm on it. IV kit, lactated ringers, and steroids."

I nodded, not taking my eyes off the man slumped over in the backseat of the sedan. Jed and Chaz began attempting to extract him from the vehicle.

Grayson joined me on the porch once it was clear that Chaz and Jed could handle Costas. He turned his solemn attention to me, assessing the damage to my face, and I braced myself. Tall and thin, with a thick thatch of white hair and bushy white eyebrows over eyes the color of slate, Grayson broke through my filters. I felt like I couldn't hide anything when I talked to him. He saw me in a way that I didn't think anyone else did, and I'd done something I didn't want to admit to him. When he spoke, his tone was controlled and reassuring, but I thought I caught an undertone of anger, his reaction to my bruised face.

"How are you holding up?"

*Forgive me, Father, for I have sinned . . .* I couldn't look him in the eye without thinking of the still form of the man I'd killed. I tried to shake the image away and build some emotional distance. I couldn't afford to be that raw right now.

"I'll be fine."

His attention didn't stray as Jed and Chaz manhandled Costas past us and into the doorway of the house and I wavered under the intensity of Grayson's regard. He could see the lie in me, I knew.

"You didn't cause this, Anna. It's not your fault, and I know that."

My eyes welled with tears and I tried to blink them back as I nodded. "I know it isn't. Thank you." It was important to me that he didn't blame me for the things I'd done. "I need to see to your friend. What happened?" I redirected the conversation, knowing he'd recognize the diversion for what it was.

"He performed the rites of exorcism." Grayson's level stare said that he wasn't letting me get away with any bullshit, but he understood that Costas needed help and that had to come first. "There was a strange moment after it ended."

"Strange how?"

"Matthew was overcome from the intensity of it, I think. He left the room. My congregant seemed more comfortable, which made me think the prayer was successful. I went to talk to Matthew and found him slumped against the wall. He said he was dizzy and didn't feel well."

"He has a ghost in him."

Grayson absorbed that before answering. "I was afraid he might."

"Did he have one before the procedure, do you think?"

"It's a rite, not a procedure," Grayson corrected me, "and I don't believe he did."

"So maybe the exorcism gets the ghost out of its host, but doesn't send it on."

"That thought occurred to me as well."

"And when the ghost left, it chose to possess Father Costas instead."

"Can you take care of him?"

"I should be able to help." *I've only killed one person banishing ghosts, so the odds are in his favor.*

Grayson followed me into the parlor where the guys had propped our houseguest on the sofa. Matthew was wearing a black shirt with a white clerical collar, black pants, and well-shined black shoes. His brown hair was so dark it was almost black and his eyes were the deep blue of the afternoon sky in summer.

Jed stood next to me, close enough that my shoulder brushed his elbow. "I'd like to talk to the spirit first," he said.

*Long lost friend?* I bit my lip to again keep from spouting my sarcastic internal commentary and hoped the gesture looked thoughtful.

"As long as we don't leave it in there for too much longer. I'm hoping that the adrenergic response won't be as severe since the spirit hasn't been in residence very long."

Adoni had been in me for something shy of five minutes, and I'd been pretty sick, but Jed had also cut me with his kilij, freeing my soul from my body. I had no way of knowing what additional impact that had. Chaz, who'd been possessed for more than twenty-four hours had been worse off. I didn't have any empirical evidence on whether the length of possession impacted the level of illness, but it was a theory I was working on.

Ty trotted down the stairs with the supplies we'd need to help the priest out. "I'm ready," he announced.

I felt my lips curve in a wry smile thinking about how nervous I'd been inserting a needle into Carrie's aunt the week before. "I'm glad you're here. Last time I had to start an IV myself."

"Dear Lord." Ty's eyes widened in horror. "Did the patient survive?" I swatted him on the arm, glad for the moment of comic relief.

"Barely." A few chuckles of cautious laughter filled the room, lightening the mood until Jed moved, looming over the priest on the sofa.

Our mirth sobered into silence as Costas' head lolled towards Jed, his eyes fixed open in a stare that lasted too long before he blinked.

"You can hear me?" Jed's tone demanded a reply and Matthew's head shifted a little. Jed took it as an affirmative gesture. "Am I talking to Father Costas or someone else?"

No answer, but the eyes narrowed a bit. Jed glanced up at me and shook his head. It wasn't Costas, but that wasn't a surprise.

"Who are you working for?" Jed tried. A small smile curved the lips but whoever was inside the priest didn't make an effort to speak. "What is it you want?"

Again, silence. Jed shifted, and I worried he was losing his temper. This wasn't a prisoner he could take more extreme questioning measures with, and his sense of what was appropriate sometimes differed with modern era thoughts on human rights. I didn't even want to know what methods he could come up with to make someone talk.

I stepped in and laid a hand on Jed's shoulder, and he stilled under my touch as if he could hear my thoughts. Costas' eyes focused on me, though it seemed like it took some effort.

"Do you know who I am?" I asked. Costas' gaze narrowed, and he nodded once. "Then you know that I'm the Magos." I used the Council's label for people with my ability, hoping that it meant something to this ghost. "You know what I can do?"

Another wary nod. I didn't like referring to myself as a witch but the ghosts seemed to understand what it meant.

"I'll offer you a deal." Jed raised an eyebrow at that but didn't interrupt me. "I can't allow you to keep the priest, or anyone else. If you answer our questions truthfully, though, I won't release you as long as you give your word that you won't possess another living being, and that you give up this body that you are in."

He glared at me but didn't respond. I wondered if the lack of speech meant he hadn't been entirely successful in taking control of the priest. I didn't know him well but Costas seemed like someone who had a strong spirit.

"Father Costas, if you can hear me, I know you are fighting." I gripped his shoulder and stared into his eyes. "I won't let this spirit stay in you. You will be free in a few minutes."

"Anna, get it out of him. What are you waiting for?" Grayson protested.

"I don't disagree with you but Jed is right. We need information. I won't let it stay there for long." My words were a promise to Grayson and a warning to the ghost.

Grayson's jaw clenched. "This isn't right."

"Please, trust me." I knew he wasn't happy about it, but he didn't protest further.

"Father Costas, if you can, let us talk to the ghost. You might have to give up a little control but you'll have it all back in a minute."

If Costas thought I was holding him hostage, he wasn't wrong. From the looks that I was getting from my friends, they thought I'd turned into a monster they didn't recognize. Jed, on the other hand, was nodding his approval, as though I'd become fluent in the language he'd been trying to teach me all along. My mouth flooded with nausea and I forced myself to swallow. If Costas being tortured for a few quick minutes gave us helpful information, I had to do it. It could save the life of one of my friends. That's what I told myself.

"Let's start with an easy question," I suggested. "Who were you, and when were you alive?"

Something shifted inside Costas and his eyes seemed to dull, the blue hue somehow a bit less brilliant. The ghost inside of Costas seemed to consider my question before answering in a voice that sounded rough with lack of use.

"I was a mother. I died in a car crash. I've been trying to watch over my babies, but then they said I could really go back."

The knot in my belly lessened a notch as I realized this wasn't a fighter. "What's your name?"

"Margaret," she spoke with reluctance, my threats hanging heavy over her.

"Hi, Margaret. I'm Anna. How old are your children?"

"Young enough they need their mother."

"You can't change the course of life and death," Jed spoke with a sudden kindness he didn't often show others.

Margaret's eyes went a little wild. "You did. Why can't the rest of us?" I didn't want to get off on a tangent about the morality of Jed possessing a soulless body. There were some arguments we weren't able to win.

"Who told you that you could live again?" I asked.

Margaret shrugged. "The one that spoke had a strange name. Adon-uh something."

"Adonijah," Jed supplied. Margaret nodded, looking a little frightened.

"Was Adonijah just a ghost, or had he taken a body?"

"He was in his spirit form." I exhaled in a rush of relief while she looked from me to Jed, and then appealed to the priest she could see, her voice trembling with fear. "He said we had God's blessing."

Grayson stepped forward, clearing his throat while he considered his words. "My child, God doesn't sanction taking life."

"I didn't kill anyone," she protested.

"You were trying to take another person from their life and their family by force. And now you have my brother, Father Costas."

"I'm not a bad person." She shook her head with such pained vigor I feared Matthew would have a sore neck. "My babies need me. I have to be able to take care of them." I blinked back a few tears, surprised by the rush of emotion her words evoked. I didn't know what it was like to be a mother but I could imagine.

"I'm sorry, Margaret, but you can't steal someone else's body. Even if you went back to your family, they wouldn't recognize you.

They'd never believe who you are and you'd be depriving another person of their own life. It's wrong."

Her hands flexed, and an expression of anger passed over Costas' face for a moment, but was quickly replaced by wide eyes filling with tears. People say love is the most powerful emotion, but anger and regret could both top that in intensity.

"What else did Adonijah tell you?" Jed inserted, distracting her from the grief my words were about to set off.

"That you would try to stop us, but that we could go home to our families if we still had them. If we didn't have any place to go, we could live as we chose."

"What happened with you?"

"It's hard, taking them over." She bit the words out in a rush of frustration. "Not easy like he said it would be."

"Because the host fights you?" Chaz asked with clenched teeth.

"That's right. I thought I chose a good one, a nice girl, but she was always fighting me, screaming in my ear."

"She wants to live her life, too." I tried to keep my tone controlled, blocking the thought of the young woman who'd fought this intruder in her own body.

"I felt bad about that. I really did. But my babies . . ." Margaret trailed off. Even while she recognized that her position was wrong, she would do anything for her children. Most parents I knew would.

"That girl you took was someone's baby, too," I pointed out, and she looked away from me to Grayson like he could rescue her.

Jed didn't ask anything else, and I didn't have any more questions. The kindest thing would be to release her, but I'd promised not to. If I didn't I knew there was the chance she'd attempt to steal another body to return to her family. While I struggled with my decision, Grayson whispered in my ear.

"I'd like to spend a few minutes alone with her."

I hesitated before answering, while I calculated the risks. With Margaret, though, he wasn't in any danger, and Costas was stable enough.

"Okay. Guys, let's go to the other room." We made our way to the kitchen and took up awkward spots along the small counter space.

"Is it a good idea to leave her alone with him?" Ty asked.

"He'll be fine. She's not violent, just desperate," I offered and Ty nodded. She couldn't take over anyone else here without me knowing, and she didn't seem strong enough to control anyone. Not when the screaming bothered her so much. I suppressed a shiver at the thought.

"How many more people are there that are possessed right now?" Chaz asked.

"I suspect many." Jed weighed in with a degree of calm that I didn't feel.

I hopped up to sit on the counter like I had when I was a little girl, letting my upper back rest against the upper cabinets.

"I don't know what the ratio is of spirits who are strong enough to control another person to those who aren't. If we knew that we might be able to extrapolate the total number of possessed based on the number of people who are known to be ill." Jed looked at me with something akin to confusion while the others were more thoughtful.

"That's an interesting idea," Chaz commented.

Ty leaned back against the kitchen counter, folding his arms in front of him. "I don't think Margaret's going to be a reliable source of information in that department. She seems to know less about this than we do."

"Jed?" I turned towards him, concerned that this was another area of the ghost world where he was going to be less than forthcoming. "If you took ten ghosts, how many of them would be strong enough to possess someone completely?"

One eyebrow lifted as he settled into his seat at the kitchen table and stretched his legs out underneath it. "There are so many differences among the dead, I don't know that I could answer that."

Chaz sat next to him and leaned in, challenging him to come up with a better answer. "I'm sure there are, but if you had to come up with an average, what would your guess be? Are there more spirits that are strong enough to control someone, or fewer?"

Jed's right eyebrow moved a notch closer to the ceiling. Any further and it would become part of his abundant hairline.

"Fewer. Perhaps two of the ten could control someone, and four would attempt but not be strong enough."

"And the ones that aren't strong enough?" Ty asked.

"Those are our hospital patients," I reminded him. The ghosts that were unsuccessful had host bodies that were visibly ill. The result was the current epidemic of an unexplainable "virus" in hospitals in the surrounding area.

"What about the rest of them? What would the last four do?" Chaz encouraged.

"Many of the dead that have stayed on this Earth are simpler than that. I don't believe they would understand the concept well enough to try."

I thought of Marnie, my sweet childhood friend who had the spirit of sunshine and stayed forever within the ruined walls of the cabin she'd lived in. She wouldn't try to possess anyone, either. The one time I'd seen her leave the confines of her home was when my life had been in danger and she'd come to help me stay with the living.

"Let's assume it's a one-to-five ratio. For every ghost strong enough to possess someone, there are five who won't be successful, or won't even try," Chaz prompted.

"And if you had one hundred thousand ghosts hell-bent on taking over the world, twenty percent of them would be able to take over a host." I looked around at the group. "That would be twenty thousand, with another forty thousand hosts that are sick, and the remaining forty thousand sitting on the sidelines wondering what the hell is going on."

Silence held the room while we thought that over. I didn't know what anyone else was thinking but I was trying to guess how many ghosts might still be on Earth and what twenty percent of that number was. Were there millions of the dead roaming the Earth? Or was the number lower than that? Five hundred thousand? What percentage of people lingered after death?

"So what if they do take over those people? Why is it our problem to fight it?" Ty asked.

Chaz looked at him like he was a stranger ranting on the street corner. "What are you talking about? We can't let them—"

"I'm not saying we will," Ty cut him off. "I'm asking a question."

"I'm answering it. If we don't fight it, we all die. We lose our freedom, just like if a rogue nation took over our country."

"Chaz is right, Ty." I tried to stay out of their arguments, but this wasn't a lovers' quarrel. "You don't have to take up arms, but I do. I'm not ready to lose our world to the dead."

"What's the worst case scenario here?" Chaz asked.

I'd spent some time thinking about it, and thought I had the answer. "The ghosts get access to the nuclear launch codes and start a war, and then everyone on the planet dies."

"They don't want to kill off all life. They want to live again," Jed said. "They won't start a war that could kill the planet. I don't think so, anyway."

"Very comforting." Ty's sarcasm was lost on Jed, who gave Ty a solemn nod and continued while I swallowed an inappropriate giggle.

"The worst case is that they spread unchecked, taking over the right people so they control your countries and your resources. This government you call a democracy would be gone. It could be a worse political situation than when I was living. If they got control of the military, then a feudal society could reemerge."

"Dictatorship at its worst." Chaz stepped in, in attorney mode. "The utilities could fail if they weren't properly maintained—we could regress a hundred years technologically. We'd also see a failure of the judicial system, reverting back to a time when the police were the judge, jury, and executioner."

I didn't feel like laughing anymore. I imagined a new society where the dead ruled the living, controlling every resource, and forcing the rest of us into a system of servitude.

"Anna?" Grayson's voice interrupted my macabre train of thought.

"Yes?" I brought myself back to the present.

He lingered in the doorway. "I believe Margaret has moved on and Matthew isn't feeling very well."

He wouldn't be, if the ghost was gone. I pushed myself off the counter, landing on my feet with a thud, and followed Grayson back to the parlor. Ty fell into step behind me, the clinician I always wanted by my side.

"What happened with Margaret?" I asked.

"She relinquished her hold on both Matthew and this world. She'll be at peace now."

"How did you do that?" Ty inserted before I could.

"I prayed with her," Grayson informed us, matter of fact, as if he cured people through prayer on a daily basis.

I didn't have any way of knowing if Margaret had gone on to

wherever she belonged, but all traces of her spirit were gone. She wasn't in the priest and I didn't sense the presence of another soul in the immediate area. The nearest ghost I could sense was the one living nearby in the old settler's cabin. Marnie's intrepid light stood out in the evening darkness like the soft flicker of candlelight.

I'd never heard of anyone else being able to send a ghost on, until today. *Did Grayson bring her to peace through her faith, and that allowed her to move on?* I wished I knew the answer. It could be a critical piece to helping us overcome this, something beyond me that might be able to help save humanity.

Father Matthew Costas lay back on my couch looking as exhausted as if he'd run a marathon, although with a gray pallor to his skin that made me worry he was preparing to either faint or vomit on the floral couch.

"I often wondered what it was like to be possessed by a demon," he informed me with an attempt at a smile, "but I underestimated how unpleasant it is."

Ty handed me his stethoscope while he fastened a blood pressure cuff around the priest's upper arm.

Margaret didn't qualify as a demon, but I didn't point that out to Matthew. I knew how awful it felt to have something inside you, controlling you.

"I couldn't have imagined it, either," I told him. I put the ends of the stethoscope in my ears and pressed the metal bell against the left side of Matthew's chest, repositioning it a couple times until I had memorized the rapid tapping of his heartbeat.

"He's a little tachy but not too bad," I told Ty as he loosened the blood pressure cuff.

"Blood pressure's a hundred and ten over seventy," Ty responded.

"Get the fluids going and let's hit him with thirty milligrams of dexamethasone. I don't want to delay on the steroids. If we get them into his system this early in the process, it should help."

I sat cross-legged on the floor in front of Matthew while he pushed himself into a sitting position. "Can you tell us what happened?"

He pressed his fingertips together, folding his hands into a pyramid, and rested his head on them. "I was performing the rites of exorcism, and they worked. I could tell . . ."

His voice faltered and I leaned forward and touched his knee. He startled at my touch. "Sorry. What could you tell?"

"You feel it, when the rites work. I could tell the spirit left that young woman and then a moment later, something slammed into me. My chest felt like it was exploding and then I lost control."

"I know what that feels like," I assured him, "and if you want to talk about any of what's happening, I'm happy to talk with you anytime. Right now your body is having what we call an adrenergic response to the spirit possessing you. We need to get you started on steroids and IV fluids to help you recover."

His brow furrowed in confusion. "Why do they call it a virus?"

"There isn't a virus," I reminded him. "Ghosts possessing people upsets their endocrine system. Since the physicians seeing these patients don't understand what's causing that, they assume it's a virus. Viruses are easy to blame."

His eyes wandered up towards the ceiling and he leaned back against the couch again like he was dizzy, or having trouble processing everything I said.

"I'm sorry that I didn't believe you yesterday."

"It's a difficult thing to comprehend." I gave Matthew a wry smile. "Even for a priest, I guess. Ty is going to get you started on the IV."

"Should I take him to the hospital?" Grayson asked. I considered our options.

"I think he's better off here, for the time being. I need to get dinner ready but I think you two should stay for a while. Do you need anything before supper?"

I'd offered the invitation to dinner earlier, but I didn't plan to let Matthew leave the house until I was confident he was improving, whether he wanted to stay or not. If he worsened, he might have to go to the hospital, but I felt more prepared to deal with him than they were.

"Thank you." Grayson accepted again on behalf of both of them and I was relieved that I didn't have to argue about it. "Is there anything I can do to help?"

"If you don't mind helping Ty with Matthew, I'll get things going in the kitchen. We'll eat in about half an hour. I hope you guys like chili."

I turned away while they were in the process of assuring me it was a favorite meal. I wasn't listening. My mind was already back on the problem of what had to be a hundred billion people on Earth who'd ever lived and died. *How many had stayed as ghosts?* I paused in my sunroom, the only place in the house that was empty, to give myself time to think.

If one out of ten had stayed, that was one hundred million spirits to contend with, and a potential twenty million who were capable of controlling a living person. It was a fraction of the world's total population, but in terms of a mass possession event, it would be overwhelming. Even a tenth of that number would be devastating.

We didn't have any indication that Adonijah had been able to reach every ghost in the world—far from it, in fact. The problem didn't seem more widespread than the immediate area. If it was, we'd have reports of the illness coming in from everywhere.

Staring out the window into the remaining twilight, I hoped my assumptions were correct. The burning question was what Adonijah's next move would be. And the Master. What was he up to? Whatever it was, it wouldn't be good. Shoulders set, I made my way back into the kitchen where Jed and Chaz were seated at the table, each with a cold beer. Jed's head lifted at my approach and he held his hand out to me.

I went to him. He wrapped his arm around me and surprised me by pulling me into his side. He didn't engage in many public displays of affection.

"Are you all right?" I asked.

"You look tired," he answered. "Share your burden with us and it won't be so heavy."

I hesitated, searching for a way to put what I was feeling into words. "When this started, it seemed like all the ghosts we ran into were bad. They all had some evil agenda, but Margaret just proved that they aren't all that way. Some of them may just be trying to go back home." Jed gave my side a little squeeze before I pulled away so I could take my seat next to him.

"There are many different agendas among the dead," he agreed.

"It changes things a little bit if they aren't *bad.* Doesn't it?" My voice wavered a little and I thought back to my conversation with

Eli about how the ghosts all had different agendas. Fighting a war against the dead where I was the one who had to choose who lived and who died was harder to come to terms with if they weren't all evil. I wasn't in the habit of releasing ghosts just because they were in our world. I'd only done it if they were distressed, or causing trouble they shouldn't be.

"Good and evil are nice distinctions to draw, but reality isn't that simple," Chaz murmured, his dark eyes evaluating me with sympathy. "Most of us have some combination of both."

"Of course we do—" I started but, Chaz stopped me.

"I'm not sure you can understand it if you haven't been in war before. I saw it on both sides when I was in the marines. The people my commanders said were the enemy—said were evil—it wasn't that simple. Those people were parents, and siblings, and someone's child. They loved and lived, and when they weren't fighting us, they were probably helping little old ladies cross the road and giving what they could to people who were less fortunate than they were.

"On our side, they told us we were the good guys." Chaz's voice dropped an octave. "Some of the men I served with weren't good people. And I wasn't always good, either, while I was out there."

"Thinking that some of these ghosts are good people doesn't make me feel any better about releasing them."

Chaz leaned across the table and covered my hand with his. "In this case, though, aren't you helping the ones that are good too, by sending them on? Don't they belong in heaven, and not here on Earth?" I sometimes forgot that Chaz had grown up Catholic, because he didn't talk about his religion much. Not because he didn't still believe, but because the church wouldn't accept who he loved and said he was sinning because of it.

"I don't know if I'm helping or not," I admitted.

Chaz turned towards Jed with his usual direct manner. "Jed, maybe you can ease Anna's mind on this."

"I do not know what comes after this world. The only ones that would are the Council members that were cast from heaven in the beginning of time."

Did the beginning of time mean when the Big Bang occurred, or when the first humanoids stood upright? Or was he referring to something more recent? My scientific questions stacked up. Since Jed didn't like to talk about the ghost Council, and his grasp on modern day science was stuck in the middle ages, I kept my questions to myself.

"Wouldn't heaven offer more peace than eternal existence here on Earth?" Chaz asked.

"Knowing that whatever lies beyond this existence is more peaceful, and being the one who makes the choice for them are very different things." I'd heard the stars sing and enjoyed that sweet silence of death. That didn't make it my right to banish peaceful spirits from this world. I'd become the gatekeeper, unilaterally deciding what happened to each soul. Chaz himself had warned me about the risk and responsibility that came with that kind of power. I didn't want to become jaded to the moral dilemma it presented. Did I have any right to make that choice for them?

"You didn't choose this battle," Chaz reminded me.

"It doesn't matter whether I chose it or not." I sounded more bitter than I meant to.

"The soldiers never get to choose." Chaz's rebuke was gentle, but the conversation was making me restless and sitting down didn't feel comforting anymore. Extracting the pot of chili from the fridge, I set it on the stove under a low flame. Aunt Ann's favorite iron skillet hung from a hook on the wall above the stove. I set it in the oven and turned the oven dial to preheat.

"Keep in mind the ghosts belong in heaven or hell," Chaz said. "They don't belong here on Earth. And if they are possessing people, no matter what their intention is, they've crossed a line."

"Chaz is correct," Jed said. "Every war has its innocents, but if you don't defeat the army, they will win."

"Margaret wasn't part of an army." I pulled out two mixing bowls, one large and one small, and started extracting the five ingredients I needed for cornbread from the cabinets.

"She was, though." Jed surrendered his chair at the table and took the two steps needed to cross the kitchen to me. He took the canister of flour from my hands and put it on the counter so he had my attention. "She is part of the army, just as much as the ghost that brought a gun into the hospital."

"That's not the same at all." My voice rose in shrill disagreement.

"It is, Anna. They are all distractions, the pieces and pawns that

Adonijah is throwing at us. He hopes that the volume of them will weaken you enough to break you."

"The only defense is to be better at offense," Chaz uttered with finality.

"They choose Adonijah's side when they take over a living being, Anna." Jed's tone softened and his words pulled at me. "They don't have to do it, but they do. That is the only act that matters to you. Once they do that, they have crossed the line and you must destroy them." I guessed that kings had to be good orators to stay in power, and Jed could be persuasive when he wanted to be.

"You're right." I knew in my heart that any spirit possessing another person had to be released, but stories like Margaret's tore at me.

"You are a warrior," Jed reminded me.

"A badass one," Chaz informed me with sincerity. I would have laughed had Grayson not chosen that moment to walk into the kitchen.

Jed turned towards the priest. "And now we have the armies of God on our side."

"As long as we are still serving God's will." Grayson's lips quirked upward in wry amusement.

We weren't much of an army; doctor, lawyer, priest, and former king, but at least I didn't feel like I was quite so alone anymore.

Tears blurred the edges of my vision as I turned back to the flour. "How's Matthew feeling?" I asked Grayson while I measured out the rest of the dry ingredients.

"He's coming to terms with the unbelievable," Grayson answered. I'd been inquiring about his physical health, but if Matthew was focused on the supernatural elements of what was happening, that was a good sign.

"The presence of ghosts can be a difficult concept to get used to."

"He's the diocesan exorcist. He'll come around quickly. This is not the first time he's faced something out of the ordinary."

"Actively seeing spirits try to take over the world, followed by getting possessed yourself is a lot to take in." I cracked an egg into a glass bowl, then added a cup of milk and a quarter cup of vegetable oil.

"Indeed it is." Grayson peered over my shoulder. "Can I help?"

"Set the table?" I nodded towards the drawer with the silverware. "We need knives, forks, and spoons." I glanced at the small kitchen table. I could squeeze six people in there, but it was tight. "We'll be eating in the dining room."

Grayson helped himself to the silverware drawer like it was his own home and I hummed a little with momentary happiness while I scraped my cornbread batter into the hot iron skillet and put it back in the oven. Grayson and I had met a few days before but it felt like I'd known him for much longer. He belonged here, in my little circle of friends.

I checked in on Matthew while the cornbread baked and found him sitting upright, the IV bag balanced above him on the back of the sofa. My formerly anthropophobic cat was sprawled in his lap, purring with satisfaction. Ty was on the floor, organizing the supplies we'd brought from home.

"How's it going in here?"

"I'm all right. Tired. I feel a bit off." Matthew glanced at the IV in his arm and Ty's box of supplies. "You all do this often?"

"Post-ghost resuscitation at home?" I gave him a tired smile. "More often than I'd like to admit."

"How long has this been going on?"

"About two months." I noted his improving color with satisfaction and laid my fingers across the inside of his wrist and felt the steady thrumming of his pulse. Rapid, but not erratic. His skin was dry and warm, although not feverish. "You're a little dehydrated. The faster we can reverse that, the better you'll feel. I'm giving you steroids as well, they help reverse the effects the possession has on you. You're getting treated earlier than anyone else has, so I'm hoping that means you won't be as sick."

"Those patients in the hospital . . ."

"Didn't get fluids and steroids right away, and many of them are still possessed. Learning how to treat this has been an ongoing process for me. Chaz and I were the first test subjects." Matthew's eyes widened a little. "Don't worry. I'll keep a close eye on you. If you'd feel more comfortable, we can move you to the hospital, but I don't think you need it, and they don't necessarily know how to treat you."

He took a moment to consider the options. "I'll stay here with you, if you don't mind."

"That's my preference." It may have sounded arrogant, but he was better off under my care for the time being.

"The authorities won't ever understand what's going on here." Matthew was talking to someone beyond me and I dropped his wrist, turning to find Grayson in the doorway.

"Most of them wouldn't be able to," Grayson agreed. "You didn't either, at first."

"No, I didn't."

"No one does, until they see someone possessed first hand and find out what it means," Ty agreed.

"That's why I need your help in this, Matthew." I took the chair across from the sofa and Grayson sat next to Matthew, careful to not disturb the IV bag. "Aside from using my power, your exorcism and whatever Grayson did with Margaret are the only ways I know to get a possessed ghost out of someone."

Matthew looked concerned. "There are strict limits on performing the rite of exorcism."

"I understand that, but these people are desperate and I can't fix every single one. There were at least fifteen more people at Unionville Regional yesterday that were possessed that I didn't get to, and I don't think this problem is limited to this area. It could be happening worldwide. We need to find a way to help them."

I didn't want to go back to that hospital ever again after everything that had happened there but I didn't have that luxury. Those people needed help and I wouldn't leave them.

"Grayson, you said you didn't use the rite of exorcism on Margaret . . . how did you get her to leave?"

"I prayed with her to help her find peace."

"Would it work with the other ghosts?"

He shrugged. "Perhaps."

"Do you guys know how Father Lombardi was doing?" I asked.

"He was recovering well this morning. He didn't seem to have any injuries from the fire." Matthew frowned. "He never did say why he was there with you."

"Can you enlighten us on that, Anna?" Grayson interjected. Ty's eyes widened a little. He knew the truth but I hadn't shared it with Grayson and Matthew yet. Grayson would believe me, but I was less certain of Matthew.

"There's a lot to tell you, and I don't know how much of it you'll believe."

"Beyond spirits of the dead possessing the living?" Matthew raised an eyebrow. "I'm willing to suspend any disbelief I might have had."

"That will help." I smiled at him. "Let's chat over supper. Ty, can you rig something for Matthew's IV bag?"

"I think I can manage that," Ty said.

"Perfect. I'll let you guys get moved to the dining room. I've got to check on the cornbread."

Jed and Chaz helped me serve dinner by ferrying bowls of chili to the dinner table. Grayson and Matthew sat next to each other with Matthew's IV bag hooked to a coat rack that stood behind him. The elevation was perfect to keep the flow going and I wondered why we hadn't thought of using it as an IV pole before now.

Despite being quiet, Matthew ate well, which I considered a good sign. Grayson made pleasant conversation about the farm and our careers while we ate, saving the talk of ghosts and war for after dinner. The thick dish was spicy and meaty, it was the fulfilling comfort food we all needed. I served bowls of seconds to both Jed and Chaz. When I'd finished scooping up the last of my serving, I drizzled honey on a well-buttered hunk of cornbread and ate it with my fork for dessert. I pushed my empty bowl a few inches away from me. Everyone else was finishing up as well.

"Tell me about the new people who showed up at the hospital?"

"Multiple groups have come to the hospital looking for help since the news reports of . . . healing." Grayson carefully avoided the word "miracle," which I appreciated. "They were told that they had to go elsewhere if they weren't patients at the hospital, or looking for medical care from the hospital staff. The hospital administration wouldn't allow them to stay on the grounds."

"I'm sorry I couldn't get here sooner. Where did they go?"

"Some are in the local motel but there were others that weren't able to afford that option."

"So, they're sleeping in their cars?" Chaz asked.

Grayson considered this, taking a sip of water. "That was my assumption."

"It's too cold for that," Chaz pointed out.

"It is, for people who are ill and unprepared. My parish is opening to them for the time being."

"That's wonderful, Grayson. Thank you." I sounded too surprised and he turned his careful consideration on me.

"Kindness is what we practice in the church, Anna."

"You said you didn't think all of them were possessed. Why are they here?" Chaz was focused on the cause, Grayson the solution.

"They are searching for healing, but what is wrong, I don't know. I saw one man who was in a wheelchair who might have cerebral palsy. There was a woman wearing a scarf over her head who might be a cancer patient."

"People who I won't be able to help," I noted. There were things we didn't have the necessary science to cure, and many things in the realm of specialists that I didn't try to manage. I was in primary care, not neurology or oncology.

Grayson sipped his coffee before he responded. "I suspect that is the case."

"The hope of a miracle when you have an incurable illness is a strong lure to dangle," Matthew pointed out.

"I'm sure it is, but I wasn't dangling cures," I reminded him. "We have the television stations to thank for this particular problem."

"They were following a story that was true," Grayson defended them in his mild manner. "You were helping people that modern medicine couldn't heal."

"Just because people don't understand what's happening doesn't make it a miracle," I reminded him.

"It may appear that way to some."

"Someone needs to convince them to go back home. Their conditions won't be improved by spending the night on the floor of your church."

Major cities lacked the necessary resources to cope with homelessness. Our small town didn't have shelters or the resources to cope with an influx of people with high levels of medical needs. Without Grayson's help, they'd be sleeping in their cars.

"The parish is making them as comfortable as we can." He leveled the full intensity of his kind gaze on me. "I would appreciate it if you would call on them. Your medical insight would be helpful, and it's possible there are some of your ghost cases too." If he could take the time to help them, so could I.

"Of course. Should we go now?"

"No, Anna." Jed put his foot down with an emphatic stomp, bumping the table and making it rock in the process. "Dark has fallen. We are safer during the day, and you can help no one if you are not rested." I was opening my mouth to argue when Grayson agreed with him.

"Tomorrow will be soon enough. My congregation volunteers have set them up with a warm meal and blankets. They are safe tonight."

"First thing in the morning?"

"That will work for me." He stacked a few bowls up and headed for the kitchen.

I turned my attention to the man in black sitting across from me. The IV bag was half empty. His face was drawn with lines and exhaustion but he looked pretty good given what he'd just been through. He'd eaten well, too.

"How are you feeling?"

"I'm tired," he admitted after a pause, "and I have a bit of a headache. Other than that, I'm all right." He nodded towards the needle in his right hand. "Is this really necessary?"

"The ghost possession seems to cause an imbalance in your electrolytes and dehydration. That's why your blood pressure is low. We're using lactated ringers—IV fluid with electrolytes—to get your body back in sync. The headache is probably due to the dehydration, and you may feel dizzy when you stand up."

"I felt like I had the flu for about a week afterward, but I had the bastard in me for a couple days." Chaz grinned at the priest and added, "Pardon my language."

"No offense taken," Matthew assured him. Grayson and Ty finished clearing the table and I started to join them but Jed stopped me.

"I'll assist with the dishes while you see to your patient."

Jed had a way of making a kind offer sound like a command, but I wasn't going to argue with anyone who wanted to do the dishes. I did as he suggested, escorting Matthew back to the living room to recheck his blood pressure. It was low, but not enough to worry me.

"Matthew, I know this seems strange, but I'd like it if you'd stay here tonight. I have an extra guest room and you're welcome to it."

He looked uncomfortable. "It's nice of you to offer but I was planning on heading home tonight."

"How far away do you live?"

He hesitated. "Towards St. Louis. It's a couple of hours from here. I did stay with Grayson last night."

"I definitely don't think you should be driving, and I don't want you that far away. Your body needs to rest, and I'd like to see you tomorrow to make sure you are recovering. You seem good now, but I've seen people have very negative reactions to possession. If you worsen, I'd like you where we can take care of you."

He looked at the site on his hand where the IV needle went through his skin and sighed. "I don't suppose my doctor would know what to make of it if I went in and asked him to remove the IV."

"That would make for an interesting conversation," Ty noted.

Grayson walked in and Matthew looked up at him, eyes pleading for assistance. I couldn't blame him for not wanting to stay with strangers.

"Perhaps you can stay with Grayson again?" I suggested.

"The guest room is all yours," Grayson hurried to assure Matthew. "I assumed you'd be staying with me again, if Anna was willing to entrust you to my care."

I nodded. "Call me if anything changes, okay? And I want to see you in the morning before we go into town."

Matthew agreed with relief.

"This bag of fluid will run out in another couple of hours. Before it does, you'll want to put the next bag in. Ty will show you how."

Matthew walked to Grayson's car without assistance, his IV bag cradled in his arm for the drive. Grayson assured me they could tie it up to the bedpost overnight so that gravity would help deliver the fluids.

We bid Ty and Chaz goodnight in the upstairs hallway. Jed and I brushed our teeth in amicable silence, elbows brushing in the narrow space of the bathroom. He handed me the hand towel when I finished and turned me towards the light to study my face.

"The bruises are darker." I felt embarrassed by the purplish marks, like I was a teenager with acne.

Jed was unaffected, agreeing with a deep-throated grunt. "They are healing. In my experience, they often look worse as they get better."

I could have told him that was because the blood cells in the area were deoxygenated, causing the red cells to darken as they started to break down, but his thumb was tracing the bruise on my forehead in a gentle circle that made my breath catch in my throat.

"It is more difficult to keep you safe than I imagined it would be," he murmured, wrapping me in his arms.

Later, after we were in bed, he told me about Ned and the gate. "There have been multiple incursions on the property." He spoke into my ear as if this was a great secret to be cherished and I stiffened in his arms.

"What do you mean?"

"Reporters, curiosity seekers. They have discovered where you live and they come down the drive as if they have some right to be here." Indignation spiked his tone.

"The drive is marked private property, and we have 'no trespassing' signs up," I noted.

"That doesn't appear to deter them."

"Did they do any harm?" I yawned, leaning back against the mountain behind me. A few curious people couldn't be too big a problem compared with ghosts.

"Ned found a man on his front porch, looking through his windows."

"What?" I tried to sit up but the weight of Jed's arm kept me close against him. "Did the guy live?" Trespassing on Ned's land and staring through his windows was not a safe thing to do.

"He was not injured, but Ned made sure he knew what would happen if he ever returned again."

"Good." I forced my breathing to slow again, contemplating the look Ned and I had exchanged when we'd pulled in. No wonder he was upset with me. "I'm glad he's putting in the gate, then." The property fencing wasn't secure enough to prevent someone from getting in, but they'd have to crawl through four rows of barbed wire, or over the new gate. It wouldn't be as easy as strolling up the driveway.

"As am I."

My thoughts jumbled together, ghosts and miracles, trespassers and priests. It was some time before I fell asleep in the solid embrace of Jed's arms with the feel of his breath against my hair and his scents of cedar and sunshine filling my mind.

That wasn't where I woke up.

# CHAPTER SIX

"**D**O YOU EVER WONDER** what happens when you die?" The voice, throaty with insinuation, resonated out of my dreams, rousing me. I blinked against the bright sunlight, and realized I'd been again pulled into the place that stood between life and death. I scrambled away from the bright hue of the ghost next to me. It was all soul. If it had a form to take, it had chosen not to.

"Eli?"

A low chuckle was the only answer I got. It didn't sound like her and the hair on the back of my neck stood up. I reached for my power, but the internal mass of heat was missing, still with my corporeal body. It hadn't made the leap with me to wherever we were.

"Who are you?"

The cavern was as I'd last seen it before meeting Eli; a vast cave without a ceiling, carpeted in a layer of lush grass. The night sky overhead blinked with serene stars, a clearer view of them than I'd seen in a long time.

"Calm yourself, little one."

Only one ghost had ever called me "little one." Jed's brother, Adonijah. Panic flared as my body remembered the sensation of strips of flesh being torn off from inside me, while I was trapped and helpless in my own body. I backed away in hurried steps and my heel caught on the ground, causing me to fall back into the grass.

"Get away from me."

"Ah, you haven't forgotten me." He was satisfied with my response and I sought to temper my fear. He enjoyed it and I didn't want to give him any pleasure. "I'm not here to hurt you." He chuckled, a low and soft promise. "That time will come, but it is not today."

"Send me back." I was on my feet again, backing up until I was pressed against the rock wall. Jed's sword hadn't weakened Adoni as much as we thought if he was able to take me in my sleep.

"Not yet, little one." He swirled closer, nothing more than incandescent light. "I've promised you your safety, for now."

He hadn't, but I didn't belabor the point with him. His promises wouldn't be worth much anyway. I glanced left and right at the solid walls of rock extending away from me, each one too high to scale. There was no escape. This place wasn't large enough to get more than a few arm lengths away from him.

"I don't believe you." I searched again for my power, for a way to hurt him, and found nothing.

His voice suffused with the satisfaction my fear gave him. "When I am here to take you, you will know it."

From one instant to the next he solidified, his body coming from the light of his soul as if he'd stepped through a curtain. In my fascination, I almost forgot to be afraid.

Was this what he'd looked like when he was alive? Five foot eight, with skin permanently kissed by the sun, features rugged as if the wind had roughened them. Dark hair brushed his shoulders, tangled with curls. I'd caught a glimpse of Jed a few days before, when he was in ghost form, but if there was a strong resemblance between the brothers, I couldn't tell.

"I ask again." Adonijah sat, relaxing on the lawn a few feet from me and lifting his face to the night sky like he was enjoying a day at a sun-filled beach. "Do you wonder what happens when you die?"

Where was he going with this? Had the spirit who tortured me called me here for a casual conversation about life after death? I couldn't use my power against him in this space, and I didn't know if he could hurt me here or not. I stood still with my back flush against the cold cavern wall and contemplated my limited options.

"I know what happens."

"You saw for the span of a heartbeat what it's like to be out of your living body. It was extraordinary, wasn't it?"

My silence answered his question and he leaned forward, caressing my cheek in a tender gesture that was almost worse than when he hurt me. I smacked his hand away, hard enough that the skin of my palm stung. He dropped his arm with an amused smile. He'd done it to frighten me. To show me he could. And I'd shown him I'd fight.

He stood again, still within arm's reach. "Do you think about the peace of the stars, Anna?" His voice curled around me, persuasive, alluring, and full of manipulation.

I did think about the stars, a lot.

He leaned closer to me, stagnant breath against my ear. I tried to pull away from him and found myself trapped against the cliff wall I'd put at my back. "It is extraordinary, the first time you hear the music of the heavens."

When I didn't reply he gripped my neck and I struck out again, an ineffective glancing blow that made him laugh. Digging desperately for the core of power inside me and not finding it, I tried to twist from his grasp, not wanting to touch him any more than I wanted to be touched by him.

"Tell me what you remember," he insisted, giving my head a quick shake.

"The stars sing," I whispered, blinking back a sheen of tears. I hadn't told anyone about that. I didn't think it was the stars that were singing, exactly, but maybe the energy from the galaxy that translated into noise we could hear only when we were dead.

He relaxed his grip, as if my answer had satisfied him, and stepped back again, giving me enough space to breathe. His smile told me he knew he had won. He knew I was afraid of him.

"The first few decades after you die, you watch those you knew. You watch them live, and grow old, and then they die. And the ones you waited for, they go on."

"You thought there was someone that would stay with you, here?"

He let out a harsh laugh. "You imagine you will live for eternity with the ones you love."

"Was it Makeda you were waiting for?" Makeda was the given name of the Queen of Sheba. She and Jedediah had been lovers when they were both alive, and his feelings for her had lasted beyond the grave.

"Then, everyone you ever had a connection with is gone." Adonijah ignored my question. "Even the grandchildren, and their children's children—all the ones you never knew are long dead."

"Do you expect me to feel sorry for you? Life is a fatal condition."

"I don't seek your pity, little one. I strive to help you understand me. We are more alike than you realize."

"You and I have nothing in common. I don't care about you. Who you are, or who you were, means nothing to me."

"If you don't know your enemy, how can you hope to defeat him?"

"I know you more than I care to."

"You remember how I felt inside you? You were delicious, Anna. I want to come back to you. We were so good together."

"Go to hell." I stood again, back to the cavern wall as I edged sideways away from him and he laughed at me.

"How did it feel to kill for the first time? Did you enjoy it? There is a rush of power that comes from knowing you hold someone else's life in your hands. Jedediah knows this. I know it. Now you also know it."

"You're sick." He was speaking to my deepest fears. Was there part of me that thrilled to use my power? Was I that ruthless?

"You are so easy to upset. You must learn to control yourself if you want to win this game." He sat in the grass near the center of the cavern. I hoped it was full of the chiggers of Missouri so he'd be covered in bites and miserable for days.

"Fuck off." I skirted around him, and walked to the far edge of the cavern, looking up at the steep walls as I walked. Maybe a rock climber could get up them, but I wouldn't be able to. Adonijah continued the conversation as though I hadn't moved, his tone amicable.

"I did what many of us do, that stay here, once they are old enough and strong enough. I took over the body of a wealthy young man, and took his wife."

Bile rose in my throat. "Were you as cruel to them as you were to me?"

Another burst of laughter that held no trace of amusement. "The man was weak. His soul all but disappeared when I took over his body. I didn't have to hurt him." He paused, and then continued, his voice bitter and introspective. "You may not believe it, but I cared for her, in my own way."

I felt nauseous contemplating what Adonijah's affection would have felt like from a wife's point of view. No one wanted to be adored by evil.

"It doesn't matter, though." He sighed with too much emphasis.

"The cycle starts over again, and in the end they all die and leave you alone."

He sounded so pathetic I had to suppress a surge of pity for him. *He's trying to manipulate you. Don't get drawn into it.*

"I tire of it, the loneliness." His voice rasped, appealing me to understand. His head was down. He looked like he was reflecting on those he'd lost, but it could have been an attempt at manipulation.

"Where do you think they go?" If I was stuck here with him, maybe I could learn something useful.

"Heaven and hell, perhaps." He tilted his head, his dark eyes were thoughtful. I was reminded that evil looks like everyone else. "Does it matter? They aren't here with us."

I kept my back against the wall of the cliff, but let myself lean against it. Adoni might try to hurt me later, but for now we seemed to have a truce of sorts. I scanned the surrounding sky and cave, looking for a doorway.

"Why do some of the dead stay here?" I asked.

"Who knows? The question is irrelevant." He paused to pick at a blade of grass next to him, then answered. "Perhaps those of us that stay have a strong attachment to something here on earth."

I'd wondered the same thing. It seemed like it had to be related to a strong connection to an event, person, or place.

"Possessing the living isn't the answer to being lonely in death." Preaching morals to this spirit was a lost cause but I couldn't let it slide.

"There is no answer, no way to change what we are. No resolution. There's nothing wrong with taking what we can."

"Don't make excuses for your pathetic lack of character." I remembered what it felt like when he'd tried to take me. "It is wrong, and you make those choices."

His voice rolled up in a sneer. "Right and wrong are false constructs. Things you create in the living world to maintain order. There is no order among the dead."

"What about the Council? I thought they were supposed to maintain some sort of balance."

"They tried to enforce their rules upon us, that is true. They have little power, now, though. Thank you, by the way, for taking care of them."

They weren't all gone but I didn't know if there were enough of them left to still be a Council that could maintain any semblance of order. I didn't even know if the ones that had survived were the ones that supported me or the Master. Either way, I didn't want Adoni to know that they weren't all gone. He'd just try to form an alliance with any that were on the Master's side, and I didn't need my enemies any more organized than they already were. I turned the conversation away from the Council.

"Why are some of the ghosts that are trying possess people unsuccessful?" I was testing him. If he'd lie to me about this then everything he said was suspect.

"They are too weak to take control of another soul."

"What makes you stronger than they are?" I was still looking for a door, but couldn't find one. Jed had said it was inside me, but wasn't this entire place in my mind?

"I was always strong. The longer I've been dead, the stronger I've become." It made sense that a ghost would gain strength the longer they'd been dead, but I didn't think that rule always played out.

"I've met strong ghosts that were younger."

"You are too simple. That is not the only factor. A spirit with the Master on their side would have an advantage. Evil is a strong ally."

"Why did you bring me here?"

"I've missed you, little one." His tone was sarcastic despite the tender tenor of his words.

"Don't call me that."

"Do you think of me?" He ignored my protests.

"No." I did. The memory of him torturing me haunted my dreams. I'd been trapped and helpless in my own body while he prepared to use my own power to release the man I loved.

"I must admit, I was surprised Jedediah was strong enough to use his kilij against you." His lips twisted in an amusement that belied the bitterness of his tone. "Then again, a man who would kill his own brother wouldn't hesitate to murder the woman he claims."

"You can't expect me to believe you're innocent of murder."

He stared at me for so long, I wanted to shift away from the intensity of it. But I refused to look away first. "I do not claim innocence, little one. But you also know what it is to take another's life."

I had to clench my teeth together to keep from responding. Maybe I wasn't any better than he was, but at least I was fighting on the right side. He smirked when I didn't reply. "Why do you think my brother used his sword on the woman he protects?"

"I asked him to do it." In the silence after I spoke, I had the uncomfortable sense that Adoni had learned something about me he found useful.

"Perhaps you have more strength than I gave you credit for." My stomach turned at the admiration in his voice. I did not want his esteem.

"I am stronger than you can imagine." I never broke eye contact, so he would know I believed every word I spoke.

"Let me ask you this, Anna. How many of the dead have you been banishing each day?"

"I don't think that's any of your business." I wasn't going to tell him the truth. Over the last week I might have released fifty spirits, though none in the last day.

"Your power grows stronger. I can sense it in you."

It frightened me to think he could see that. Could every ghost? But he was right. My power had grown over the last few months. I'd always been able to see ghosts and release them, but now I could see them from farther away, and I could use my power dozens of times each day. It replenished itself faster, and it didn't hurt quite as much. Or else I'd gotten used to the feeling of fire singeing through my veins.

"How long will it be," he pondered, "before it consumes you?"

*What is that supposed to mean?* I schooled my features. "It's my power. It's a part of me and I control it."

"Everyone with your gift has believed the same. And yet, so few of you survive."

"We don't survive because ghosts like you keep trying to kill us." The Council's tactics to overpower me had involved throwing things at me from a safe distance—beyond the reach of my power. If I'd been injured enough, they'd be able to possess me, or execute me.

"It's true that the dead don't appreciate being sent on, and we have had to stop the different Magi on occasion."

"On occasion?"

"Some of you have felt it your mission to release every spirit on the planet and send them to the next world. Those of us who are peaceful don't appreciate your meddling."

"You hardly qualify as peaceful." It was unfortunate for me that none of the previous Magi had gotten to him before now.

He ignored me. "If the dead don't find and eliminate the Magi first, then it is your own power that destroys you. You cannot use it too much, for too long, before it incinerates you."

I couldn't tell if he was lying to me. I stayed silent, not wanting to reveal my ignorance.

"Didn't Jedediah tell you?" His lips curved upwards. He was enjoying this conversation too much.

"Keep your brother out of this," I ordered. If it was true, and if Jed knew, he'd kept it to himself. One thing was clear to me—if Adoni could drive a wedge between Jed and me, he would. "If that's the case, all I can do is make sure I take you with me when I die."

"Your mother tried, but failed."

"She died in an accident." The response was automatic. I didn't let my expression change, but his remark had shaken me. *What does my mother have to do with this?*

"A fiery one," Adoni pointed out.

My anger flared, but I kept my tone calm. "Lying to me isn't helping your cause." He was attempting to use my mother against me, but I refused to give him the satisfaction of reacting in anger.

"What would I gain from making this up?"

"I don't know but I'm sure you would enjoy upsetting me."

"I'm trying to help by telling you things about yourself that you have a right to know. Things my brother would have told you, if he cared for you."

"You weren't with my mother when she died, and you probably didn't even know her." Nothing he said would make me believe his motives were altruistic, but his dig about Jed's feelings for me struck an insecurity of mine.

"Not many women are as remarkable as Makeda, but your mother had a strength I admired." His voice had a ring of sincerity, which upset me more. "There was little she feared."

"Trying to make me angry won't work." I had a tight handle on my temper, and was glad for it.

"While antagonizing you is enjoyable, I assure you that I have no reason to lie."

"Prove it."

He sighed. "If you are determined to disbelieve me, then nothing I can say will convince you."

That much was true. "Where was she when she died?" I challenged him.

"Guatemala." His lips curved in a smile.

He was correct. She'd died in Latin America while she was doing missionary work during the Guatemalan civil war. I'd grown up thinking she loved her god more than she loved me, and that was why she'd left me with her sister when I was young. It wasn't until I'd met Jed that I'd learned she had the same ability I did. That still didn't mean she'd been down there because of it.

"She was a fierce woman. So righteous in her determination to save the world." He spoke as if he were reminiscing about someone he'd known well and been fond of. It was difficult to maintain my doubt when he sounded so earnest.

"Why was she there?" I couldn't stop myself from asking.

"To quell the war."

The civil war in Guatemala had lasted thirty years. We'd been told she was volunteering with a humanitarian group when she was in some sort of accident and died. My aunt had told me we never knew exactly what happened. "I thought you said she was fighting the dead."

Adoni shrugged. "We get bored. Sometimes starting wars makes for an entertaining decade."

"You started a war in Guatemala because you were bored?"

"I know you would like to believe I am the cause of all villainy, but it wasn't me." He held his palms up, the picture of innocence. "A spirit took over the leader of the country and started a war against his own people."

"That's a bit beyond possession for the sake of living again."

"It was part of the Master's plan."

"Why was the Master interested in Guatemala?" It was a small country compared to the States, how could it be that important?

"With one war, they destabilized that region of the world for decades. Where there is instability, there is darkness in the hearts of men. That is what the Master ultimately wants."

"Darkness?"

"Chaos, little one. You don't know much about it yet, but you will." His words sounded like a loving promise and I ground my teeth together, wishing they made enough noise to drown out the sound of his words. "Your mother was trying to get to the possessed, to stop it."

"What role did you play in that?" My words were tinged with the bitter taste of anger.

"Ella era mi amante," he announced. He shifted in the grass until he was on his side, head propped in one hand

*She was my lover.* I translated automatically, noticing how Spanish flowed off his tongue like a native speaker, which added some credence to his claim.

"You were not," I objected in English. This was a ploy, Adonijah trying to upset me. It was working.

"You understand Spanish." The glint in his eye told me he was thrilled to be getting under my skin. Amidst my anger was a smidgen of relief. He didn't know everything about me, even though he'd been inside me.

"A little." Not as well as he appeared to, but I knew enough to get by with my Spanish speaking patients.

"Yo también soy tu padre."

I let out a choked laugh. "You are not my father."

"Well, my body is long gone, that is true. But the one I possessed at the time is the same one that your mother took to her bed." He made it sound dirty and real and I shuddered as a wave of revulsion rolled through my stomach.

"You said you were in Guatemala with her, but I was five when she died. She was here when I was born."

"We were lovers for some time. I went to Guatemala with her after you were born." I'd learned a lot about how to tell when someone was lying to me. People told their doctors half-truths and outright lies all the time. If we couldn't detect them, our patient might suffer. I didn't think he was lying, as much as I hoped it wasn't true. Aside from that, his story was too crazy to make up.

"You tricked her, then." Him telling one truth, though, didn't mean it was the whole picture of what had happened. One true thing could lead you a long way down a path of lies.

"I didn't have to, little one. I didn't have to."

"We aren't having this conversation."

"I told you before, the cycle continues. She was not the first lover I watched die, and you are one of many offspring. I will outlive you as well."

"She would have known you were a ghost. She wouldn't have slept with you; she would have released you."

"As you have released Jedediah?"

"He didn't steal a body from someone who was using it."

He shrugged. "A technicality of no matter."

I thought it mattered very much. "She would never have loved someone like you." Whoever my mother had been, she couldn't have been involved with Adonijah. I protested the thought even as I believed him.

"Loved?" He shrugged. "Love is a relative term. It's of little matter. She had use for me, as I had of her. We were united in our own way."

I swallowed the thick strands of nausea in the back of my throat at the thought of anyone letting this man touch them, and my hatred for him burned brighter. If Eli was right, I carried some piece of him inside me. I couldn't imagine anything worse than that.

"And then she died. What did you do to her?"

"I did not hurt her, little one. I enjoyed her company and was quite affected when she left me." Despite myself, I was starting to believe him. Even monsters must have mothers and lovers. And children.

"Tell me more about Guatemala."

"There was a war, an uprising. Another time, little one, perhaps I will be able to tell you everything. Today we do not have time. I spoke of your mother for one reason. You need to know that your power will destroy you if you keep using it."

"That's ridiculous." My protest fell flat. Wouldn't Jed have warned me if I was at risk of killing myself?

"Your power has grown too strong, and you don't control it. It will consume you." He spoke with emphatic clarity. "That is what happened to your mother."

A charming thought. Was I going to burst into flames in accidental self-immolation? Then again, I had no reason to believe he was telling me the truth. Whatever his history with my mother may have been, what he wanted most was revenge on his brother, and the easiest way to do that was through me. I knew he hadn't told me all this out of the kindness of his heart.

"Why did you bring me here?"

"Is it wrong of me to take an interest in my only living child? I did promise your mother I'd look after you."

"If that was true, you wouldn't have been able to resist tormenting me sooner. She didn't tell you how to find me, did she?" He didn't have a ready answer and I knew I was right. She'd hidden me away on a farm with her sister, and never told her ghost lover where I was. "She knew who you were, and she never trusted you."

"It is ironic that my brother found you before I did. Convenient, though. I need you and your power. Getting to use you against my brother is an unexpected gift."

"I appreciate how you prioritize your family." My sarcasm wasn't lost on him.

"Three thousand years of boredom, little one. You can't blame me for seeking out entertainment. Sadly, our playtime has come to an end." He looked genuinely regretful, his lips lowered in a pout. "You should be waking soon, and you can't do that if I don't send you back."

"I'm surprised you don't want to keep me here to annoy me further." *Why is he suddenly so eager to send me back?*

"As much as I've enjoyed myself, I know we will meet again soon."

"There's one thing I want to know, Adonijah."

"Yes?"

"What was his name, the man that you possessed?"

"Ah. She kept him a secret from you as well, then." He giggled.

"She died before she could tell me much, and it's pretty clear she didn't trust you." I tried not to sound defensive, and failed. Had Aunt Ann known? If she had, she'd kept it to herself.

"A bargain. I'll answer your question, if you'll answer one of mine first."

"It depends on what you want to know."

"You murdered the envoy I sent for you. How did it feel to take a life?" He leaned forward, eyes eager like a child at Christmas.

"I should have known you were behind that."

"Clever, wasn't it? Getting him to come find you?" It's unfortunate the Council got to you before I did."

Hatred swelled in my chest. "You killed him. Not me."

"No, little one. I put the pieces in place is all. He died by your hand."

"Because I had no choice."

"You could have gone with him."

"He would have died anyway." Adonijah wouldn't have let him live.

"I don't murder as lightly as my brother does. It was interesting though, watching you choose."

"You were there?"

"Close enough."

"I'm done talking." I stood, brushing the grass from my jeans and turned my attention back to the cavern wall. It was rough and cool under my hand, the texture of real stone after dark.

"You haven't told me what I want to know," Adoni cajoled, his face bright with playful energy. He was enjoying this too much.

Not playing his game was the one way I could win; depriving him of my reactions. I ran my hands up the rock face and tried to see what was beyond it, but that wasn't a gift I had.

"Then the name you want will remain in the realm of the dead."

"Ask me something else." The words slipped out and I leaned my forehead against the stone. I'd given away the fact that I was willing to trade a bit of my soul to my father's murderer so that I'd know whose DNA I shared. It had been too long since I'd had a family. I'd never known my mother, and her extended family was gone. The sudden hope that my birth father's family was still out there was too great.

He tapped his tongue against his teeth, chiding me. "I don't think so. Did it feel sweet, little one? Did you hold on to him as your power drove the life out of him? Did you feel powerful?"

"Stop it!" The valley seemed to shake with the force of my words and Adonijah sighed with pleasure. I pulled my emotions back under control. He liked it when he was able to frighten me and when he provoked me. When I spoke, I tried to embed my tone with the dangerous reminder of what my power could do. "I was angry, when I released him."

"And do you regret it?"

"That's two questions."

"Answer it," he commanded, like his brother might have once done. Adoni might not have been the king, but he was used to being obeyed. "Otherwise I won't tell you what you want to know."

"I gave you your answer."

"You would do it again, wouldn't you?"

"What I will do is release you," I promised.

He gave a low chuckle. "William Lawson."

"What happened to him?"

"That's more than one question." He raised his eyebrows in challenge and I wondered if I'd be able to do him any harm if I punched him in the face.

"I answered several of yours."

"He wasn't valuable to me after your mother died." He brushed a blade of grass off his knee.

"You killed him."

He glanced up, confused. "Death isn't the end. It's another beginning."

"I'm not sure William Lawson would agree with you."

"Nor would Marcus Wilson," Adoni countered, rising to his feet. "It's time for you to go back. When you wake, tell my dearest brother how much I look forward to seeing him again."

That wasn't a conversation that would go over well, but if Adoni was telling the truth, then Jed had been withholding critical things from me. He was going to have something to worry about other than his brother.

"I don't think I will."

"The next time we meet will be under different circumstances, little one." That sounded ominous but I wasn't going to let him think he frightened me.

"I daresay it will." My words were part promise, part threat.

"Goodbye, Anna." He disappeared in a burst of light and my vision blurred into darkness. I blinked and found myself in my bed, eyes matted with sleep. Jed stood over me, concern etched in his features.

"What are you doing?" I cast my senses out, but there weren't any ghosts, other than the one in front of me. It was disorienting to come back from Adonijah and wake up to his brother.

"I have been unable to wake you. Where were you?"

"You know where I was." Resentment tinged my words. How much of what Adonijah said was true, and how much of it did Jed know but hadn't bothered to share? He wasn't particularly forthcoming, but if my power was going to kill me, wouldn't he have mentioned that? Had his brother been possessing the body that fathered me?

I sat up in a bolt of anger and registered the daylight outside. "Shit. How late is it?"

"Past eight." Jed was staring out the window, his hand gripping the curved wood at the end of my bed. "The others will be here soon."

I was late. We didn't have time to talk about what had happened, and I was angry enough that I needed to think about what I wanted to say first. "I need a shower."

"Someone from the Council survived and reached out to you?"

"No."

"Then who? Eli?"

"It was your brother I was chatting with." I didn't try to keep the irritation out of my voice.

Jed roared what sounded like a long string of curses in a language I didn't know. I ignored him, throwing back the covers and heading to the bathroom.

"Did he hurt you?" Jed's hands were clenched into fists and he looked angrier than I'd seen before, but I wasn't ready to talk to him.

"I need to take a shower."

"Tell me what happened," he insisted.

"I'm not going to discuss this with you right now." I closed the bathroom door between us with a thump. The door didn't lock but he wasn't dumb enough to barge through after me. I drowned out his angry muttering by turning on the shower.

# CHAPTER SEVEN

I UNDRESSED while I was waiting for the hot water to make the long trip from the hot water heater through the old pipes to the second-floor bathroom. My reflection in the mirror gave me pause, lending truth to some of Adoni's words.

*You're starting to look like you're starving yourself.* I had lost some weight in recent weeks, maybe more than I realized since I didn't keep a scale at the farmhouse. My hipbones, once hidden by a healthy layer of muscle and fat, jutted against skin. My lower ribs were visible and my breasts seemed smaller than they had been a few weeks before. I'd noticed my clothes were loose on me, but I'd been ignoring it, telling myself it didn't matter, that it was the stress. Maybe it did matter.

My cheeks looked thinner, too, and my hair hung in limp brown lengths over my shoulder blades. I glared at the early streaks of gray clustering at my part, and wondered what had happened to my once shiny hair. I didn't think there was a miracle shampoo that could cure this. My power might not incinerate me, but if Adoni was telling the truth, it was consuming me from the inside. My body might be using my own energy reserves to keep itself from burning up.

No wonder Carrie and Jed were handing me plates of food every time I turned around. I was always hungry and I'd figured that the nuclear core inside me was burning more calories than it used to, since I was using it so much. I'd thought Adonijah meant that my power would consume me in a fiery blaze, but maybe he meant that it literally would devour my own body.

I contemplated the biology of what was happening. I still had good muscle tone, and my energy levels had improved over the last few weeks as my body adjusted to how often I was using my power. I might be losing weight but I wasn't in imminent danger of death, I didn't think. Maybe if I ate more and used my power less often

I wouldn't look so disheveled. It might be wishful thinking but I couldn't afford the luxury of wasting away. Everyone needed me.

The front door opened and then slammed shut while I was in the shower, the commotion unmistakable in the confines of the aging farmhouse. I showered fast, dressed, and left my hair wet because I didn't have time to dry it. I opened the bathroom door to the smell of bacon, and knew eggs and toast would follow. Hash browns, if I was lucky.

I trotted down the stairs, sending Luna scuttling for the dark safety underneath the dining room table. She peered out at me from under a chair, licking her lips with what looked like satisfaction. She had an uncanny sense for knowing when Jed was going to cook bacon and she'd probably been in the kitchen waiting for him.

Jed stepped into the dining room from the kitchen and tried to guide me into the sunroom, Ty following him.

I shrugged Jed's hand off my shoulder, feeling like a herded cow. "Good morning, Ty."

"Morning, sunshine." He raised his eyebrow and I knew he'd registered my rebuff of Jed's attention.

"You're upset," Jed noted.

"Yes," I agreed. I didn't want to fight with him in front of Ty any more than I wanted an audience for the conversation Jed and I needed to have.

"They took her again, this morning. I couldn't wake her," Jed explained to Ty before resettling the full force of his attention on me.

"I don't want to talk about it," I spit out, cutting off any comment Ty might have made. For some reason, I wasn't as anxious as everyone else about the fact that I was difficult to wake when I was in the cave. Maybe I should be. What if they kept me there and I couldn't ever get back? I added it to my list of things to worry about when I had time.

"That's not cool." Ty wasn't going to let it rest. "You've gotta figure out how to get out of there, or keep yourself from going in."

On that point, Ty and I agreed. "I wish it was that easy."

"Which ghost lured you away from us this time? That new one or someone different?" Ty asked.

"Adonijah," Jed whispered his name like a curse. "My only regret is that I didn't do a more thorough job of killing him."

"I don't know how you could prevent a soul from staying on earth after they've been murdered," I pointed out, unable to keep the irritation out of my voice. I could speak for myself, I didn't need him to answer for me.

"Did he hurt you?" Jed ignored my snide comment and asked the question I hadn't answered before.

"He just wanted to talk, but it sounds like he plans on coming back for more than a conversation," I said. I watched Jed with concern for the well-being of the coffee mug that he gripped with fury. How much force could the ceramic vessel withstand before shattering in his hand?

"Ty, would you see if there are any newspapers in the kitchen? I'd like to light the fire." I didn't take my gaze from Jed and the mug.

"Sure. I'll be right back."

Ty walking out was a distraction that helped break the tension. Jed took a deep breath and eased his death hold on the mug. "Did you try to release him?"

"I can't access my power in that place. If there's a way to do it, I haven't figured it out."

"How did he trap you there?"

"I don't know," I half-lied, but Jed guessed the truth.

"The Council controlled that realm. Without them, he is free to use it."

"That's one theory."

"The Council could have been a powerful ally." Jed's tone was reproachful and I objected to his comment, mainly because I'd been thinking the same thing. I was also still furious with him for hiding things from me. I bit my lip to keep that to myself, though. This wasn't the time for that argument. They were starting to stack up. Was this what marriage was like?

"If they hadn't been trying to kill me, yeah."

His expression turned grim. "I was wrong."

This was surprisingly close to an apology, which took me by surprise, though it didn't lessen my fury any. Still, I didn't think that kings in Jed's world ever admitted they were wrong.

Ty walked back in with a folded up newspaper in his hand. "Wrong about what?"

"Anna's instincts for Christiana were correct," Jed explained to

Ty without turning away from me. "I let my prior history with her cloud my judgment. I didn't trust you, and I should have."

Three days had passed since the night Christiana and her friends kidnapped me and Jedediah nearly died trying to save me, and he was apologizing now?

*Better late than never, Anna.* The little voice inside my head tended to get me into trouble, but sometimes it was right.

"Apology accepted." My voice was still cool.

Jed grunted, recognizing the dangerous tone of my voice for what it was. He proceeded with caution. "What did happen last night?"

"The usual. He threatened me, I threatened him. He tried to convince me that I should join his little takeover of the world and tried to make me doubt you."

"Did it work?" Jed's gaze met mine and I looked away from the depth in his eyes.

"Which part?"

"Making you doubt me." My silence stretched between us like a taut rope. "What did he use against me?"

*How many things are there to use?* "That you can't be trusted since he feels like you betrayed him."

"He didn't mention her?"

I knew he meant Makeda, but it was my mother that was on my mind. "Of course he did."

"Do you doubt my devotion to you?"

I didn't point out that devotion and trust were different things. How could I doubt his devotion? He'd given up his body to follow me, had saved my life several times, starting with the moment we'd met. But if he wasn't going to tell me everything I needed to know then I wouldn't be able to trust him.

"Makeda was a remarkable woman," he interjected into the silence. "Like none I had ever met before."

Jed apparently needed more than three thousand years to learn about women, because talking about how wonderful your ex had been wasn't the best way to calm a discussion with the woman in front of you.

"I'm sure she was fantastic." I was pleased at how neutral I kept my voice. The queen of Sheba bothered me a lot more than a woman dead so long should. I turned my attention to the fireplace. It was too cold in the sunroom to continue talking in there without more heat.

"It was a long time ago. And now I have you."

"I don't belong to you, and I'm no queen." I shoved some wood into the stove with more vigor than was necessary. Ty squatted next to me, handing me a few sheets of newspaper, his eyes meeting mine with a cautioning glance.

"You are so much more. Anyone can be born into royalty. You are a healer and a warrior. Skills you have worked hard to learn."

"I'm not much of a warrior." I wadded up Ty's newspaper and tucked it under the logs, wishing Jed would go away.

"You just defeated my brother for the second time, did you not?"

"He sent me back. I wasn't fighting him." And if that was a battle, then I hadn't been the victor. I struck the match down the rough side of the box and the flame sizzled to life. When I held it under the edge of the paper the fire caught and flared in a satisfying rush of heat.

"You have to tell me what happened."

"I don't have to, Jed." Anger rose in my voice but if we had this conversation now we'd do it in front of a crowd. I was well aware of the group gathered in my kitchen. "When I'm ready to discuss this with you I'll let you know." I cracked the door on the fireplace, and turned to face him. His eyes were wide open, expectant, inviting me to disclose more. "Was there something else you wanted to talk about?"

He settled into one of the armchairs in a deliberate movement that made me wonder if he was feeling okay. He had to still be suffering the effects of re-possessing his current body, brain dead or not. If he was feeling weak, his voice didn't betray it.

"There is. You didn't destroy them all."

"I'm sorry?"

"You didn't banish everyone from the Council. We have to discuss what to do about the rest of them."

"We knew that already." The exhaustion I felt from months of fighting ghosts swept through me and I felt my legs shake. I locked my knees, forcing my legs to continue supporting me. "How many of them are still out there?" I hadn't been able to count the swirling mass of ghosts in the shabby farmhouse they'd chosen to meet me in. "I know that Dakini and Christiana are gone." The blue dragon goddess hadn't been on Christiana's side, but she'd fought against me and lost. Whatever her allegiance had been, it hadn't been with me.

"The dragon goddess was strongest," Jed said.

"It's too bad that the strong ones aren't ever on our side." It was a dig at him, but he didn't take it that way.

"Morality, that which is good versus evil, becomes less clear to the dead."

"How so?" Ty asked, taking the armchair across from Jed. I kept my position next to the fire, standing with my backside to the growing heat.

"Once you are dead," Jed explained to Ty, pleased to have an audience more engaged than I was, "the moral choices that affect life seem less meaningful. Consequences are non-existent and that which is acceptable can shift without the living world exacting discipline." It was a strange logic, one that almost made sense to me.

"You don't seem to have that problem," Ty pointed out.

*Except when it comes to telling me everything you should.* I bit my lip to keep from voicing my thoughts out loud. My patience was waning but I needed to get Jed away from the crowd in my house to be able to say everything I wanted to.

"I had few enough scruples when I lived." Jed said it in a lighthearted tone, like it was something he found more amusing than sad. "I struggled after my death to understand why God left me here and what I needed to do to redeem my soul."

"Did you ask Him?" I couldn't keep myself from sounding snarky.

Jed lifted his dark eyes to meet mine, and I was struck by the sadness in them. "It's been some time since God spoke to me."

"You're in the Bible." Ty sounded like he couldn't believe that Jed didn't call God up once a week.

Jed shrugged. The fact that the Bible told his story was of little importance to him. "That book does not always speak the truth," he reminded Ty.

"So, which part is wrong?" I couldn't stop myself from asking. "You didn't have seven hundred wives?"

He answered with a half-smile. "I was never a magician."

"That's unfortunate. I'd imagine that would come in handy." Jed agreed with a laugh. He was either ignoring, or oblivious to my overt sarcasm.

"What else?" Ty prodded the conversation away from the argument he couldn't know I was skirting around. I understood his curiosity—Jed had been reluctant to discuss his first life. I had a lot of questions, too, but I'd grown tired of having to ask them.

"It was long ago. That time is of little consequence now."

Ty wasn't ready to give up, perhaps as tired of Jed's reticence as I was. "What was it like? Being a king?"

"Treacherous," was his initial answer. We waited for more since he appeared to be mulling his words over. "When you are wealthy and powerful, everyone wants to take your place. They all believe they will be a better ruler, or that the power will help them." He paused. "In the end, power corrupts all who have it."

"Is that what happened to you?" I was quick to ask.

"Yes." Jed stared up at me, acknowledging his sins like he was in confession.

"If you could have that power again, would you take it?" Ty asked, probing for more.

Jed redirected his attention to Ty, and I found myself missing his intense gaze. I couldn't help but wonder if he'd been this captivating when he was alive in his own time.

"I would like to tell you that I wouldn't, Ty."

"But?"

"It's too easy to delude oneself into believing that this time you will be better. That you've learned from your mistakes. That now you will use your power for good. It corrupts you, nonetheless, every time." We considered that for a long moment and then Ty asked his next question.

"Do you miss it, then?"

"The era, or being a king?" Jed asked but went on without waiting for clarification. "There was no healthcare to speak of, by your standards. Women often died in childbirth, men in war, from minor wounds that you would cure today in your clinic. There was no dentist and we didn't have running water. Travel by horse is not the same as a pleasure ride through your woods here.

"Later in life, as my morals declined, so did my empire. I was embroiled in wars, attacked from every direction. I lived in constant fear of losing everything, and never knew when someone close to me would try to kill me, to take all I had."

"Like Adonijah." I hadn't forgotten my anger, but it was interesting, imagining the era in which he'd lived.

"He wasn't the only one." Jed's grim tone spoke of other betrayals, but he didn't name them.

"You make it sound less glamorous than I'd imagined," Ty admitted.

"I was a king because my mother wished for me to be one, not because I deserved it. Here your rulers are chosen by you. They must earn the privilege to rule."

"That doesn't always work out well for us in a democracy, either, but you make a good point," Ty agreed.

"This country has made some interesting choices," Jed's lips twitched with wry amusement, perhaps referencing a singer who'd been president a few terms ago.

"That's one way to put it." Ty was troubled by the current administration. The once-charismatic Iowan that he and I had both voted for had been acting erratically of late, enough so that many in the medical community wondered if he was suffering from early-onset dementia. I feared he was possessed. If he was, though, I wouldn't ever get close enough to find out.

"Magnetism has always been a valuable asset in a leader, but in my case it wasn't enough."

"Charismatic people aren't always good leaders," I agreed. "Sometimes they're just charming."

"As may have been the case with me." Jed was intense, but charming wasn't a word I'd use to describe him. I kept that to myself.

"So you wouldn't go back, if you could, and be the person you were then?" Ty pushed, ignoring the question of charisma.

Jed studied his empty mug for long enough that I thought he wouldn't answer.

"Death brought me many regrets. I wish I had lived a better life, that I could go back and change my selfish behavior. When you draw your last breath, though, it is too late. I spent centuries ruminating over that life and the things I should have done differently. It took me all of that time to realize that my afterlife could serve a purpose." He turned his attention to me in a long-considered look, and I braced myself against the determination in his expression. "I found a way to atone for my sins, but I never hoped to love again."

I stopped breathing as if I'd been shocked by electricity. Our relationship, a few months in, had been intensified by our near-death experiences; first mine and then his. We hadn't said the "love" word yet, though it hadn't been worrying me. I accepted our relationship as it was, other than my lingering doubts about how I could ever measure up, long-term, to one of history's most amazing women. The fact that he chose this moment, when he knew I was angry with him, to all but say he loved me, was a sneaky move. It wouldn't work.

"It was not my intent," he broke through my contemplations, "to seduce you. I didn't plan for this to happen between us."

I could almost hear Ty trying to blend into the upholstery. He hadn't bargained on being part of a conversation this personal.

"I never thought you planned it." I turned away from him, staring out over the snow-covered field and the wooded hills beyond it. "And I'm mad at you, so don't think you can distract me from that with this conversation."

"You have yet to tell me what wrong I committed."

"I didn't want to argue with an audience, but I would think you'd be able to figure it out." I threw another log on the fire and then walked back into the dining room. I was long overdue for a cup of coffee. Ty followed me.

"Are you okay? What's going on?"

"Too many secrets. I'm tired of it. I'm supposed to be able to trust him, and I don't know if I can."

"What caused this?" Ty pulled me into the parlor, away from the dining room so that we were out of earshot, both of the kitchen and Jed. Jed followed us as far as the dining room. He stopped there, his eyes on me. The message was clear—he was giving me enough privacy to talk to Ty, but wasn't going to let me out of his sight. I shifted my position so the wall blocked my view of him and kept my voice low.

"Just a few things Adoni told me last night."

"What's the one thing Adonijah wants most?" Ty was looking at me like I'd lost my mind and I focused on my scuffed house shoes, shuffling them against the aging throw rug.

"To hurt his brother."

"And the easiest way to do that?"

I hesitated before admitting, "Is to make me doubt Jed."

"Then explain to me why you would listen to that psycho?"

"He said some things, Ty, that seemed like they might be true."

"Like what?"

There'd been more than I had time to talk about. I tried to filter all of the details down to the most important pieces.

"Adoni knew my mother. He possessed my biological father, and she knew—she knew he was a ghost."

"And this is somehow Jed's fault?" He shook his head, as if he despaired of me ever learning. "Anything else?"

"I can't believe you don't think this is a big deal." My voice strained with the effort to keep quiet. "But yes, there is more. He said that my power will kill me if I keep using it this much. He said that's how my mother died. Her power consumed her."

Ty let go of my arm and turned back to Jed with his lips pressed into an angry line.

"Did you know that?" he shouted across the room. Jed's blank expression signified confusion. I sighed and took a few quick steps after Ty, stopping him before he got back to the dining room. Jed was the bigger man by far, but Ty was tough enough to cause some damage if he wanted to. I hadn't seen him angry enough to punch someone in a long time, but he looked like he was there, now.

"Ty, we are not talking about this right now." I pulled him back to the parlor before Ty extracted his arm out of mine, jaw set with rage. "It's a conversation for me to have with Jed and I'm not doing it in the middle of this house with everyone around. This is neither the time nor the place." I could tell the conversation in the kitchen had quieted into an awkward silence as the commotion we were causing caught their attention.

"If you get hurt because of him . . ." He left the threat hanging.

"I'm mad too," I whispered. "But even if he withheld what he knew, he didn't cause this. It's not his fault I have this power."

Ty didn't turn his gaze from Jed, who stared back at him, unfazed but looking a little perplexed. I met Jed's eyes and gave my head a shake, hoping he wouldn't engage. He nodded.

"I know I need to talk to Jed about this but I need to find some privacy. Since I don't have that option right now, I'm going to settle for a cup of coffee. Care to join me?"

My attempt to distract him didn't work. Ty's jaw was clenched and the taut set of his shoulders said he wasn't done yet.

"Do you think it's true? That your power could kill you?"

I thought it might be, but I didn't know how to admit that. "I don't know, Ty."

"Fine," Ty agreed. "Let's go get caffeinated, and then you and he are going to talk."

That was the exchange, then. Ty wouldn't say anything else, but I had to talk to Jed sooner rather than later.

"You're blackmailing me."

"Pretty much." His mouth pressed into a grim smile and he linked his arm through mine, drawing me past Jed and into the kitchen.

Aside from Ty and Chaz, there were four extra people in the kitchen. Ned's wife, Carrie was a little taller than I was. She looked at home tending to my stove in well-worn leggings, winter riding boots and a roomy pullover that fell to her upper thighs. Her dark brown hair was shiny. Her sweatshirt hid the small swell of her first pregnancy. Ned leaned against the far end of the counter in dark jeans and a thick red sweater, and watched his wife. He'd spent half his childhood in that same spot and I wondered at how things changed, and yet didn't. Grayson sat at the table with Matthew, his eyes crinkling in greeting when Ty and I walked in with Jed on our heels.

"Good morning, everyone." I forced a smile and contemplated the comparative serenity my place in the city had. I was no one there. Just another face among two million people. What it lacked in friendships, it made up for in anonymity. I could shop for groceries—and cook them—alone. Here at the farm, my friends felt free to come and go as they pleased. I'd be lying if I said that I hated it, but there were times when I wished for the privacy the city offered. The way things were going here, I was going to have to add on to the house, because eight people in my little kitchen were several too many.

Ned paused in his conversation with Chaz long enough to give me a nod of greeting, and I chastised myself for being inhospitable. Everyone in my kitchen had played their part to help me. Chaz was helping with our legal problems, and Ty had acted the part of my unpaid nurse the night before. Ned kept us safe, Carrie kept us fed, and Jed . . . *lied to me.* I wasn't going to start an argument in front of others but I couldn't let this be for long. At this rate, my anger would consume me long before my power did.

"How are you feeling, Matthew?" I distracted myself by tending to my clinical duty. Both priests were in their standard uniforms and I wondered if they ever got a true day off when they could wear anything else. Surely they didn't wear their white collars to bed and the grocery store?

"I'm a bit shaky, but I think I'm on the mend." I glanced at Ty and he nodded in confirmation.

"Blood pressure's one forty over one hundred and he seems to be rehydrating quite well."

I laid a hand on Matthew's and noted that the skin felt cooler and more supple than it had the day before. "Any dizziness?"

"I was a little unsteady when I got up this morning, but it's better now."

"Let's pull his IV," I suggested to Ty. "Not too much caffeine today." I gestured to the cup in Matthew's hand. "And stay focused on drinking lots of clear fluids. Sports drinks are your friend right now." He nodded and I turned my attention to the rest of the group.

"So, what's on our agenda today?" I stepped past Jed to the coffee pot without acknowledging him. My espresso machine sat unused next to the drip coffee maker, which had a half-full carafe. I didn't feel like offering to make espresso for eight, so I poured a cup of the standard fare and mentally promised my Italian-made beauty that we'd make wonderful coffee again soon.

"I'm continuing to work on gate installation," Ned informed us as I poured him a refill on his coffee. "We had another reporter yesterday, despite the 'no trespassing' signs."

"What do you mean, 'another' reporter?" Ty asked.

"It's not the media that are the problem." Ned was staring into his coffee cup like it held the answers he was looking for. "They started it, though, when they reported Anna's name. We've had multiple incursions on our property, all from people trying to find Anna." He looked up at me and his eyes held mine, his voice astringent with frustration. "I don't know if they're dangerous or not. I can't tell if they have ghosts."

"The gate is a good idea." I hoped my agreement would calm his irritation. Ned had found his role in the defense of our mutual properties. If keeping curiosity seekers and the possessed away from our front doors was becoming more difficult, then he could help with that, even if he couldn't tell who was possessed. Ned liked his privacy and had never cared for extra vehicles on our private road. The way things had been the last few months, every stranger was a threat, to all of us. Besides, if my power was going to turn me into a little inferno, it was better if they had a way to keep themselves a little safer. The gate and fences wouldn't protect them from ghosts, but maybe it would help keep the possessed at bay. I needed to start thinking longer term than my own life. If I was gone, how would my friends stay safe?

"I'm glad you approve." Ned was being sarcastic but Carrie looked up from the skillet where she was frying eggs and gave me a nod of thanks. "I'm going to set the posts today—should be able to get the whole thing up by the end of next week. It's six feet tall, so it isn't inconspicuous but should be effective."

A six-foot-tall metal gate would prevent cars from turning up the drive. If someone climbed over it, or crossed over any of the rest of our fence-lines, they'd have to walk over a mile to get to my place. We were far from impenetrable, but intruders would be easier to spot.

"When it's done, there'll be a keypad that controls the gate. The three of us," Ned nodded at Carrie and me, "Will have remote openers, and we can give everyone else their own codes so they can come and go. The gate won't open without a code, and we'll be able to track whose code opened it."

"Fancy." I wondered what it was costing us, but it didn't matter. We needed it. Like all the improvements for the general farm upkeep, Ned and I would split the cost, though this was one I should offer to pay for on my own. My dwindling checking account was another concern I needed to figure out, though. It had been too long since I'd had a paycheck. I added the gate topic to my list of things I needed to talk to Ned and Carrie about when no one else was around.

Grayson set his coffee down with a thump. "I haven't been by the church this morning but I understand a few new groups have come in. I think we should go there and check on them."

"Of course, as soon as we're done with breakfast." I was more than willing to go in with him if he thought it would help, but food was a priority.

"I don't want Anna going," Jed informed the group. I was so startled that I had to grip my coffee to keep from dropping it.

"You don't get to make those decisions," I reminded him.

Jed crossed his arms over his broad chest and puffed himself up like a territorial grizzly.

"It isn't wise. Someone has to protect you since you won't take care of yourself."

My eyes narrowed into slits and I set my coffee mug down on the counter with more force than I needed to. Jed looked surprised, like he hadn't caught the nonverbal cues I'd been giving all morning about how mad I was at him. That fact alone added fuel to the fire.

"Let's go to the barn and feed the horses." It was a pretty sad state of affairs when you couldn't find the privacy in your own home to have an argument, but that was my reality. I didn't want an extended audience for this particular conversation.

"I already checked on them, Anna. You don't have to go out there," Ned interjected. Carrie jabbed him with her elbow to shut him up. She could tell I was trying to get some privacy, why couldn't any of the men figure it out?

"Will you join me in the barn?" I asked in a tone that said it wasn't a request.

Jed evaluated me with an irritating degree of calm, his tone descending into condescension. "It would be my pleasure."

It was all I could do to not slam the door in his face as I stepped into the mudroom and grabbed my jacket. I kept walking, not bothering to put it on before I stepped outside. The cold winter wind took my breath for a moment, and then my lungs accepted the rush of icy air, warming it enough that when I exhaled my breath hung in a fog. I realized I hadn't changed out of my house shoes. They detracted from the commanding air I was trying to project, but it was too late to go back. The door to the house closed, indicating Jed was following me. I marched towards the barn and didn't look back.

The barn door slid open with a gentle squeak and I stepped through into its soft light, absorbing the smell of fresh alfalfa and grain. The mares nickered gently at me as I entered. I stopped walking for a moment, overwhelmed by the urge to bridle one of them and take off for a ride, disappearing into the woods where no one could find me.

Ned's stallion threw his head over the stall door, stomping to protest the intrusion, ears flat back against his head. The horse had an attitude problem that only castration could fix. For some reason Ned was determined to keep breeding him. I hoped that Charlotte and Hattie's sweet natures would outweigh Demon's nasty temperament in their offspring.

Jed stepped through after me and leaned back against the wood slats of the mares' stall, well out of reach of Demon's teeth. Hattie draped her head over the top rail and nuzzled his shoulder. He held her nose and rubbed the side of her face absently, never taking his eyes from me.

"I think it's time you told me the truth." I tried to keep my tone of voice level and failed.

"Such as?"

"Maybe something to do with my power?"

His right eyebrow twitched in surprise. "What is it you think I have been keeping from you?" He kept stroking the horse; his tone of voice said I was being unreasonable.

"I don't know, Jed." I bit the words off. "Everything, apparently."

"What did my brother have to say?" He enunciated the word brother like it was a rare poison he didn't want to get too close to.

"He told me a lot. For starters, that my power is going to kill me. I'd like to know why you didn't think that was an important thing to mention."

The eyebrow twitched again. "You are too strong to let your power control you. I could tell the first time you used it that you weren't in danger."

"If that was even a concern," I started shouting, and Demon snorted his displeasure at the decibel, "if there was even the slightest risk, you should have told me."

"And have you worry about a terrible thing you need not be concerned about?"

"How do you know I shouldn't be worried?"

"The fact that we are having this conversation means I am correct."

"You mean I'd be dead by now?" He nodded. "Then how did it kill my mother so late in her life?"

Jed was better at schooling his emotions than most doctors I knew. Training to be king must require even more emotional self-control than medicine did. "I've no reason to believe that her power bested her. You told me she died in an accident."

"According to your brother, she died when her power turned her into a fiery tornado."

"How would he know?"

"He says he was there. With her." Jed's absolute stillness was the only clue he gave as to how much my statement surprised him. *Is that because you didn't know, or you're just surprised I found out?* "Why don't you tell me what you know about that."

"Very little, I'm afraid."

"That's not going to cut it."

"I'm unaware of an association between Adonijah and your mother. It is possible he's lying."

Driving a wedge between Jed and I would make Adoni happy, but I didn't think he'd been lying to me, at least not about that. Something in his voice, his expression, had been sincere. At least it had when he was talking about his relationship with my mother. Either Jed was lying, or the Council hadn't told him the whole story. Maybe they hadn't known either.

"You aren't aware of a relationship between your brother and my mother?"

"I wasn't aware they had ever met. How would I know if they had?" He paused and then asked, "What kind of relationship did he claim to have?"

"Don't be naïve, and answer my question." It was the most irritating habit Jed had. He acted like knowledge was to be protected, not shared. As if his secrets were the greatest power he had.

"I did answer."

"He said they were lovers. United in some common purpose, although he didn't say what."

His clenching jaw was the sole indicator of his indignation. "You believe him over me? Adonijah is not known for his honesty."

I forced my own jaw to relax a notch. "Adonijah doesn't always tell the truth, but that doesn't mean he's lying to me about this. And you aren't always as forthcoming as you should be. Besides, this is too complicated a story for him to have made up."

"Which should not mean he's incapable of it."

"I'm sure he's capable." I glared at Jed, thinking about how they'd been raised together. Jed stiffened and folded his arms. I got a rush of satisfaction that he was getting angrier too. "What I don't understand is why I had to hear it from him and not from you."

"I told you that I knew nothing of them being together. What you should ask yourself is, if you will not trust me, then why am I here with you?"

"You make it hard to trust you when you keep things from me. I don't know whose side you're on."

"I see." His lips, set in a bitter line, told me he certainly did not see. "In my era saving someone's life on multiple occasions must have been worth more than it is now."

"Was it your custom to trust people who kept important secrets from you?"

"I've had good reason for not telling you certain things."

"I'm an adult, not some child to be kept in the dark. I'm not one of your concubines that you can keep like a pet." My voice was a thin treble, ire beating in a palpable pulse through my jugular vein.

"When have I ever treated you as less than my equal?" His roar of indignation had Charlotte stamping her hoof against the wooden floor. He lowered his tone. "You are more demanding of my obedience than any queen I ever knew."

"Don't start comparing me to *her.*"

"I compare you to no one, Anna. You are the one who does that," he growled.

I bit my lip because that part might be true. Jed had never brought up the Queen of Sheba. His brother and I had done that. And Adoni had only done it to make me jealous. It was wrong of me to let his brother's machinations come between us.

I backtracked. "You're right that I let your brother get under my skin about her. But you let him interfere every time you keep something from me that he can use against me. You make me weaker with your secrecy. Information is the only thing that helps make us stronger together."

He glared up at the rafters and didn't answer. The silence stretched between us, filling the barn until the only sound was the gentle rush of the horses breathing. The few minutes before he uncrossed his arms and turned his eyes back to me felt like an eternity.

"You may be right," he conceded.

"Thank you." I exhaled some of the tension I'd been holding. "I have some questions and I'd appreciate you answering them." He dipped his head in what looked like agreement. I took a breath to ease more of the anger out of my limbs. "Could Adonijah be telling the truth about having a relationship with my mother?"

From the way his body went rigid, I knew that it was the last time he'd be answering that particular question.

"I don't know."

I was pushing my luck if I thought he'd tolerate me accusing him of dishonesty again, but I was satisfied that he was telling the truth.

"I'm asking you if it's possible."

Jed looked away from me into Demon's stall, answering after a long pause. "Many things are possible, even when they are unlikely."

"He says he's my father."

"That is not possible." Jed furrowed his brow at me as if he thought I'd forgotten how babies were made.

"I don't mean biologically." Jed shrugged, as if the distinction didn't matter.

"He also told you that your mother's power destroyed her."

"Yes."

Jed crossed the wood-planked space between us in two long steps. He stood in front of me until I looked up at him and then covered my shoulders with his hands. His grip strengthened, emphasizing his words.

"If he knew her, I think it more likely that he killed her himself when he found he couldn't control her."

My stomach twisted as I realized Jed was right. Tears filled my eyes in a rush of emotion I didn't expect, anger turning to anguish.

"That's possible." I started shaking and Jed led me to a wooden stool next to my uncle's workbench. I sat as the tears took control of me, my voice cracking between sobs. "As crazy as it sounds, when he talked about her, it sounded like he cared for her."

"Perhaps he did," Jed offered, "in whatever fashion he's capable of. How many in this day and age hurt the ones they love?"

"Murders are most often committed by someone close to the victim."

"It has always been so," said the man who'd killed his own brother.

"I suppose." Adonijah murdering my mother was possible. After all, he'd tried to kill me too. If she had kept him from possessing her power, then he could have killed her some other way. It was impossible to know, though, what had happened. The one person left to tell the story was a ghost intent on taking over the world. It didn't seem like his goals would have changed much in the last thirty years. That span of time was nothing compared to the thousands of years he'd been around.

"I don't understand how she could have let him get close to her."

"There is much we do not know about your mother. And my brother could be charming, when he chose."

"Charming is not a word I'd use to describe him." Terrifying, evil, and sociopathic came to mind as more reasonable descriptors, but I didn't voice them.

"Death seems to have brought out some of his less appealing qualities."

I snorted. "From what you've said, I can't imagine there were many good ones."

"I never cared much for him. It never occurred to me that when I killed him, I'd create a monster that would haunt me for the rest of my days."

"And may have created the circumstances that led to you staying here too."

"That may be," Jed agreed with solemn dignity.

I wiped my tears on my sleeve, wishing I had a tissue to blow my nose.

"Am I going to die?"

He chuckled and stroked another tear from my face with his thumb.

"We all die. I told you, though, you are strong. Your power will never destroy you."

"How can you be sure?"

"I have seen you banish a thousand ghosts and walk away. Not every Magos would survive that."

I took his hand in mine and rubbed my thumb in a slow circle over the ridge of his first knuckle. "How did you die?"

Jed drew the other stool towards mine and perched on the edge of it, as if concerned it might not hold his weight.

"It may surprise you to learn that in the end, it was the ailments of old age that finished me."

I contemplated that, wondering what Jed had been like, in his own life. Would I have loved him then? He didn't give me the impression that I would have.

"Where were you buried?"

"In English, I believe you call it the City of David."

"I guess I've heard of it, but I don't know where it is."

"It's not there anymore. One of many places I knew that have disappeared with time." I waited to see if he would provide more information without me asking for it and he added, "It's south of Jerusalem, inside Palestine."

"It's Israel now," I pointed out. Jed replied with a non-committal noise. So many names had changed over the years, it was difficult for him to keep track. I knew where Israel was, but was a little fuzzier on the exact location of Jerusalem. I needed to spend more time with a world map. "This is a weird question, but do you ever go there?"

"To visit my own grave?" His lips twisted in amusement.

"Well, yeah." I contemplated the current state of my boyfriend's original body and decided that no good came from that particular train of thought.

"I did a few times, in the years after I died. I have not been there in some time."

"Anna?" Grayson was calling me from outside.

"We're in the barn," I hollered before I realized it wasn't necessary, Grayson was sliding the door open.

"I'm sorry to intrude."

"You aren't intruding. We were just talking." I was lying to the priest again, because it was an unwelcome interruption. Jed didn't often share anything from his past. Delaying the conversation might mean he'd be less than forthcoming later, once the reconciliatory mood had passed.

"Ned asked me to let you know there's a car coming down the drive."

"Oh Lord," I murmured. I pushed to my feet and stretched my senses out. There were two souls in front of the house, so the car had made it in. It had come in so quietly neither Jed nor I had heard it. "I see three souls."

"Are they possessed?" Grayson asked.

"I can't tell." He gave me an odd look and I glared at him. "I'm not magical. They're too far away."

"Then we'd better get you a little closer." Jed stood and then braced his hand on the workbench like he was dizzy. I offered him a hand and he growled something unintelligible. I suspected he was fighting the urge to tell me to stay back and let him handle it, knowing that there was no way I would, and that he wasn't up for it either way. When it was clear he wasn't at risk of fainting, I led the way out of the barn and around the side of the house, ignoring the snow that melted into the edges of my slippers.

Everyone in the house had spilled onto the front porch to see the newcomers. I registered the fact that Ned was holding a shotgun, barrel pointed to the ground, but still a tangible threat. *Why the show of force?* I wondered, even as I recognized the mass of wild red curls emerging from the passenger seat of a red sedan. Armella was quite possibly the only other person in Missouri who could see ghosts. She couldn't release them, though. I'd ascertained that when I met her and banished the ghost possessing her brother.

My breath caught when her dark-haired companion turned around and caught sight of me. His handsome face broke into a grin and I understood why Ned was brandishing his twelve gauge. Was I dreaming?

My senses told me the man was, without a doubt, possessed again. His host body was as handsome as ever; unscathed, despite his proximity to the gas explosion. He'd been lucky to be far enough away to avoid harm. The Saint of Sebaste had already left the Italian priest's body when I pulled it away from danger three days earlier and I couldn't imagine how he'd survived. The last time I'd seen him, he was fighting a losing battle against the dragon god.

"Blaise," Jed hissed, closing the distance between them with a few broad strides. He grabbed the trim man by the shoulders before I could muster the wherewithal to utter a warning or try to stop him. Jed pinned him against the red car, wrapping one hand around the slender man's throat. Armella backed away from the commotion with a squeak of alarm.

I brushed past the redhead while I considered how to intervene, and held a hand up to keep anyone on the porch from joining me. The saint's face was turning red, his hands pushing against Jed's chest. I could tell from the bead of sweat running down Jed's forehead that he was exerting more energy than he had. Even so, Blaise might as well have been trying to hold back a locomotive. I didn't know if I'd ever seen Jed this enraged before, and I had no doubt that he was capable of breaking Father Lombardi's neck if he decided to, even when he wasn't at full strength. It wasn't Lombardi he wanted to kill, but the ghost inside him. Jed had good reason to be angry. The last time Jed had seen Saint Blaise of Sebaste, he was in the process of abducting me.

Blaise choked under the hold but managed a benevolent smile. I guessed he either didn't mind being assaulted, or he'd expected it.

"Jedediah, so good to see you again."

"Release him, Jed," Grayson commanded, with enough authority that I was almost surprised Jed didn't oblige. I quieted Grayson with a hand on his arm, hoping the gesture relayed as much reassurance as I could offer him.

"Jed." I kept my voice calm, hoping it would help remind him that I was safe. "Don't hurt him. The body isn't his, and remember that Father Lombardi isn't to blame for Blaise's actions." If Jed heard me, he didn't act like he had. Maybe an appeal to his ancient sense of honor would be more effective. "I'm the one he harmed, and I'm the one who should get to release him. It's my right."

Blaise's eyes widened in alarm but Jed's grip had tightened and he couldn't emit more than a grunt of protest.

Jed's jaw clenched and then relaxed in slow stages as he forced himself to gain control of his temper.

"Why have you come here?" He loosened his grip enough that the man was able to draw in air with an audible gasp.

Blaise clawed at the hand on his throat and then dropped his hands in defeat. His acceptance of the situation made me more suspicious.

"Don't kill him, but don't let him go," I suggested.

"I do not intend to," Jed answered, and I hoped he meant that on both counts. His voice did have a measure of control to it that both comforted and frightened me. My heartbeat quickened. If he was going to kill a man with his bare hands, it wouldn't be from an out of control rage. It would be a premeditated act, a decision that to him, was a logical one.

"I thought you were dead, Blaise." I gave a short laugh after I said it, because of course Blaise was dead—had been for a long time. "Again," I added.

"We can discuss that later," Blaise suggested in a hoarse whisper. "I have come to offer my assistance."

"We do not require your help," Jed rebuffed with a squeeze of his fingers. Blaise relaxed against the car like a defeated dog showing his subservience.

"The Council is in disarray. They can no longer help you," he managed to choke out. I folded my arms.

"I didn't find the Council very helpful before they were trying to kill me. And you're the one that delivered me to them."

"A mistake," Blaise whispered, pushing against Jed for a little leeway so he could squeeze a few words out. "I believed they were on our side."

I shuddered with the remembrance of the shabby, ice-cold room, swirling with powerful ghosts. And Blaise's voice in my ear, *I shouldn't have brought you here. Run.*

"He did try to get me out of there, Jed, once he realized that the dragon ghost wasn't going to protect me."

Jed ignored me and gave the slender man a rough shake. "Why have you come?"

"To offer my assistance," Blaise repeated in a grunt.

"It is not required," Jed spit out.

"I can still be useful," he pleaded.

"You have yet to be."

"I saved Anna," the saint protested, and Jed gave him another rough shake.

"She would not have required your help if you hadn't delivered her to them."

"You both helped, but I saved myself," I reminded them. I'd been the one that defeated Christiana.

"I did that which you were tasked with, Jedediah. At one time were you not prepared to deliver her to the Council?"

Jed's fingers tightened again in response, his expression darkening with righteous anger.

"I don't think he's in a position to hurt us right now, Jed," I intervened, fearing for the priest's windpipe. "You'll have to hash this out with him later. Let's find out what he knows."

Jed released him with a suddenness that made Blaise stumble. He collapsed back against the car, rubbing the red skin of his throat.

"I will have my reckoning," Jed promised, his words heavy with danger. He turned and stalked away. Many other men on the receiving end of Jed's fury would either have crumbled or retaliated once free. Blaise smiled, seemingly unconcerned about the big man with a grudge.

"We have much to discuss." Blaise pushed himself upright again. He brushed out the wrinkled cloth of his jacket and turned his attention back to me. "You look a bit worse for wear, Anna."

I reconsidered letting Jed have at him right then.

"It's not polite to tell people that they look like shit, Blaise." He responded with a guileless smile that I wasn't buying. "Search him." I gave Ned a pointed look. "Last time I saw him, he had a gun."

"I assure you, I am no threat," Blaise protested, but Ned and Chaz descended on him. They held him fast while they went through the pockets of his coat and patted down his waistband before stepping away empty-handed.

"He's clean," Chaz said with reluctance. I evaluated the Italian again, wondering what he had planned this time even while I accepted the unreasonable fact that I was pleased to see him. We'd fought together and it gave us a shared bond.

"It's odd, but it is good to see you," I told him. He gave me another cheeky grin.

"High praise, indeed. Come, we have work to do. Do you remember Armella?"

"Of course I do. Why do you have her?"

"I've done nothing to the child," Blaise protested. Armella's eyes narrowed into slits at being referred to as a child but he spoke again before she could say anything. "We have work to do, Anna. There are people that need your help, and hers." I didn't buy his angelic act. I might not know what it was yet, but Blaise had an agenda.

"Bring him in," I directed to Chaz and Ned. "It's too cold to talk out here." I ushered Armella ahead of me, hoping to keep her away from Blaise. There was a reason he'd found her and brought her with him, and I was concerned he was considering switching bodies. He was strong enough to choose another host and take them whenever he wanted.

Armella could see ghosts like I could, and if she could do that much, he might hold out hope she could do more than she knew. I wasn't planning on letting that happen, which I tried to convey with a warning glare that Blaise ignored.

Ten of us crowded into my little parlor, and I suppressed a tinge of claustrophobic panic.

"I have a gift for Jedediah," Blaise announced once he was settled in a chair next to the fireplace, Chaz on one side and Ned on the other. Jed was in the doorway, blocking the entrance. Now that Blaise was in he wouldn't be able to get out without our permission. Carrie perched on the edge of the sofa, as if ready to flee, Armella sat beside her, and Matthew squeezed onto the sofa on the other side of Armella. Ty and Grayson lingered in the doorway to the library. There wasn't any place else to go.

"What game is this you play?" Jed folded his arms over his chest but he didn't need to do anything to look more formidable. He was radiating animosity and strength.

"No contest is afoot, Jedediah. As I said, I've come to help. You still need me."

"You have nothing we need. I should have killed you. I still can."

"I knew you would be angry with me." Blaise's head turned down in an act of humility but the way a clever smile played at the sides of his mouth made me doubt the veracity of his remorse. "I seek redemption."

"I don't have the power to grant that."

"Anna." Blaise's pretty, dark eyes turned to me. "I helped save you. Tell them I can be trusted."

"I don't trust you, Blaise. If you're helping us, it's because you think you can gain something from it. If you have something to offer us, maybe I'll let you live. If not, Lombardi gets his body back sooner rather than later."

"Check the boot of the car," he rushed to interject, even though I was too far away to release him without hurting his host.

"What have you brought?" Jed demanded.

"Could be a trap," Chaz voiced. Ned shifted off the mantle, his shotgun on a loop over his arm. "I'll go see what it is."

"No," Blaise objected with too much force. "It is dangerous to all but Jedediah."

Jed turned on his heel and walked out the front door, and I wondered what was out there that would harm the living but not the dead.

"I swear to God, Blaise, if anything happens to him, when I release you, I'll make sure it hurts. Keep him here," I ordered Ned and Chaz like they were mine to command, and followed Jed out the door.

"Stay back, Anna. I don't know what he has brought." Jed approached the car like he might a wild dog.

I couldn't imagine an ancient saint crafting a bomb, and despite his competing loyalties, I didn't think Blaise intended to harm me. But it was Jed he'd sent out.

Jed released the latch on the back end of the car. I flinched, but nothing happened. Whatever was inside had Jed mesmerized. He stood over the open trunk, staring.

"What is it?" I demanded, stepping off the porch to join him. Jed reached into the trunk and withdrew a length of steel with reverence.

I stopped short. "How the hell did Blaise get your sword away from the police?"

Jed answered with a sinister smile. "I can think of only one way."

He must have possessed a police officer to get to it. I wondered if Jed would have done the same, given the chance. I decided I'd rather not know.

Jed stomped up the porch steps and walked back into the house, the sword tucked safely by his side. I opened my sixth sense as easily as blinking and swept the surrounding area with it. Nothing. If this was part of some plan against us, it hadn't started yet.

"Why bring it back to me? What is it you want?" Jed was demanding when I walked back into the entryway, shutting the door behind me with a gentle thud.

"It was a gift from the Council," Blaise explained with an altruistic smile. "You will have need of it yet."

"How much of the Council is left?" I interjected before Jed could ask any more questions. I'd worry about how—and why—Blaise had returned the sword later. I needed to know how many more of them were against me, and how many of them might be on my side. A few of the ghosts that night had helped me, but the ones trying to kill me were in the majority.

"It will take time to determine new leadership. These are things that can take decades to resolve, but there is no time to wait for them. We must act."

"Why?" Jed demanded.

"What reason would anyone have to sow such chaos among the Council that they were able to divide it?" Blaise countered.

"The best way to cause confusion is to create a vacuum of leadership," Chaz suggested.

"Indeed." Blaise kept his eyes on Jed, who was inspecting his sword blade to ensure it hadn't been damaged.

"Christiana—" I started.

"Is not intelligent enough to craft such a plan on her own," said Blaise.

"You think someone set her up?" I asked.

"Who do you think has such power?" Blaise had the irritating habit of answering a question with another question.

"Adonijah?" Chaz asked.

"Jed's brother is a convenient pawn. He is not the true danger." I disagreed with this assertion, but I knew who Blaise was talking about.

"The Master." I gave Jed a cautious glance since the first time he'd heard that name from me he'd reacted with violent anger. Other than his hand caressing the hilt of his sword, he was as still as the wood doorway he stood next to. Blaise gave a convulsive swallow, his Adam's apple bobbing up his throat.

"Without the Council's intervention, the Master will be free to bring chaos to reign in the living world," Blaise said.

"We're already seeing that, aren't we? There's a mass possession event going on right now," I pointed out. Blaise dropped his eyes from the sword long enough to turn his attention to me.

"My child, you have no idea who you are dealing with. This is just the beginning."

"Then why don't you tell us."

"The Master is the antithesis of God, the source of evil."

"That's a bit melodramatic," I protested, but Father Costas interjected one word.

"Satan."

Blaise regarded him with intense blue eyes. "Indeed, but you will not find the devil spouts horns and a tail. The Master will not be that obvious or easy to identify, but he is here, among us." I glanced around, sensing nothing but the ten of us in my parlor. Blaise chuckled at my ignorance. "I don't mean in this room, but you are right to be cautious. He could be anywhere. Anyone."

"You believe the spirit everyone calls the Master is, in fact, the devil?" I couldn't believe the words I was saying but Blaise's face had the fervent ardor of honesty.

"The devil as written by man isn't accurate. As I've said, you won't find horns on this beast."

"So what is he? A devil or another nasty ghost?"

"Don't mistake the source of evil for a man. The Master is one of the fallen."

"An angel?" Carrie asked.

"Why wasn't I aware of this? Which one of the fallen is he?" Jed demanded.

"Jedediah." Blaise crossed his arms, his tone one he might use with an errant child. "You were at as much risk as any of joining him."

It was hard to talk down to someone who towered over you. Jed took two steps closer as if to emphasize that fact.

"I worked for the Council for centuries. How could you doubt my devotion?"

"We did not trust each other, much less those who helped us. Deception was the reason they were thrown from heaven to begin with," Blaise murmured. "And remember," he chastised, not wanting to get thrown under the bus with the rest of the Council, "I am not one of them. I was human, like you are."

I ignored his sudden bid to distance himself from the Council. "You're the Council as much as any of them, Blaise. Don't try to pretend otherwise. Why is the Master focused on me?"

"Evil seeks opportunity, and it has found that here."

"Why would Missouri be at any more risk than the rest of the world?" Carrie argued.

Blaise relaxed into his chair, crossing one leg over the other.

"Mankind is an easy host. This is where the Father of Lies has found root today. He never wastes an opportunity to sow the seeds of malcontent."

It was a little more complicated than that. They were here because I was. I was one more link in the chain of people with the genetic ability to banish ghosts.

"This isn't the first time that ghosts have started possessing people, is it?" I asked.

Blaise stiffened as if his suit had been starched with him in it. "No. There have been many such episodes in the history of this Earth. Have you heard of the dancing plagues that started in the eleventh century?"

I took a moment to dig through the random bits of medical history I had stored in my brain, and then nodded. "I heard about that in school. It's considered to be a case of mass hysteria."

"Or mass possession," Ty noted.

"I guess that makes sense." I wondered how many other events that were medically inexplicable were caused by ghosts, and guessed a great many of them may have been. "Where does Adoni fit into this?"

"He's a recruit, as was Christiana. They may have been tasked with finding you and killing you."

"I'm sure they were. And when Adoni found Jed with me, he couldn't resist attacking us."

"His hatred of his brother is his weakness, but don't underestimate him."

"I'm not the one that's been underestimating him. That was the Council."

"How so?" Blaise's look of confusion was genuine.

"That's why you failed," I explained. "You designated yourselves as the protectors of mankind, but all you cared about was your own self-serving goals. Each of the fallen wanted to go back where they came from. By protecting your own interests, you guaranteed you couldn't succeed. You left the Council open to be infiltrated by the Master so he could get to Christiana. And the rest of them."

"Pride and envy," Matthew murmured. Blaise clenched his teeth together, body still rigid in the chair like he was welded to it.

I changed tactics. If he wasn't going to give us useful information, then it was time to free his host from the prison he was in.

"One of them came to me yesterday."

"One of who?" Blaise's black eyebrows furrowed together like a sleek caterpillar crawling across his forehead.

"One of the Council. She claimed her name was Eli." His expression was blank, so I went on. "She's a little shorter than me, dark short hair. Young. But she could take any form she wanted to." I remembered Scipio, shifting to appease me, and the dragon ghost who'd run the Council. I felt suddenly foolish for describing her to Blaise.

A shake of Blaise's head indicated that he didn't know who I was speaking of. "Did you get any other name from her?"

"No." Would she have given me a fake name?

"Be careful, Anna. Not everyone can be trusted." Blaise's patronizing timbre was back and I bristled.

"I noticed."

"Excuse me," Matthew Costas said, and our attention swiveled towards him. "It's pretty clear this isn't Roberto Lombardi, but who exactly is he, and where is Roberto?"

"This is Father Lombardi, but he's possessed right now. By the patron saint of snowy days or something like that," I told him.

"Sore throats," Blaise corrected me with crisp offense.

"Whatever."

"You can't let him—" Costas began and I finished the sentence for him.

"Stay possessed? No, we won't let him keep Lombardi," I promised. "Blaise needs to start making other plans."

"Yes, of course." Blaise agreed with too much haste and I turned on him.

"You will leave the living alone. Armella included."

He shrugged, a gesture that might indicate agreement but didn't commit to it.

"For now, though, there are other things to be worried about, Anna," Blaise reminded me. "Armella, tell them."

"How did you wind up with Blaise?" I asked the redhead. "He's dangerous. You should stay away from him."

"I ran into him again at the hospital," she answered. Her eyes were the color of lilacs and seemed to gaze through me. The color clashed with the wild mass of red curls that she didn't attempt to control.

"I was surprised to see you here, but I'm glad we got to meet again." I was grateful. Having someone else who could tell if a person was possessed would be helpful, but she also added to the list of people I was responsible for, someone else that I had to keep safe.

"We heard there were people at Father Grayson's sanctuary that needed help," she jumped in as if she'd been awaiting this very moment. "I picked up some second-hand blankets from the thrift store and took them there, but I didn't bring enough for everyone." She looked around with concern.

"Thank you for your kindness," Grayson replied. "My parishioners are also gathering supplies for them. We will make sure no one is left out in the cold."

Armella nodded impatiently in his direction. "While we were at the church I noticed there were a couple people with ghosts in them. Only a few, though. Most of them are just sick." She was excited about the ones that were possessed and found the ill boring.

I glanced at the clock on the mantle next to Blaise. It was half past ten. I'd only managed one cup of coffee so far, and nothing to eat. "Right. Let's get some breakfast and then we can go up there."

I wasn't sure if we had enough food for everyone but I shouldn't have worried. Carrie had my kitchen well enough stocked to feed dozens. I left the priests in the parlor with Jed to watch over Blaise while the rest of us split up. Chaz retreated upstairs and I brought Armella to the kitchen with Ned and Ty. She declined coffee, choosing a mug of green tea instead.

"I'll have your breakfast ready for the road," Carrie promised and I realized she was making individual sandwiches with egg, bacon, and cheese wrapped between slices of her homemade bread. I shot her a grateful look, she knew we shouldn't take the time to eat at home.

"Do you want me to come with you?" Ty asked. I nodded, refilling the coffee maker with water.

"Please. I don't know how much medical care we're going to need to provide, but I may need a nurse."

"Can he ride with you?" Chaz asked, rejoining us. He'd changed into a pair of slacks and a blue pinstripe shirt. "Ned and I need to head up to Unionville and talk to the sheriff." He looked at Ned. "I just learned that the formal inquest is tomorrow, where they'll tell us how Marcus Wilson died."

Ned's jaw clenched at the news. I wondered what the finding would be. Would the coroner be able to tell that the cause of death wasn't from the gunshot wounds? The bullets were the obvious explanation for death, but a good medical examiner might find other evidence.

If my power had similar effect to a lightning strike, Marcus's arm—where I'd gripped him tight and blasted my power through to him—might have a pattern etched into it like the branches of a tree. Pulmonary edema wouldn't be explained by a gunshot wound, and neither would alveolar hemorrhage. Laboratory screening might show high levels of myoglobin, potassium, and troponin. He'd have the same electrolyte imbalance that the possessed patients demonstrated.

Maybe I'd get lucky and they'd assume he had the same "virus" that the other possessed hospital patients were diagnosed with. But me not being associated with the cause of death meant the responsibility of it fell on Ned, even if some of the histological findings were inconsistent with a gunshot being the cause of death.

"Thank you for defending him." I gave Chaz a one-armed hug and he shrugged. He acted like he hadn't taken yet another week vacation from his job and put himself at risk by being near me.

"Since Ned hasn't been charged with a crime, I'm not defending him, technically. If it gets to that point, which I don't think it will, we'll have to get some help on that front. It's not my specialty."

"Whatever it takes." I tried to set aside my surge of remorse to be dealt with later. There was no doubt my power had killed Marcus' spirit, but Ned shooting him might have sped the process along for the body. Either way, Marcus was dead without his soul. Ned had shot to kill but I'd beaten him to it. If they decided to charge Ned with a crime, I could confess, but it would be impossible to convince the police that I'd killed him. I promised myself that I'd deal with it later, if I had to.

"We should get going, too." I needed to grab my medical kit, but other than that there wasn't any reason to delay our departure. "Armella can fill us in on the way." I stepped past Ned to get to the dining room. My bag was on the buffet where I'd dropped it last time I came home, and my medical kit was sitting in the parlor.

Ned stopped me with a hand on my arm, his voice a low whisper that was still loud enough to be overheard.

"Don't go. You don't have to do this." Jed followed him and the two tall men towered over me in the narrow space. I scooted back against a chair to give myself room to breathe.

"Of course I have to go out there. Why wouldn't I?"

"You can't single-handedly deal with this anymore," Ned argued.

"Who's going to if I don't?" The room was pressing in on me, the edges blurring.

"Let the priests deal with it." Ned's voice was low persuasion, his hand massaging my upper arm with familiarity I hadn't forgotten. "They've proven they can."

My head spun and I gripped the back of a dining room chair. What was wrong with me?

"This won't ever end if I can't figure out how to stop them. They'll kill me, too."

"You heard Blaise. This has gotten bigger than you, Anna."

I would have laughed but my mouth was too dry. "It's always been bigger than me."

"There's no point in risking yourself anymore. Let the priests go. We'll stay here with you."

"Close your new gate against the world and to hell with everyone else?" I tried to argue but it sounded like I was talking through a tin can and expecting them to hear it reverberate down the string.

Ned ground his teeth together again, his mind made up. "Yeah. We protect ourselves. Here."

My vision grayed out for a moment, and I braced another hand on the table to cope with a new surge of dizziness. I knew Ned was right next to me, but it seemed like he was farther away, the table appeared to elongate. The room was stretching.

"Are you well, Anna?" Jed asked, his voice filled with concern. I felt myself slipping but wasn't sure if I was falling. It felt like I was being pulled away.

"What's wrong with her?" Ty's voice, even more distant. I watched myself, as though through a dirty glass door. Ty shouldered in between the two larger men and lowered my body to the floor. He kept mouthing my name, but I couldn't hear him anymore.

# CHAPTER EIGHT

**I BLINKED** and Ty's blurry image was replaced with darkness. I tried again but I still couldn't see. My mind swirled like I'd had too much to drink, tilting on an axis I couldn't control. Had I fainted? I didn't recall feeling ill earlier but now the sensation of movement without being able to see caused my stomach to churn. I clamped my eyes tight and tried to find something to hold on to, but the darkness surrounded me like a cloud. I retreated into my mind, focusing my efforts on being still and breathing through the nausea.

I wasn't sure how much time had passed before I realized I was able to focus again. I was lying on my side. My right arm was stretched out overhead at an awkward angle. I tried to shift and realized I was stuck, my wrist caught tight in cold metal. I tried to pull free but it held me fast. My fingers wrapped around the links that trapped me. I could feel dirt beneath my backside, and the wind whispered across my chest. I ran a hand down my torso, and my fears were confirmed. I wasn't wearing anything.

My ribcage constricted, trapping my breath as I realized I couldn't see because there was a cloth over my face. Someone else had been here. I had to repress the urge to scream with a forceful swallow. I couldn't give in to fear.

I opened my second sight, but I was alone. Whoever had been there with me was gone. I ripped the cloth covering my face off with the hand that wasn't chained down. The darkness was complete, still. It was as if I was locked in a windowless room. Based on the dank, earthy smell, I was back in the in-between cavern. I'd just been here with Adonijah a few hours before, and I didn't think Eli would bring me here like this. The Master could have. Or anyone from the Council.

I backed against the cavern wall, where some enterprising soul had managed to anchor a chain into rock that didn't exist. It felt real enough now, and when I tugged on the chain, willing it to give, it didn't budge. My bare back ground against the rough rock wall as I sat in the dirt, knees pulled up against me while I tried to figure out how to use the heavy length of chain as a weapon. It was about two feet long, not enough to do much with unless my captor was close.

Despite being naked, I was sweating. My heart raced inside my ribcage, drowning out the sound of my own thoughts. *Breathe, Anna. Panicking isn't helping.*

Maybe it was the Council again. The good members of the Council weren't likely to tie me up, though. Which of the surviving members hated me enough to drag me here against my will and chain me like a dog? The last time I'd seen them, they'd tried to kill me, so tying me up seemed like a step down on the hostility scale. It didn't make sense. What ghost was strong enough to call me here while I was awake?

The fact that this place wasn't real didn't help. I should be able to rescue myself but until I figured out how, I was stuck, waiting for whoever did this to me.

The heavy chain scraped across the dirt floor when I shifted, pulling tight when my fettered wrist tugged against the length of it. I tried to squeeze the bones of my hand together to slide out of the manacle, but it fit the curve of my wrist too well. The metal was rubbing against my skin, and it was beginning to hurt.

*How long have I been here?* In the sensory deprivation, I had no way of knowing. At least my heartbeat was calmer now. With my fight-or-flight instincts triggered, I counted it as a victory.

*You don't have to sit in the dark.* I reminded myself. I'd created light here once before, so I should be able to do it again. I focused my thoughts on being able to see, on having light around me. When nothing changed I closed my eyes and calmed my breathing, focusing all of my will on light. When I opened them the cave was filled with a low light, as if dawn were breaking.

After another series of slow breaths, I looked again for the door in my mind that controlled access to this dream world. All I found were the shifting sparkles of spots on the insides of my eyelids. I tried to convince myself that next time I opened my eyes I would be back in my dining room with Jed and Ty, but the still cavern and the pungent smell of dirt stayed with me.

I focused my energy on the chain around my wrist, imagined it vanishing, or changing into something with the consistency of paper. Here, too, I failed. The metal rattled when I moved, unaffected by my will.

If relaxation didn't work, maybe pain would. I dug my fingernails into the palm of my hand until they cut through the skin and turned red. I kicked at the chain in the wall with my bare heel until it was bruised and there were tears of pain in my eyes. Pulling with all my might, I tried in vain to pry it from the wall. If there was weakness in one of the metal links, I didn't find it. My only achievement was making myself sore, breathless, and refilled with a sense of panic because I was tied like a hog waiting for slaughter. I shouted my frustration until I couldn't breathe anymore, coughing in shallow gulps that echoed back to me from the cavern walls.

Consciousness left and returned in timeless intervals while I leaned back against cold rock, cradling the coiled length of chain in my arms like a shroud.

"The time has come." The voice slid around me like snake scales rasping on the ground, and I woke with a start. My other sight focused on one spark of light, another soul, sharing the space around me. It was too close. I tried to pull away but the rock wall against my back and the chain around my wrist held me. The spirit brushed against my bare shoulder and I let out a gasp at the sudden cold.

It drifted around me, a dank fog of ghost I couldn't get away from. I shivered. I couldn't hurt it but feared it wouldn't have the same restrictions.

"It's time, Anna." I recognized Adonijah's voice, which solidified as his body did. The linen tunic and pants he wore emphasized the power gap between us, that he was in control while I was not.

He squatted in front of me, lips set into a congenial smile, and settled his hand above my knee in a possessive grip. I was backed against the wall, with no place to run. I braced my hands on his torso and shoved, but he was immovable. His hand stayed, tightening into a vice that I couldn't budge.

"Get your hands off me." I used my most commanding voice, a tone that I'd spent years perfecting. He laughed, a mocking sound that echoed around us. I wasn't in a position to demand anything and we both knew it.

He squeezed my knee. "It doesn't have to be the end. You could change your mind and join me."

I couldn't help wonder if he had touched my mother this way. Had she liked it? I automatically reached for the nuclear core of my power, but it was still locked inside me. I ignored his hand on me and focused my energy on my surroundings. Anger fueled a different kind of power. It pulsed through me and the half-light shifted into a bright sun in the sky. It wasn't much but I could better see the bearded face next to mine.

Why didn't my power help when I wanted to get the chain out of the wall? I couldn't get rid of Adonijah by making the sun come out. He wasn't a vampire.

Adonijah chuckled. "You are strong, little one." The pressure on my thigh lifted and he brushed his fingers across my cheek and hair in what would have seemed a tender gesture if I wasn't tied up. I refused to flinch because I knew he'd enjoy that. "It's unfortunate you were never trained to use your power. I could help you with that."

"I don't want your help, Adonijah." I stated his name in a flat curse and he let out a satisfied sigh.

"Don't be cross, little one, I promised you we would be together again soon." His hand caressed down my arm and across my hip. I shifted so I could free a leg, and kicked. My bare foot struck his midriff. He grunted as my foot sank into his middle like I'd struck a pillow instead of a solid being.

He stood and waggled his finger at me. He hadn't solidified enough for me to damage him. The dead were hard to hurt, which had me at a distinct disadvantage when I couldn't use my power. I wished we were in my world so I could destroy him.

"Let me go," I enunciated, each word clipped with anger. They'd taught me to control my tone in medical school, so my voice wouldn't give my emotions away. I hoped he didn't have a nose like a dog's, or he'd be able to smell the fear on me. I was determined not to show it, but I remembered what it felt like to be under his control. He'd managed to turn possession into a bonus package of violation and torture. I'd sworn to never let him hurt me again, but in this place, I might not be able to stop him.

"I don't think I will." Adonijah's smile lingered, lazy and insolent.

"Why am I here?"

"We can rule the world together. I can make you a queen."

"Tempting, but I think I'll pass." My Aunt Ann used to warn me that my smart mouth was going to get me into trouble. So be it. I didn't have it in me to temper my tongue, though it might be safer for me if I did.

"Everything you want will be yours," he continued.

"All I want is for you to die. It's nice of you to offer."

"My brother is weak." He leaned closer to me, pressing me against the cliff and I felt his breath on my ear, his voice a dangerous whisper. "He contaminates you. I can make you stronger."

"Your brother," I fought to get the words out as my jaw clenched in anger, "is a far better man than you could ever hope to be."

His hand squeezed my shoulder in warning and I tried to pull free.

"Without the Council guarding you, this space is mine to have." He chuckled as I absorbed the implication. By killing off Christiana, as awful as she'd been, had I allowed Adonijah free reign inside my head?

His fingers drifted across my clavicle and I slapped his hand away before it could move farther down.

"What do you want with me?"

"The question isn't what I want, it's what I will have."

"You are never going to have me." I tried to make my voice sound bored.

"I am more powerful than you know." His throaty voice crawled across my skin and I had to resist the shudder of revulsion that accompanied his words.

"Good for you," I taunted, but he didn't take the bait.

"If you joined me, we could have everything. I could give you the world, Anna. I would protect you far better than my brother could."

"I would never give him up for you."

"You are already mine, little one. You always have been."

"Never," I protested, but he ignored me.

"What makes you think you understand anything? Do you think my brother is sane? He murdered his own flesh and blood. Can you be sure he won't hurt you, when the time comes?"

"You won't turn me against Jed. It's a waste of your breath to try."

"His heart will never be yours. He gave it to Makeda. In his eyes, no woman could ever be her equal."

"He loves me." In a moment of weakness, I lost control, and the defensive tone of my voice gave away how I felt about the woman Jedediah had loved long ago.

"He is my brother. I knew him in the flesh my entire life. How long have you known him, little one?"

A couple of months, but I wasn't going to admit that. I stayed silent.

"She was a remarkable woman, unlike any I've ever known. Not to say that you aren't attractive, little one." His tone turned clever again, his lips played into a smile that bordered on cruel flirtation. "But if she returned to him today, who do you think he would choose?"

His implication was clear. I couldn't hold a candle to the Queen of Sheba.

"She's dead," I reminded him.

"As am I, yet here we are."

"She's not still here," I pointed out.

"Are you sure of that?" he asked.

My silence betrayed my sudden uncertainty. I didn't have any way of knowing if she was or wasn't. I'd assumed she was long gone. *If she wasn't, and she wanted to be with Jed, wouldn't she have been able to find him by now?*

I cut off my own wayward thoughts. "This conversation is pointless."

"I could help you defeat the Master." Adoni dangled the one thing I needed help with.

"You work for him. Why would you do that?"

He stood and took a step back as if I'd slapped him. "I'm no one's lap dog, but there have been times when our plans aligned."

"And that's changed now?"

"I can coexist with him, little one. The only reason for me to work against him is if I can have you."

"I won't let you have my power. I'll kill us both first. You know this."

"You are stubborn, like your mother. The moment is fast approaching when, like her, you'll realize how much you need my help."

"I would never ask you for help and you will never have me." I reiterated, even as I doubted my ability to keep that promise. Had my mother tried to kill him, but failed?

"You are a troublesome thing, but one that can be controlled, as you and I both recall." He came towards me again, voice lilting with innuendo, and stretched his hand out to touch me again. I kicked again and this time my heel connected with soft flesh over bone. Adoni let out a grunt of pain and indignation. I kicked again but he stumbled back out of reach.

"If you could take control of me here, you would have already done it." I realized it was true even as I said the words. Although he enjoyed taunting me, he didn't have any power here either. Beyond the ability to get me here, and tie me up like an animal. Assault me, maybe. This wasn't my physical body, but it felt real to me, in whatever construct of my mind that we were in.

"What are you waiting for?" I challenged him and he lurched forward, grabbing my free arm and digging his fingers into the skin as he pulled me up to him. I stumbled, trying to gain my footing. He had me off balance, rendering me defenseless.

"The Master promised you to me." His breath touched my ear, smelling of death and decay. I gagged in response. "I assure you, it won't be long. Even now he has gathered your friends. You will meet him soon, and then you will be mine. If you'd come of your own accord, I would have been kind to you, but you've made your choice. Now I make mine." He avoided another kick by dematerializing so my foot struck air. He rematerialized enough to push me to the ground, face first. My manacled arm stretched out against the full length of chain. In that position, I couldn't fight.

"You will be mine," he promised as he knelt over my back.

"Stop touching me, you pervert," I hissed. I tried to scramble away but he pinned me to the hard-packed earth. The knowledge that his body wasn't real didn't help when I could feel the detail of his genitalia through the thin cloth of his pants, pressed against my thigh. I already knew that it excited him to hurt me. I didn't need that disgusting bit of proof. I closed my eyes and focused on using my anger to channel my ability to affect the realm we were in. Adoni shifted his pelvis against my buttocks and I lost control of my fear.

I latched on to that strange fury-fueled power, so different from my ghost-killing nuclear core. The ground shuddered, and I felt the vibrations through my chains. Adonijah lifted off me in alarm as the earth rippled beneath us.

"What have you done?" he demanded, I rolled, slamming my knee into what I hoped was his groin. Ghost he might be, but the corporeal body he'd taken on was solid enough right then that he groaned with real pain. I felt him collapse to my right, heard the tell-tale sign of agony laced with profanity.

His arm slammed against the side of my face. Pain exploded through the rim of my orbit and my cheek split against my teeth. The taste of blood filled my mouth. He hadn't wasted any time retaliating. My wrath kept me connected to the power and the earth shook again. I felt the ground fracturing beneath me. Adonijah, still in his corporeal body, tried to stand and fell to the ground next to me.

"What are you doing?" The first hint of uncertainty filled his expression.

I didn't respond as I envisioned the ground opening up and swallowing him. The hard dirt underneath me was replaced by empty air. Adonijah grabbed ahold of me, wrapping his arms around me as we dangled from my manacled wrist. I screamed from the pain in my hand before the bones of my palm folded together, breaking as they slipped free of the manacle with a sickening crunch that resonated down my arm. We fell, entwined together as one.

We dropped through darkness so complete the only light was the one from Adonijah's soul, visible to my sixth sense. I could feel him against me, could hear his screams in my ear. The only way I knew which end was up was from the air rushing against my backside. My cries were lost to the wind.

Realization dawned that I was going to die, here in this in-between space while Adonijah would survive. There were benefits to already being dead. *The door.* My inner voice spoke with focus my conscious mind hadn't been able to achieve. *Find the door or you're going to die.*

I closed my eyes again, not that it mattered in the darkness, and focused my energy on relaxing. It wasn't easy in a free fall, but I clutched Adonijah closer. I vowed to myself that if I didn't kill him in this world, I would in the next.

Envisioning a doorway on a quiet plane, under a great oak

tree, full of its summer leaves, I found a moment of peace inside me. There wasn't fear in the finality of death, any more than there was in living.

As if formed from the sense of acceptance inside me, a doorway flared into existence beneath me, the outline orange like the ball of fire I carried inside me. Adonijah clawed at my arms, trying to pry my body away from him as if he recognized the door for what it was. I knew what I had to do.

The door opened for us and I wrapped my legs around Adonijah's, my arms holding him close. His form was shifting under my hands, losing substance at an alarming rate as he turned back to his spirit form. He wasn't fast enough. We fell through the doorway, landing inside my body with a thump that knocked my hold loose. It didn't matter. Adonijah's spirit was inside me, in the real world.

He twisted as he realized his predicament, the sinews of his soul grating against my visceral organs as he struggled for control. How had I forgotten how strong he was? He entered my mind, clouding my ability to reach my voluntary nervous system. I couldn't feel anything, and my hand clenched without me telling it to. My voice let out a victorious laugh that said the action had been Adoni's, and I knew he controlled my central nervous system.

I grappled, clearing a path in my mind before Adoni covered it again. I found another synapse he wasn't in yet, and the advantage was mine. My familiarity with the convoluted paths of my nervous system was better than his, and he hadn't had time to suppress my access yet.

I found the pathway that accessed my nuclear core and released it in a glorious rush. The roar of energy flashed like an explosion. Adonijah's scream of rage was cut short, his essence bursting out of me like the dust from a blast of dynamite. My fire burned through me, a welcome agony. It was mine, part of me, the one thing I could control.

The knowledge that I was safe enveloped me in a cocoon of recognizable warmth. I was back, inside myself. Relief filled me as I realized that the cavern the ghosts took me to was external. It wasn't in my mind, that was just how I got there. They could call me away from myself, but at least they couldn't use my mind to get inside my body while I was sleeping.

I refocused my thoughts and turned back to the door in my mind, memorizing the location, so I could find my way back to it. There wasn't a door there at all. Instead a tree stood over me, white blooms and green leaves sheltering me from a strange bright light. Satisfaction filled me. I knew where I was, and I knew I could find it again.

When I opened my eyes, I found Jed standing by the door of my room, kilij balanced between his hands as he watched over me from a safe distance. I scrambled upright, with my back against my solid wood headboard as I checked for ghosts. Not a wisp of Adonijah's soul remained.

I might have been able to convince myself it was a bad dream, if it weren't for the wary stance of my lover and the tell-tale signs of my power still scorching through me. How I'd gotten to my bed from the dining room, I wasn't sure, but Jed could have carried me there.

"I released your brother." The words tasted like a strange fruit that I wasn't sure I liked.

Jed shifted his stance and then acknowledged my words with a curt nod. "It is well done, then. I wasn't sure what was happening when you passed back into your body." He hefted the kilij to show me he remembered his promise to me; that he'd kill me before he let another ghost take control of me. I hadn't forgotten.

"I'm glad you weren't in the way. I could have hurt you."

"I have no wish to get caught by your power. Are you all right?"

"I'll be okay." It was at least half true. My voice shook with doubt.

"It was a battle only you could fight, Anna. There is no shame in winning it. He would have taken you, if he could." He paused, let me absorb that strange string of words. He was right. My only hope at survival had been to release Adonijah.

"I hope he did not damage you."

I looked at my right hand and saw it looked and felt normal, no torn skin or broken bones.

"I'll be fine." *Would I be?* I thought it was true. Maybe not tomorrow, but someday.

Jed looked me over, and I had the uneasy feeling that he saw more than I wanted him to.

"Yes. You are strong." He understood that the healing would

come with time but that right now I was not okay. He was wise enough not to mention it.

Hearing him call me strong helped, even though I knew it was true. I didn't want to dwell on what had just happened. I'd have to at some point, but right now I needed something to distract me, something else to focus on. I needed something to be normal.

"What time is it?"

"You were gone for several hours."

"So it's . . ." The light outside suggested it was mid-afternoon. I wondered how he'd kept everyone away from me.

"It's past noon." Jed had an expensive-looking watch on his wrist but he didn't take his eyes off me long enough to look at it.

"This isn't done yet. Adonijah taking me—I think that was the beginning of something." It wasn't the same sensation as I got from my sixth sense and ghosts, but I felt something, an uneasiness. Like the way the air feels before a bad thunderstorm sweeps through. Too still, with undertones of violence.

"Our enemy stirs," Jed agreed. "I also feel it."

"Where is everyone?"

"Ned and Chaz have gone to see the police. It took some encouraging but I convinced Carrie to go with them. I thought she'd be safer with them than here. The priests and the young girl are tending to the needs of those at the sanctuary."

"They went without me?" I forced myself upright.

"Given your situation, I thought it best to have them gone." He paused. "It was difficult to persuade them to go but I did not know how long you would be." He made it sound like I'd run to the store for milk. "Having them here was not helpful."

"They're in danger." I was already out of bed, relieved to find that I could in fact stand on my own. The alien dizziness I'd felt in the dining room was gone. The only tangible remnants of my encounter with Adonijah was in the power that coursed through me as if it was swept along by my beating heart. *Did that make it less real?* "Where's Ty?"

"Downstairs. He would not leave you, no matter what I said."

"Adonijah said something about the Master gathering my friends. I don't think he would care about Ned and Chaz, but the priests . . ."

"The priests have some power of their own and may be at risk." Jed threw the bedroom door open and evaluated the hallway for unseen danger.

I brushed past him, taking care to not touch him. It would be a while before I was ready for contact. I knew there weren't any ghosts in the corridor.

"Let's go."

# CHAPTER NINE

**T**Y MET ME in the dining room, peppering me with questions and barking orders all at the same time.

"Are you all right? What happened? Go sit down so I can check your blood pressure. You shouldn't be up."

"Adonijah is dead," I announced while I tried to sidle past Ty towards the kitchen. I didn't want to spend too much time in the dining room. Part of me was a little worried that whatever Adonijah had created to pull me into the other world was still around.

"You released him?" Ty's voice shot up an octave and he clutched my hands in his, looking me up and down to make sure I was okay.

"I did."

"You'd better eat something." He drew me into the kitchen, morphing into the Italian grandmother I never had.

My stomach rumbled in agreement. It liked this side of Ty. I ignored it, and the fact that I needed to eat.

"I've got to get going. I have to catch up with Grayson and the others."

"Carrie left extra breakfast sandwiches in the fridge. I'll reheat them." That was merciful news. I decided a few more minutes wouldn't matter.

"I'll drive you to the church," Jed spoke into my ear, alarming me by his sudden proximity. I stepped away from him. Part of me wanted to go alone. I could tell from the set of Jed's jaw, though, that that argument wasn't one I'd win. Not after I'd spent some quality time with his brother, and Blaise had shown up. Plus, he had the sword and we might need it.

"You can come with me, but I'm driving," I insisted, sliding into my chair at the table so I could rest a moment. Ty put a platter of sandwiches in the microwave and then turned his clinical eye back to me.

"You passed out, Anna. You shouldn't be driving." He had the blood pressure cuff around my upper arm before I could protest. He might be right about me driving, but I didn't want to admit it. I needed to be in control and I wasn't going to explain why. I pulled the Velcro sleeve off my arm before he could get a reading.

"I didn't pass out because of low blood pressure, I was pulled to another place. The ghost who did it is gone now. If you don't feel safe riding with me, you can stay here." It was a shitty thing to say but Ty ignored my tirade, folded the blood pressure cuff and set it in front of me on the table in reproach.

I stepped to the counter so I could get a cup of coffee, grumbling to myself about how I didn't need a damn chauffeur. Ty's pointed look said I was being a jerk and he didn't understand why. I didn't explain myself.

When I stepped outside I was struck by how it felt almost balmy, despite the drizzling rain that was melting the remaining snow. I thanked the weather gods for giving us temperatures that were above freezing for the first time in months.

Jed draped his long coat over his arm and I caught a flash of steel from it. I was glad we had the sword, but I'd better not get pulled over. At some point, the cops were going to realize they were missing some evidence from the scene and go looking for it. It would be difficult to explain how Jed had reacquired it.

Ty loaded a crate of the medical supplies we'd liberated from our Kansas City office into the back while I started the car. Jed slid into the passenger seat and laid his coat and sword against the door. Ty buckled himself into the seat behind Jed.

My sandwich was still warm when I unwrapped it. I handed the brown sack of goodies to Jed for further distribution before smashing my bread down so it would fit in my mouth.

"Grayson's church is on the far end of town but it shouldn't take longer than ten minutes to get there," I spoke through the bite in my mouth and steered my Subaru uphill through the rain. "Hopefully we can convince people to go home and won't be there too long." I wanted everyone back at my place where Jed and I had a chance to protect them. Either that, or separated and sent away. Far away, where evil couldn't touch them.

I set my sandwich in my lap for a moment, holding on to the

wheel with both hands as we crested the hill and began our descent. The drive was more mud than road. We needed a few loads of gravel to turn it back into a driveway, but it would have to dry out before we could get a dump truck up it with enough gravel to do any good. If Ned was right and the ghost apocalypse continued, we might not be able to come up with any gravel at all.

We drove past the white clapboard farmhouse that Ned had grown up in and now belonged to him and Carrie. Purple crocuses, flowers so hardy they often poked through spring snows, bloomed in a bright clump at the edge of the drive and around the front end of their house. It looked like the normal beginnings of spring, not the end of the world. I wasn't permitted normal anymore, not since Jed had saved my life and embroiled me in a war with ghosts who were tired of being dead and wanted another chance at life.

I took another one-handed bite of my breakfast and evaluated the area where the new gate was going in as we pulled up to it. Ned's desire to wall us off from the world scared me, but it made sense. Our world had changed, and everyone but me seemed to understand the full impact of that. I'd refused to acknowledge it, but this rash of ghost possessions wasn't something I could stop. If Adonijah had told the truth, I was at risk of killing myself if I tried.

I corrected the vehicle's trajectory as it slid from the muddy drive onto the paved county road. The windshield wipers made a thumping sound as they flicked back and forth. Mud and gravel flew off the wheels as I accelerated, assaulting the underbody like an upside-down hailstorm.

"You're scaring me." Ty gripped the overhead handle as I took a curve too fast. I slowed down a little, because he was right. I was being reckless. "What the hell happened to you in there?"

"It's not important." It was important but I didn't know how to explain it. I wasn't ready to.

"If I'm going to die because of it, I'd like to know the reason."

"I think the Master may be after our priests."

"Why?"

"I'm not sure—maybe because he knows we have a chance to stop this. We know that Matthew was able to get rid of a ghost. I think Adoni taking me today was a way to distract us. To separate us."

"You won't be very useful to anyone if you don't get us there in one piece."

"I'm not speeding," I protested. "Not much," I added after a glimpse at the speedometer.

Grayson's church was on the edge of town, right next to the cemetery, with its aging oaks lining the drive. Saint Michael's looked like they might be having a mid-week event based on the cluster of cars in the parking lot. Not enough for Sunday Mass but more than I expected to be there in the middle of the week. We parked next to the red sedan that Blaise had been driving.

"Are there any people who are possessed here?" Ty asked as he opened the door and hopped out into the light rain.

I listened to the buzzing of souls with my second sight.

"Armella said there were a few. It's hard to tell when there are so many people around." I stretched my senses further, searching for ghosts around us and didn't see anything. If the Master was here, he was hiding. Maybe inside someone.

"Let's get our supplies and see what we can do here." I didn't voice my concerns. If the Master was here, then my best chance was to release him before anything else happened. If I could release one of the fallen.

Ty pulled the plastic crate out of the back.

"If there are people who are possessed, is there any chance you can avoid releasing them? Let the church do its thing?"

"I'm not sure if that's an option or not."

"But if they can do it, you'll let them?" I hesitated and he added, "If it won't harm the possessed to wait a little longer."

"You know I can't promise that." I didn't understand why I had to tell him that.

"You may need your strength for other things. Let the priests do what they can. Let me do what I can. Let Jed watch over you."

I closed the trunk lid and locked the doors while I thought about the possibility that the Master was waiting for us inside.

"I'll try."

The interior of the church was dark and quiet. Even though I could tell there weren't any souls in the immediate vicinity I half-expected something to jump out at us. We followed the murmur of voices down a corridor that went past the administrative offices. At the end of the hallway, we reached a large room that looked like a multipurpose space. I imagined it could be used for everything from coffee hours to church school classes and cub scout meetings. Right now it was a strange sort of indoor campground.

The three priests who had been in my parlor were easily identifiable in their clerical collars as they moved among the crowd. People were clustered everywhere, sitting on metal church chairs and camp loungers that they must have brought with them.

Despite the heated building, the room was cool and most had a variety of jackets, blankets, and sleeping bags wrapped around them to keep warm. No one was in danger of freezing, but it was far from an ideal solution. I spotted a man in a wheelchair, one that tipped back to relieve the pressure on his backside. He wasn't possessed, but having been out on a rainy day in near-freezing temperatures wasn't helping him any.

The woman with a mass of fiery red curls made her way to my side.

"They all want to see you," she stated—though unnecessarily. The group was fixated on me, murmuring to one another. Those that could walk were edging closer. There were more than a few in the crowd that were possessed, but too many of the people here had ailments I couldn't help with. For a moment I wished they were all just possessed, so it would be something I could fix. I found it hard to imagine that anyone in this bedraggled group could be the Master.

"Don't get too close to Blaise," I warned Armella again while I tried to figure out who in the crowd was possessed. They were packed so close together that people's spirits overlaid one another and I was having trouble isolating which of them had two souls. Grayson and Matthew stepped among the groups, laying hands on shoulders, offering blessings and conversation.

"Father Blaise won't hurt me." She sounded confident, but I wasn't as sure.

"I don't trust him with you. He may just want your power."

She shrugged, with the same concern for her safety as a teenager headed out with their friends. "I'll be fine."

Arguing with her was going to be futile. "Have you figured out who's possessed?"

She pivoted, scanning the group. "That one, with the green

jacket, and there's a man sitting past him, with a brown blanket." Her descriptions matched more than one person in the room and I strained my eyes looking at each of them to figure out who was affected. "And then we have to go to them, in the woods." She gave me a patient smile, looking far older than the young woman she was.

I checked her again, to make sure Blaise hadn't possessed her while I was out of the way, but she was alone in her body.

"Go to who?"

Her bright eyes widened into large violet orbs of surprise. "Don't you feel them?"

I focused all of my energy on my second sight, and sensed nothing beyond the energy in the room.

"Not here, farther," she instructed, like she could tell that I was having difficulty locating what she saw.

*Can she see farther away than I can, or is she imagining things?* Then I caught a glimpse of something swirling at the edge of my range of perception, several specks of brightness.

"There they are."

"They want us to come see them."

Were ghosts visiting Armella in her dreams too? I admitted her sixth sense must work on a wider range than mine did.

"Did they tell you that?"

"I can feel it." The edges of her lips shifted in a dreamy smile. She wasn't possessed, but she was so ethereal, it seemed like she was from another world.

I glanced back at Jed, a few feet behind me. He appeared to have taken his self-imposed duty to watch my back literally.

"I'll go see what's out there in a few minutes. For now, I need to see how we can help these people."

It had to be the Master, didn't it? Adonijah had said he was close. And if I couldn't destroy the devil himself, then it would be my life on the line, along with the rest of the world.

"I'll come with you," Armella stated with an easy smile, like we were headed for coffee.

"We'll see." I wasn't interested in exposing any of them to more danger, but getting away from the group would be tricky.

"You think that by keeping everyone else away from the demons you can protect them."

I studied her young face, surprised by her ability to read my thoughts. It was a rare gift to be able to interpret people's intentions even when you didn't know them well.

"I have to try."

"It isn't working, though, is it?" she asked, and I paused to think about it. Chaz being away from me hadn't saved him, and all the people in the hospital who had been possessed, they'd gotten that way without any connection to me.

"Not as well as I'd like it to."

Armella nodded with a little hum. "There's a gentleman over here that I think you could help."

I needed to talk to Jed before I did anything else.

"Give me a minute."

I pulled Jed into the dark hallway, suppressing a snort of amusement when he had to duck to get through the doorway.

"Do you feel them?"

"I do not sense anything unusual." He reached for the hilt of his sword and I stayed his hand.

"You don't need that yet. I couldn't see them at first either, but Armella can. Her sense must be stronger than both of ours." And mine had grown stronger than Jed's. It was interesting information, but I didn't know what it meant. "There's a cluster of ghosts out there, past the cemetery. Can you watch for them? I need to make sure they don't come any closer while we're getting these people out of here."

"We should leave."

"No. I'm not running away."

"You may not be able to defeat the Master."

"I know that." I gripped his arm tighter, hoping he'd understand. "I have to try. If I don't, they'll continue taking over the world."

Jed rubbed the sword hilt like it was a lucky coin. "I will protect you for as long as I can."

"No one is sacrificing themselves," I said with a degree of certainty I didn't feel. "Before we go out there, I'm going to help these people and try to get them someplace safe."

"It is what you do." Jed reached out and caressed my cheek with his work-roughened thumb. "Still, I would have you from harm's way. You need to heal."

I placed my hand on his and rested my cheek against his palm for a moment, seeking strength and finding it.

"I'm strong enough." I almost believed myself.

Armella and I stepped into the crowd, who parted to let us through. A few fingers touched the sleeve of my jacket as I walked by as if I were some blessed relic that could heal. Murmurs followed me. I was the one they were hoping to see, the one they hoped was a miracle doctor. They were going to be very disappointed.

"Dr. Roberts?" a tentative voice asked. I stopped, turning to a middle-aged woman who was even shorter than I was. She was wrapped in a quilt to stave off the chill.

"Yes?"

"My husband, will you help him?"

The man sat on a chair next to her. He was balding, with gaunt cheeks and no eyebrows or eyelashes. He wasn't possessed. The ghosts preferred healthier hosts. I knelt in front of him, lowering my voice in an attempt at privacy.

"I'm Anna." I held out my gloved hand to his and he evaluated it for a moment before taking it and giving it a squeeze. "What do your doctors say you have?" I asked.

"Pancreatic cancer." His voice was dry and raspy, as if the chill air was in his throat too.

"Where are you from?"

"Up by Des Moines."

"You're in treatment?"

He gave a curt nod. "Ain't helping."

There wasn't much to be done, as far as I knew, for pancreatic cancer. It was renowned for being asymptomatic, so we didn't usually detect it very early, and aggressive. I was a primary care doctor, not an oncologist, and though I'd heard that new treatments were coming, I didn't know the details on them.

"I'm not going to lie to you. I can't cure this disease." I stared into his eyes. He didn't look surprised. He'd come because his wife had hope, not because he did. "I wish I could help you."

"Will you pray for him?" His wife pleaded and I hesitated before nodding, feeling every bit the fraud that I was. I glanced around and caught Blaise's eye and gave a mental shrug. Maybe praying with the saint could help them.

"Father Blaise?" I asked, and his lips quirked at the name. I couldn't very well address him as a saint in mixed company and I wasn't going to call him Lombardi. "Will you join us?"

"It would be my pleasure." He waited for a nod of consent from Jed, permission granted to approach me. Blaise bowed his head, standing over the couple, one hand touching each of their shoulders while he prayed for the man to find healing in God and the saints. I prayed too, silently, wishing with every fiber of my being that this man live the rest of his life free of pain, and able to cherish whatever time he had with his family.

When Blaise finished, the woman thanked us both, eyes filled with despair. She'd been looking for a miracle and I knew we wouldn't be able to deliver one.

"Go back home," I suggested to her, "where you can both be comfortable. Spend time with your loved ones." We stood, and I realized we had the attention of the entire group. I pulled Blaise away from them so we could talk without being overheard.

"We need to do this for every one of them. They've come so far and you have a far better chance of helping most of them than I do." It was clear that caring for the soul was better than trying to fix a body that couldn't be healed. Emotional health in the end of one's life was a critical component in finding peace and dignity in death.

"I hope you understand, I cannot perform miracles on demand. God doesn't work that way." Blaise chastened me.

I didn't point out to him that I didn't believe in miracles at all.

"I do understand that, but these people don't need the kind of miracle you are thinking of. They need peace and acceptance." I might not qualify as an atheist anymore but that didn't mean I believed in God. Most of these people probably did.

"Belief in itself is a powerful tool for healing. You should have more faith."

"That's cryptic."

"Sometimes the miracle comes from the person and their belief in its ability to occur, Anna. Not from the person the miracle is ultimately attributed to."

I knew, of course, about the theoretical placebo effect of prayer, but it wasn't something I'd seen in practice.

"Give them a chance," he argued, his voice smooth persuasion.

"It's what you want for them, isn't it? You being present may help them more than I can."

"I won't pretend that I can cure people when I can't."

"You can pray for them, though, like you just did. With your sincerity and theirs. It may not heal their body but it may very well help repair their spirit. And yours."

Was it that obvious that I felt like I was damaged beyond salvation? I hoped not.

"These people came here looking for me, and they'll get whatever I can give them." Even if I didn't know what that meant for each of them. It didn't matter what I thought it meant. "Are you going to help?"

Blaise's beatific smile said that he was happy I'd come around to his way of thinking. "It is my pleasure to be of assistance."

"Grayson, Ty, Armella?" I called for them and they joined me. Matthew followed Grayson and Jed stood so close behind me that we touched. He didn't like me being in close proximity to Blaise, but I didn't think Blaise would try to harm me, though I wasn't dumb enough to get in a car with him again, either.

"We need to get organized here. There are a few people with ghosts, but most of the people here aren't possessed." I turned to the priests. "Everyone that wants them gets prayers, and while you're doing that, evaluate them for what they need. If they have homes, we need to convince them to go back there, unless they need urgent medical care. Then they should go to the hospital. Ty can help evaluate that part."

"We have much to offer them," Blaise protested, and I suppressed an eye roll. His sense of self-importance was irritating but sometimes the best way to get someone arrogant to do what you wanted was to praise their inflated sense of worth.

"You more so than me, Blaise." His lips curled into a smirk and I hoped he didn't make the mistake of thinking he knew what was best for them. He wasn't the only person in the room that was supposed to be favored by their god.

Matthew exchanged a brief glance with Grayson, and I took a deep breath.

"You guys all know there's more here than meets the eye but we haven't told you all of it. Father Lombardi isn't the only one of us that's possessed. You may remember Armella mentioning that, the day we met her." I pulled the edges of my jacket tighter together, hunching into its protection. "I'll let Jed introduce himself."

Jed inclined his chin to me a notch. "I was once a king in Judah."

"A king named Solomon, if I'm not mistaken," Grayson murmured, and I wondered when he'd figured Jed's history out. Jed gave another curt nod.

"That's not possible," Matthew uttered, a response that, while out of line with his role as a priest and his recent experience with being possessed, wasn't at all unreasonable.

"We shouldn't let our knowledge of modern science get in the way of that which is possible," Grayson said, and I wondered if he was trying to convince himself or Matthew.

Matthew made the sign of the cross in front of his chest, and I wasn't sure if he was trying to protect himself from our heresy or was invoking his astonishment at meeting such a notorious member of the faith. Maybe both.

"So that's it. No more secrets. These people that need help are our first priority, but we need to convince them there aren't any miracles that I can give them and get them out of here before they get hurt."

"They are waiting for us," Armella reminded me.

"We've got some ghost friends nearby that want to chat. Let's get these people to safety first." I hoped I'd have all of them out of there before I was forced into a confrontation with whatever was waiting for me.

"What do you want us to do?" Matthew asked with a degree of reluctance that made it clear he would follow along if it went with his sense of what was best, but not if it didn't.

"I want you to take the one person here who's ever been credited with a miracle, and I want you to pray for the people here. Take Jed too. Will you?" It was a long shot, but it was the best hope I could offer them, and our time was limited. I didn't know how long the ghosts would be willing to wait. "They came here for miracles, and we aren't likely to have any of those. From what I can tell so far, modern medicine can't help them. They deserve any comfort you can offer them."

It felt like a long time before Matthew nodded. "I'll do as you ask because it won't cause any harm."

"And convince them to go back home," I stressed. "If they don't have a home to go to, then we need to try to help them figure something else out. I'll leave that to Grayson. If you need my help, tell me."

"They came to see you," Grayson leveled me with a stare. This was the whole reason he'd called me back here in the first place.

"I know. I'll come by and see everyone but you and I both know that I can't help most of them."

"Your presence may be useful." Grayson's gray eyes fixed on me from under his white eyebrows and I nodded so he knew I understood. I took a deep breath and turned to Armella, waving Ty over.

"You two isolate the ghost cases. I'll deal with them separately. I'll release them here, then we can convince their families to take them to the ER for treatment."

"Do you want IVs started?" Ty asked and I took a steadying breath while I considered what was best.

"I don't really want to be liable for that, but yeah, if someone crashes and we have to do it to save their life, obviously we will." I hoped nobody went down the tubes on us, but we weren't very far from the local hospital.

I wasn't sure how the ghosts possessing people knew who I was, but they always seemed to, and made it clear they didn't like me.

When Armella had sequestered the possessed into a small group of four surrounded by their families, I approached. Three of them roused from their somnolence, the threat of my presence enough to stimulate them to action. *If these are the people possessed by the weakest ghosts, where are the ones who were strong enough to take a healthy host?*

I feared the answer to that question, because they could be anywhere, scattered into the far corners of the Earth and inserting themselves into society. Doing whatever they wanted to do and had the ability to get away with.

As long as they stayed away from me, I'd never be able to find them. Instead, they'd left me on cleanup duty with the weakest of them, distracted by the supernatural trash that I could see.

The next two hours were a blur of activity. I released four unhappy ghosts and dispatched their victims to the hospital. A conversation with the Trenton Emergency Department physician ensured that they'd be given the proper treatment of fluids and steroids when they arrived.

The people who weren't possessed were more difficult to deal with. I had to tell each family that I had nothing to offer them, all while shaking from the effort of releasing ghosts and hoping I didn't self-combust in the middle of the church.

I listened to each story, and looked a couple people over whose illnesses I couldn't cure. I prayed, with the Saint of Sebaste, two priests, and a king from the Bible. I found a curious sense of peace from our prayers and I hoped that our words helped. I found I wanted there to be a god who was listening, one who cared about these people. Most of all, I hoped they found their way to safety.

I took a moment to breathe, and tried to shake the aching remains of my power from my arms. Grayson and Ty were helping a couple load their mother into a car. The parking lot was emptying, there were only a few cars left.

Blaise and Matthew were bent in prayer with a young woman, and Jed was watching Blaise like a hawk. Armella had drifted away from the group and was standing at a side door, looking out at the cemetery. She had a distant look on her face, like she was listening to music and couldn't figure out where it was coming from. I heard it, too, but I'd been trying to ignore it, wanting to get everyone out of danger first.

# CHAPTER TEN

"**THEY'RE STILL WAITING FOR US.**" Armella snagged her thumbs into the belt loops of her faded jeans and gazed into the woods beyond the cemetery. A gravel road intersected the neat rows of tombstones, branching a smaller path in the general direction where the ghosts were. Was there more cemetery back there, or just trees? I didn't know. I couldn't tell how far away the ghosts were, but I didn't think I could sense ghosts that were more than half a mile away. The sensation was faint, so I thought that must be about where they were, right on the edge of my vision.

I pulled my jacket hood over my hair and stepped off the patio steps and into the gentle rain, Armella beside me. I felt the others follow, a gathering of living souls drifting after me. When I swiveled on my heel to face them, they stopped again.

"You can't all come with me."

"Where are you going?" Ty demanded, looking like the parent of an errant teen.

"We're going to visit the ghosts in the cemetery," Armella offered as if it made perfect sense.

"Who are they?" Grayson asked and I shook my head, drops of water falling off my face.

"I'm not sure, but I think they may be bad."

"I'll come with you." Grayson stepped closer to me.

"It's not safe. I can't protect all of you." I appealed to the Saint of Sebaste. "Please tell them."

"There may be danger," he admitted, "that you cannot save her from." He straightened like a proud soldier. "I will accompany her."

Jed arched one eyebrow and looked down at the saint with a forbidding glare that would have stopped most people in their tracks. Blaise ignored it.

"They want me to come, and I'm going." Armella's voice was bright with curiosity, but this wasn't a stroll through the park.

"It's been three days since a group of ghosts abducted me and tried to murder me," I reminded them all, glaring at Blaise. He gave me a bright smile as if he enjoyed the part he had played in my story.

"You put your lives in peril if you join us," Jed predicted with his usual degree of practical calm. I didn't want to put him in danger either, but I had to admit that I needed him. He might know the ghosts that were out there, and he had the sword, hidden in his jacket. Blaise had a stake in this too, but I didn't have the right to risk Father Lombardi's life.

"If you don't come with me, I don't have to worry about you. I can focus on doing what I need to do." My announcement didn't seem to sway anyone and I wasn't their mother. I didn't want to stand in the rain and argue about it anymore. I turned towards the cemetery.

The first part of it was new with neat symmetrical stones, identical in size, altered only by the etchings on their fronts. Plastic flowers in bright reds and unnatural blues dotted the landscape amid patches of snow and mud.

I paused when we reached the tree line. The gravel path forked to the left and then ended underneath the branches at a large padlocked gate that led to a utility shed. This had been a cleared pasture, once, but had been left unkempt for so long that the trees had come back. Maple, locust, and cottonwood stretched overhead in gaunt clusters.

I stepped off the gravel and found the rain had softened the first inch of earth. My feet sank through the mud until I hit the deeper layer, still frozen from winter, and slipped. I grimaced and took another careful step. Icy rain trickled around the edges of my hood, dripping down my neckline. I was grateful I'd had the foresight to wear boots that were waterproof.

A breeze full of winter's chill blew through my supposedly windproof jacket, making my wet shirt feel colder. I heard the others behind me, squishing into the muck and brushing rainwater off their sleeves, but I didn't turn back. The ghosts were waiting for me.

We didn't have to walk much more than a quarter mile to find them, but slogging through the mud without a path to follow was hard going and it felt farther than it was.

I stepped through an invisible perimeter ten yards from the ghosts and the wind stilled. Stale air replaced the earthy wet smell of the woods as if this space was a room left closed too long. The forest around us closed in with a disorienting layer of fog that would make finding our way back difficult. I didn't think the fine mist had appeared of its own volition, it was an unnatural creation of one of the ghosts, a first act of aggression meant to disorient us.

Watching the pale glow of spirits swirling through the bare branches above us, I clutched the core of my power close, ready to use it but mindful of the living behind me. I had to be careful—if my power arced in the wrong direction or one of them stepped into the path of it, they would die.

I heard the footsteps behind me stop and turned back to see what was wrong. Costas clutched a black prayer book to his chest like it would protect him, and Grayson was staring above him like he sensed that something else was up there. Ty and Armella were right behind Jed, which was a pretty safe place to be.

"Be sure you stay behind me. If you get in the path of my power, it will kill you." I spoke loud enough to make sure all six of them heard me. I hoped they'd heed my warning because I couldn't bear to hurt any of them.

The ghosts rattled the branches overhead as if my words had threatened them, causing a shower of cold raindrops to fall on us.

"Stop that!" I ordered. "Making me wetter and colder isn't helping my mood any."

"Some of them want you to use it on them." Armella had ignored my warning to stay back and was standing again at my right side.

"How do you know that?"

"Can't you tell?" she asked. I stared at her a moment, searching her face.

"I don't know what they're feeling. How do you know?"

"Some of them are unhappy here." She contemplated the bustling trees above us and I had the feeling she was listening to a pitch outside of my range of hearing.

"That's what they want? That's why this group is here, because they don't want to be on this land anymore?"

"Not all of them." She searched the bows of cottonwood and oak for answers. "There are a few that aren't as simple but they aren't ready to die again." She paused, listening to some whisper I couldn't hear. "They are conflicted." She turned her attention to her right where a cluster gathered in the boughs of a tree. "Some seem angry. I don't know what they all want."

"If you seek me out to be released, I will help you," I spoke into the trees, into the cluster of souls, amorphous specks of light reflecting against the clouds. I saw Costas looking up into the sky, expression guarded, and wondered that the others couldn't see them when they were so clear to me. "If you want to talk to me, then come talk. If you came here to challenge me, you'll be released with the rest."

Stillness and silence were my answer. What were they waiting for? I could hear the wind whipping in the trees beyond us, but it didn't reach us, stopped by whatever invisible force the spirits exerted on the space around them. The barometric pressure was dropping so the air had the feeling of stillness, like before a bad storm. Why were we out here in the woods? Where was the Master?

Grayson cleared his throat and spoke into the eerie calm.

"If you seek peace, Father Costas and I will pray with you. We can't see you, so you'll have to come to us." He backed away, stepping to the edge of the mist to confer with Costas, his voice a low murmur.

"I'll pray for them, if that's what they need," Blaise assured me.

"Join Grayson," I suggested. I didn't care who did the praying. If the souls were content when I released them then that was nice, but not necessary. They'd be gone soon enough.

Costas' voice began in a soft murmur and Armella gave a happy hum. "They're going."

Some of them were splitting off from the main group and joining Costas and Grayson, swimming around them, disturbing the air like currents of water that caught at their clothes. Costas stopped speaking, a moment of fear crossing his face and then his expression neutralized into one of distant kindness. Maybe it was the armor he wore, along with the white collar. It might be enough to distance him from his congregation during mass, but in that moment I was afraid for him.

"Don't," Armella breathed as I started forward.

"He's not safe."

"None of us are." She was staring into the sky.

"What do you see?"

"Their feelings."

I swallowed an impatient growl. "All I see are the ghosts, Armella. Can you interpret it for me?"

"They're afraid of something that's coming." She held up a hand, pointing into the forest. Masked by the litany of souls overhead, I'd missed the spirit on the ground, approaching with the slow careful steps of a human being walking over uncertain terrain. The fog shivered like waves rippling as the being passed through.

Three spirits took advantage of my distraction and dropped down around us. I caught two of them with a one-handed burst of my power and heard Jed's sword slicing through the air, ridding us of the other.

It happened so fast that Armella's startled cry at my right shoulder came a moment after the attack ended. The other spirits stayed high above us, wary. Jed stepped up on my left side and I sucked in a breath in frustration. *Did they both have a death wish?*

"Please stay behind me," I reminded him. He didn't react and I tried again. "If I release my power, I'd prefer you not be in the blast radius."

His lip twitched as if I'd amused him, though his gaze didn't waver from whatever was coming towards us. Maybe I shouldn't try to explain how my power worked to someone who knew more about it than I did.

"I can't lose you again," I let the truth out in a rush.

Jed's eyes turned to mine, dark with an emotion I didn't recognize, but pulled me in. "You will always have me." His tone was heavy with intent and for a moment I forgot to breathe.

"It doesn't matter." Armella's breathy voice behind me solidified into a statement of fact that broke the moment between us. I addressed her with reluctance.

"What doesn't matter?"

"Your power." She blinked her eyes twice, giving me time to catch up with her conversation. "I don't know if it will work on this one."

I caught a little shake of Jed's head indicating he didn't think she was right, but if it was one of the fallen, then she might be. Could Armella tell the difference between a ghost and the fallen?

"Why do you think that?" I asked.

Eli stepped around an evergreen wearing a green army jacket and skinny black pants, her pixie hair styled around the curves of her ears. She was wearing dramatic dark eyeliner that didn't belong in the woods of Missouri and should have seemed out of place with the army jacket. Somehow she made it look hip. If any teenagers saw her, they'd be copying the look and Trenton would be overrun with youth sporting neat pixie haircuts and pairing camo with their eyeliner.

Jed was clenching his right fist around the hilt of his kilij and a tight band clenched my stomach. Eli had sought me out again. Whatever she was, I'd caught her attention. I didn't think it was a good sign that she was here. I glanced back at Ty who was huddled between Grayson and Matthew, staring at Eli and looking like he wished he'd stayed behind. I wished he had, too.

"That one is different," Armella whispered. "It's not a ghost."

Her spirit looked the same to me. I didn't know how Armella could tell the difference but she seemed to have some capabilities I didn't.

"I know she isn't. She told me she was something else. Something older."

If there were things out there that couldn't be destroyed by my power, then there wasn't any way for us to protect ourselves, not against spirits that could leap inside your soul and destroy it, take your body against your will.

"Anna. Armella." Eli named us as if we were meeting for lunch instead of standing in the woods with a bunch of ghosts hovering overhead like large snowflakes.

"How do you know Armella?" I asked.

"All are known to me." Her answer made me shiver. Did she think she was a god, too?

"Be very careful, Anna," Jed warned in a tone so low I didn't think anyone else could hear it.

"What are you doing here?" I preferred to keep the more powerful creatures in my dreams. As much as I hated being called to that in-between space, I really didn't like them showing up miles from my home. No place was safe if they could get to me this quickly. No wonder Jed had wanted us to leave.

"They called me." She looked up into the agitated swirls overhead with a fond smile, as if the souls were mischievous pets that had run away from home. "And then I called you." Her voice lilted, reflecting accents from languages I couldn't pick up. English wasn't her first language, but it wasn't foreign to her either.

"Are they Council too?" I asked. Jed shifted next to me. He didn't like this being, and it seemed like he was more than a little worried.

"No. These souls waited too long to find peace. They belong to me."

"You can't own another being."

"Ownership is a concept of the living," Eli spoke in a rebuke, as if my level of ignorance surprised her. "When I say they are mine, I am not talking about something that can be given away again. Even if I didn't want them, they would still be mine."

"You're talking in circles." I was confused but Armella stared upwards as if she saw Eli's words in the swirls of the dead.

"These are not concepts I expect the living to understand. Even with your sight, you cannot comprehend the depth of the universe."

While it would be interesting to talk to a creature who might have a greater understanding of the universe, the conversation had gotten too ethereal and I tried to pull it back.

"Who's left from the Council? Where are they?"

"Those that answer my call are here with us." She waved up to the sky. "Your Council ran, though, when they saw me coming."

The skin along my spine tingled in warning. "I thought you were one of them."

Eli laughed. "You are so trusting. Such an endearing quality. You believe what you want to, Anna. It is the curse of mankind. Your egos and pride are what bring all of you to me."

I tried to swallow against the sudden dryness in my throat. A thing who wasn't a ghost and wielded the power to control the dead . . .

"You're the one they call the Master."

"Now you begin to understand, Anna. Your naïveté was touching." Her cold eyes held something dark in them that frightened me and I backed up until my back touched Jed's front. Jed was still, like he feared movement would draw the viper's attention.

"I know your true name, Belial," Blaise spoke from behind me, his voice full of caution.

"I tired of that old sobriquet, Blaise. Why are you here? Must I remind you that this conversation is not your concern?"

Blaise's answering silence frightened me more than anything else. He'd been scared of the dragon goddess but he'd still challenged her. Blaise had said Dakini's power came from the people who prayed to her. Who was praying to Eli that made her so strong? She didn't seem like goddess material. Having met only one self-proclaimed goddess, I assumed all of them must have blue skin and extra appendages.

"Who is Belial?" I asked and Blaise answered me in a quiet tone, as if he hoped Eli wouldn't overhear him.

"The angel of darkness. Instigator of the angel rebellion and cast from heaven with the rest of the fallen. Now self-proclaimed master of immorality on Earth."

"Another demon," Armella whispered. They were all demons, to her.

"Why did you want to meet here, in the middle of the woods?" I forced a calm tone, one that belied my increasing heart rate. I hoped Eli couldn't smell fear, because I would stink of it.

"You are here because I commanded it." Eli stretched her arms out as if she was giving all of us a benediction and the mass of souls rustled with agitation.

"I don't follow your orders," I pointed out.

"Yet you are here, all the same." Eli's smile was chilling because it lacked emotion. It was a costume she'd put on to seem human, like the clothes were. She stared past me with her disconcerting eyes, dark orbits of dilated pupil.

"You are the one they call Jedediah?" She hadn't seemed that dangerous when I met her before. Today she shimmered with power I hadn't noticed. Maybe she'd hidden it from me.

"I am." Jed stepped around me, as if he thought his kilij would be enough to protect us. I doubted very much that it would, and hoped I was wrong. If he cut her, would she bleed?

"I've been looking forward to meeting you." She stared at him as if she could take the measure of his soul deep inside his physical body and I pulled the edges of my jacket tighter against a sudden chill. "You have tried to atone for it, but you still have my darkness inside you," she informed him. "You have taken lives, deceived the ones you love." She tilted one ear towards us, as if listening to the energy of his soul. "Hatred runs through your heart." Had she seen inside me the same way? What had she learned?

"Why are you here, Belial?" Jed's voice was calm and steady. If this being scared him, he didn't show it.

"This time, I came for Anna." My heart started racing at her words and I feared she would be able to hear its percussive staccato.

"You cannot have her."

"You belong to me, Jedediah. I could call you to me and you would have to follow."

"I answer to God, not to you."

"Your spirit speaks against you." Her head tilted again and a queer silence fell as her pack of souls quieted. "In this you have no choice."

"Perhaps not," he admitted, "but I would fight you every step of the way."

"God will not give up on him so easily," Armella spoke up, her voice bright and clear. Eli's attention swiveled to the redhead like a hawk swooping through the forest on silent wings, seeking its prey.

"I know your name but I don't know you, child." The body Eli had chosen was as young as Armella's, but I didn't think she saw the irony in calling someone her own physical age a child.

"And you never will." Armella spouted a saucy challenge that made me fear for her safety.

"You think yourself immune? Free from darkness?" Eli's benign demeanor made her more frightening. She had the confidence of someone who knows they have the most power. "I enjoy innocence. The pleasure that comes from one moment of anger or frustration is all it takes for you to start your journey with me."

"I don't dance with the devil," Armella snarled, surprising me. I hadn't imagined she was capable of anger.

"I'm going to enjoy playing with you." Eli licked her lips, like she knew she'd just won and was ready to taste the fruit of her labor.

"Why are we out here in the cold, Eli?" I intervened, hoping to redirect Eli's attention. I didn't know if I could protect Armella from her, I didn't know if I could protect anyone.

Eli's attention flicked from Armella back to me, a lion choosing her prey.

"Some of them are scared." Armella pointed to the spirits above us, interrupting anything Eli might have been preparing to say.

"Scared of what?"

"Of being stuck here. They want you to free them."

"What they desire is irrelevant." Eli was adamant. Armella gazed at her and didn't answer, her lack of response a question in itself. "They belong to me," Eli reiterated, speaking up to the throng above us. "You cannot be freed. If she releases you, you will go to hell for eternity."

"Life here on Earth may be an eternity just as terrible for them," Grayson's voice called out, some distance behind me. "They deserve our blessing." A flicker of something crossed Eli's face. Did that suggestion disturb her? Did she fear the priest's ability to release a spirit through prayer?

"You cannot save the damned." Eli met his challenge with confidence I wasn't sure she felt. What about this made her uneasy?

"Then you have nothing to fear, do you?" I managed to keep my voice steadier than I'd hoped for. *Small victories may be the only ones you get.*

Eli's laugh said she feared nothing, and the spirits overhead churned through the branches in response, showering us with another round of cold raindrops.

"Father Costas, Grayson?" I didn't like to turn my back on Eli but I wanted my conversation to be as private as possible. Costas seemed frozen to the ground, and Grayson had his fingers twined around a cross necklace he'd pulled out from his collar.

"Give those you can peace."

"What would you have us do?" Grayson kept his voice soft and his eyes glued to the petite form in the army jacket.

"Do what you do. Pray. Offer them absolution of their sins, or last rites, or something like that."

"That's something reserved for the living," Grayson informed me, his attention never wavering from Eli.

"This might be a good time to change that policy," I suggested, keeping my frustration in check, right next to my fear. "Don't these souls deserve one last chance to atone for their sins?" I wasn't an expert in the salvation of the soul.

"Forgiveness, not atonement," Matthew corrected me.

"Everyone deserves forgiveness," Grayson spoke with hesitation, showing me again how unnerved he was. I guessed it wasn't every day that a man of God met the devil.

"It's unusual." Costas was willing, but cautious.

"They're ghosts, Matthew," I pointed out, hoping we could move things along. I didn't know how much time Eli would give us. "Of course it's unusual. Why don't you hear their confession, or whatever it is you normally do?" I asked and Costas pried his gaze from Eli.

"You want me to take the confession of a ghost."

"Would it work?"

"What do you think will happen?" he countered.

"I don't have any way of knowing, but Grayson got rid of your ghost through prayer. I'm hoping they find enough peace that they move on to the next world, and that I don't have to use my power to release them."

"Why?" Costas looked perplexed.

Grayson answered for me. "She's afraid she'll deplete her power too much. She knows she'll need everything she has to deal with *that*." I didn't have to look behind me to know Grayson was talking about Eli.

"Take Armella with you. Go back towards the shelter and then do what you can for them. Armella can be your translator, since she can hear them."

Armella looked both surprised and unhappy with my suggestion.

"Where will you be?" she asked. I glanced back at the slim form of the woman standing in front of us. "Dancing with the devil is dangerous business," she warned, as if I didn't already know that. "Don't do it."

"I have to try to end this." I didn't know if I could kill Eli, but I knew no one else could do it.

Grayson unclasped the gold chain from around his neck.

"Take this." I considered the cross for a moment and then took it from him, and secured the clasp around my neck. Grayson was speaking, a blessing or a prayer of protection, but the buzzing of the souls had gotten so loud I had trouble making out the words.

"Go," I urged them.

"I'm staying." Armella's lower lip scooched out in a slight pout.

I could see her purity the way Eli might, the bright light of her soul untarnished. Mine wasn't that way anymore. "Go with Father Costas and Grayson. Help them. If they can save some of these souls, we all win."

Was it possible to win in a battle with the devil? Eli was something deeper and darker than any soul I'd come across. Christiana had been a devotee, and she'd come close to killing me.

Eli lunged for Armella who made a strangled sound as Eli vanished inside her. Jed reached for the redhead, grabbing her by the arms and pulling her away from me with enough force that she stumbled and fell on the ground. How Eli had made the jump into her if she wasn't a ghost, I didn't know, but I was certain that it was her essence I sensed clouding Armella's bright light. I leaped after her, reaching for Armella's wrist before Jed had her out of reach and pulsing my power into her. It was an instinctive response I didn't have time to think about before I did it. Jed dropped his hold on her before my power could slide from her body into his.

Armella's body quivered, and her eyes fixed on me in what seemed like amusement. Her dreamy expression was gone, replaced with a degree of focus I hadn't seen in her before.

My mouth filled with a brackish flavor as I realized my power hadn't even touched Eli, and I recognized it as the taste of fear. I'd used more than I'd intended, but it hadn't had an impact.

"She warned you that your power wouldn't work on me. Didn't you believe her?" Eli's words sounded strange in Armella's breathy voice.

"Leave her alone," I demanded while I debated what to do. I could try to blast her again, but it hadn't worked the first time and I risked killing the girl.

Jed hefted his kilij and I grabbed his arm while I tried to stay away from the blade. The blue fire in that sword had released whatever it was that bound my soul to my body, just as my power did for others. I didn't intend to lose Armella.

Eli raised Armella's arms up like a dancer and the souls in the sky, a hundred of them, fell to the Earth, landing in solid form. They looked like they'd just crawled straight from their graves. Stringy clumps of hair clung to skulls half covered by decaying flesh. Skeletal hands reached out from arms strung with dead tissue that somehow still held them together. What clothing they wore was in tattered rags and they smelled like death. I wondered if that was how Eli planned to best me, because the stench was overpowering.

Eli walked Armella through her army of the living dead, out of reach and then stepped out of Armella's body, her foot crushing a clump of purple crocus peeking out from the snow. I'd never seen a ghost go in and out of someone so fast, and return to a physical form like they'd never left it. Armella's body collapsed into the snow.

I heard Jed's sword striking bone behind me as he engaged the first of the ghosts to reach him, squeals of spirits dying a second death following each clash.

I ran into the ring of skeletons after Armella. A bony hand gripped my arm and I released it with a quick burst of power. The ghosts were a distraction—the kind of distraction that could kill us—but Eli was the end game. She grabbed Armella's neck and lifted her to her feet. I was relieved to see Armella's hands go to her throat. She was alive.

Eli's hand morphed, fingers elongating to an inhuman length with claws that lengthened, embedding themselves into Armella's pale skin.

"Why are you doing this?" Armella breathed through the hand around her throat.

"I came here for Anna. Imagine my pleasure when I found you."

A nasty ghoulish thing, with little resemblance to something that might once have been human grabbed me and I sent a surge of power through to it. It disintegrated with a squeal. I hoped that would be enough to warn them off but most of them were looking at me with what I thought was interest. I was having a hard time interpreting facial expressions from the skulls.

"You found me. Let everyone else go."

"No one leaves here."

*That's going to put a damper on my dinner plans . . .*

A dizzying rush of air swirled around us and I had a sudden headache as the barometric pressure changed. I blinked once, saw Eli still holding Armella with one clawed hand, and then in an instant we were in the cavern. Armella dangled in Eli's grasp, feet struggling to touch the ground. It looked like she was having trouble breathing and I worried her windpipe was compromised.

How had she gotten Armella here? Could anyone be brought, or only those of us who had a gift? I didn't know the answer, but there was Armella, thrashing for air like a fish on a line.

"Let her go before she dies," I insisted. "If there's something you want from either of us, you won't get it if she's dead."

Eli didn't react to my words, her brow furrowed in concentration. I realized I had to look up at her now. She'd grown in proportion, half guileless woman, half monster. Armella's kicks were slowing as she weakened, the loss of oxygen getting to her. I had no way of knowing what would happen if she died here, but I feared it would be permanent.

We'd left Jed and the priests with an army of ghost skeletons in physical form, ready to attack. I needed to get back so I could help them. Armella's body and my own were there, too.

Fear and anger blurred my vision and I stomped in rage, power striking out through my leg. The cavern floor beneath us shuddered and Eli turned back to me, astonishment crossing her face before her eyes narrowed and her mouth closed into a scowl.

"Put her down," I ordered again and Eli lowered the girl to her feet in a deliberate motion, though she maintained the predatory grasp. Blood seeped down Armella's neck in tiny rivulets from where Eli's claws had punctured her skin.

As Armella's legs supported her weight, she gulped air in relief, gasping so much she started coughing. Her legs were shaking but she was stronger than she looked and they held her. The claws didn't appear to have done more than superficial damage, but if they sank much deeper, I feared they'd reach critical vessels.

I needed to distract Eli, and get her away from Armella. Buy myself some time to figure out how to get us out of there. I knew I could find the door to my mind again, but how could I get Armella back to her own body where she belonged?

"What's Armella to you? She's barely an adult. Send her back and let her live her life. This is between us."

"The girl has a rare gift. It will be a nice addition to my abilities," Eli breathed. She scraped one long fingernail across Armella's face and then licked her finger with a flourish, like she was tasting a fine wine.

Concerned Eli might devour Armella in front of me, I tried to distract her.

"Why are you so threatened by me?" I asked. Eli's lips twisted in what looked like amusement. It was hard to tell. She looked like a grotesque parody of a human being. "You could have taken over Europe and I'd never have known. Why seek me out?"

"I do not fear you." She dismissed me with a laugh. "Your course and mine were set when *they* decided to seek you out."

"They? Do you mean the Council?" Eli didn't respond but that had to be it. No one else had been looking for me—that I knew of. Eli'd already had her hands in the mix with the Council, through Christiana if not through any other means. "The theory being that if you destroyed the Council, there wouldn't be anyone left to challenge you. Is that it?"

"No one of any import." Eli gave Armella a little shake, proving her point that mere mortals were no match for her strength.

"Christiana wouldn't tell you where they were? Was she not as loyal as you expected her to be?"

"She was no different than Jedediah and Blaise. The Council did not answer to her. The information they gave her was limited."

"This is happening so that you can get together with your little group of fallen angels and have a reunion?"

"Not entirely," Eli responded. Armella gripped the clawed hand that held her like she hoped to diminish the pressure in her neck by holding on.

It didn't make sense. The Council had been trying to find me, while Eli was trying to find the Council? Or was she pursuing Jed? She'd been interested in him in the woods, but I didn't think that was it. The fact that it was Armella and me in the in-between, and not Jed, was proof enough that he wasn't the one she was after. What threat did we present Eli that he didn't?

I could see ghosts and banish them, but I couldn't even contain the incidents in Missouri by myself. Eli could have gone anywhere. The fact that she hadn't meant something here threatened her. If I couldn't destroy her, then who could?

"Can't you hear them?" Armella croaked out, wincing as Eli's claws sank deeper in.

"Hear who?" Eli demanded.

Was the girl hallucinating? I didn't hear anything either.

"Them," she insisted, waving at the air around us as she ignored the wounds in her neck and chest. Her pale blue sweatshirt was turning dark at the neck as blood seeped into it.

I closed my eyes against Armella's discomfort and centered myself, trying to concentrate on what was beyond us. My second sight showed me our three souls. I strained, listening for something that I wasn't sure was there.

Eli let out a curse and flung Armella from her with as much effort as it took to toss a wet towel. She landed with a thud against the cavern wall.

I ran to Armella and bent over her still form, keeping a cautious eye on Eli.

"They're very close," Armella murmured and something stirred at the edge of my sixth sense.

"Are you okay?" We might be in another plane but she felt as warm and alive as anyone ever had in the real world. She tried to roll off her side and let out a soft moan of pain. "Stay still. You could have broken something." Eli's claws had torn the skin even more, but the wounds on her neck were starting to clot.

She stilled, her porcelain skin making her look like a broken doll. The illusion of frailty ended when she spoke, her reedy voice chilling me.

"You have to call them to us. I can hear them but I can't bring them here."

"Who are they?"

"Don't you know?"

Maybe some of them were Council, the fallen angels that were trying to redeem themselves. Some of the spirits in that shabby house had tried to kill me, but another group had decided to save me. I didn't know which were which, and I didn't know who was coming for us now.

Eli started towards us and I planted myself in front of Armella. Whether Eli was a devil or not, she looked the part. Her eyes blazed with dark urgency in a face that had transitioned into a monster's. The huge clawed hands had grown hair and her arms were bulkier. If she'd ever been an angel, no trace of that remained, unless their true form was more demon than beatific creature with wings.

I concentrated, harnessing my fear and anger like I had with Adonijah. It took me a moment to find that other ability, hidden deep inside and far from the heated center of me that I was used to relying on. I directed a pulse of that other power through me and the floor rippled, knocking me down next to Armella. Eli staggered on the swaying ground but stayed on her feet.

"That won't do, Anna." Her voice shook with anger and I guessed she wasn't used to being defied. "You aren't strong enough to hurt me, I've already told you that." With one great leap, she was on me. Great claws wrapped around my torso and she picked me up like I weighed nothing. I felt each of the ten nails that dug through my clothing into the skin on my chest and back. It felt like I was being shredded and I pushed against her hands with ineffectual force. Demon or not, she had the strength of one.

"Call them!" Armella yelled. I used a pulse of rage to send a shockwave through the cavern ceiling and rocks pelted down on us. Armella rolled out of the way of a falling boulder but Eli took a blow that knocked her to the ground with me, her big arm pinning me underneath her.

I kicked the beast holding me with no more effect than a fly biting a horse. She gripped me tighter in response, squeezing the air from my lungs. I dug my fingernails into her wrist, and the skin changed, morphing into a tough scaly substance I couldn't get my nails through. Her face was too far away for me to get to her eyes, where maybe I'd have a chance.

Whispers echoed around me, but I couldn't figure out where they were coming from.

"They can't get in here." Eli sounded sure of that but she released her hold on me and I dropped to the ground. Her head cocked sideways like a suspicious dog as she listened, and I wondered if she could understand what they were saying.

I edged towards Armella but Eli swept me backward with one swipe of her great arm. I felt a moment of weightlessness and then hit the opposite cavern wall, crumpling to the floor. I gasped, cold air hitting my lungs with a shock, as if I'd just stepped outside from a warm room. Eli grew longer, her legs and torso matching the grotesque arms. Her clothing stretched with her, the green army jacket incongruous on the monstrous form. I'd have laughed under different circumstances.

"Let us in." Voices ricocheted around me and I couldn't tell anymore if they were nearby or if I was hallucinating. Armella was getting to her feet and moved back against the wall, as far from Eli as she could get. She cradled her right arm in her left and I feared she must have broken it.

"Now!" The whispers escalated into an off-key chorus, decibels above what was comfortable. The sounds echoed in my skull, sending me to my knees. Armella lurched, grabbing her head with her good hand.

"Let them in," she begged me.

I tried to open a hole in the sky, but all I managed to do was dislodge another chunk of rock from the cliff.

"Now I know where they are. I can find them." Eli's laugh was more roar, her words distorted by the shape of her jaw and the large teeth now jutting from her jowls like a boar with orthodontic problems.

We were bait, drawing in whoever sought to breach the domains of our cavern. They'd fall into her trap just as I had.

"Don't listen to her. You can do it, Anna. Let them in," Armella called across to me. Had she never known failure? I couldn't understand her confidence in me.

The creatures beyond our world scrambled along the edges of the sky like roaches scuttling along the kitchen walls at night, out of sight.

"Are they Council?" I yelled, backing out of the way.

Armella shook her head, answering me with enough volume to cross the void.

"I don't know, but we need them." Again, the surety of her words struck me. With my sight I could sense their presence, but she knew something about them. Could I trust her ability to predict their intent?

I didn't have a choice because Eli was on her feet again, advancing on Armella like a great cat tracking a rabbit.

I used my fury and fear to tap into my ability to affect the world. Behind the sky, beyond the crumbling cavern I felt the invisible barrier. Bolstered as I was by the energy of my connection, it sundered with the ease of cloth. Creatures squeezed through the hole I'd made, their bodies morphing into existence.

The beings I'd let in swam to the floor on my side of the chasm like it was an effort for them. Gravity must not apply to the fallen, they had to work to join us at ground level. To me they looked like pulsing ovals of fire, orange instead of the typical white souls of the living and the dead.

They made a humming noise so vibrant it was indiscernible from the sound of sunshine, and I wondered when I'd begun to hear in color. From the way Armella was gazing at the subtle sunbeams, she was having a similar experience.

They were giants, every bit as big as the beast in front of me. I'd expected Eli to shrink from them but she stepped forward, resplendent in her bestial confidence.

Eli swept an elegant low bow of greeting, which was an odd gesture from such a beast.

"Welcome, my brothers."

The orange spirits moved as one into a bow, albeit one brief enough to hedge on respectful, at least in the human world. I wanted them to attack Eli, but it looked like they were getting ready for a cordial lunch with a cousin they didn't much care for.

"You have grown troublesome," they informed Eli. Their voices blended together so I didn't know which ones were talking.

"I have always been so." Eli's answering smile was mischievous.

"This is not yours to have," they intoned, with a gesture so broad they might have meant the living world. I hoped they were including Armella and me in it.

"All things are mine." Eli jumped the gap with one easy leap and stepped into their circle, scattering them backward. They resettled in a wider arc, buzzing with discordant disapproval. Eli stood in the center with a satisfied grin. "Even you do my bidding."

"We have come to stop you."

"No one can. Not even you. Do you think you can kill me?"

"We cannot allow you to continue, Belial."

"I tire of your attempts to contain me," Eli challenged, confident in her abilities.

Their humming intensified to a steady burn of indignation. One voice broke above it.

"We have given you much latitude. You have played here, made and broken your kingdoms of men, but you have gone too far."

*So much for the Council keeping the balance between the living and the dead.*

"Why have you been hiding from me? Do you fear what I will do to you? It took some time to find your Magos, but I knew you would be close to her."

For all that any of them registered my existence, I might as well not have been there, but I was close enough that any of them might have stepped on me, if they'd had legs and feet.

"Why do you interfere again in the balance, Belial? You toy with the Council, and bring your armies to us. It is against the bargain."

*What bargain do they have with Eli? One that allows her to do what she wants in the living world, as long as she doesn't bother them too much?*

Eli leaped on the nearest creature and seemed to grow until she surrounded it. They fell to the ground together, an undulating mass of orange light and pale beast. The others screamed, their agonized cries ringing my ears and sending sound waves across my visual field like waves of water in the ocean.

The screaming dissipated into agitated humming. I dropped my hands from my ears and wondered when I'd covered them. The creature was gone, and Eli was on her hands and knees, licking her lips like she'd swallowed it whole.

The remaining cluster of orange lights paused in a moment of horror, and then rushed Eli in a great mass. They covered her, and their terrible singing escalated into a noise so great I backed as far as I could from it. The orange mass writhed, and a bestial leg wrapped around an orange creature and pulled it back in. Eli disappeared into the orange haze again but I thought she'd gotten another one.

A great roar emanated from Eli, and the keening dissipated a notch as she finished swallowing what might have been an orange colored head. The rest of the fireballs pulled away from the fray and darted upwards, disappearing through the hole I'd opened in the world. Eli growled in victory, and then bent forward to the ground, her chest heaving with exertion. The jacket was gone and her hip jeans were in tatters. Something like blood streamed down her face and she rubbed it away from her eyes with a swipe of her hairy forearm.

She was tired. This might be my only chance. I ran towards her and used my connection to the world to shake the earth again. Eli fell backward and then caught herself. She came to her feet and lifted her arm to strike me. Armella grabbed it on the backward swipe and Eli growled in frustration.

Eli twisted to follow the path of her arm and grabbed Armella by the throat. Armella coughed, gagging and pushing at the hand choking her. Her face was turning an alarming shade of red. Eli was done playing. She meant to kill her.

I risked killing us both, but that would happen anyway if I didn't do something fast. It was better for me to tear the world apart now than to let Eli shred us to pieces, one at a time.

Pouring everything I had into the effort, energy burned through me with destructive intent. The walls fell, rocks disintegrating as they hurtled down upon us. An earthquake shook the floor, spreading the chasm between us. We were all knocked off our feet, but Eli didn't let go of Armella and I didn't stop. The only way to save us was to destroy everything.

I directed my energy up and the night sky disintegrated into a thousand raindrops that showered into our skin. I absorbed each bit of moisture that fell on me. It streaked my body midnight blue and melded into my bloodstream. It flowed through my cells and back into my energy core, like a new kind of fuel.

The air shook with a bellow, reverberating in a sonic boom that I didn't cause. Eli flew backward, somersaulting into the remainder of the cavern wall. Armella forced herself to her feet, her skin as blue as mine was, red hair streaked purple with bits of sky. I wondered at the fearsome midnight of her previously pale eyes. What had she done to Eli?

Eli staggered upright with a yowl that was inhuman. Wind raged with the force of her anger, stinging my eyes and whipping my long hair into frenzied tangles that covered my face.

Armella pulled her hair back with one hand and turned on the beast that had lost all semblance of human form in her transition into a nightmare.

"Armella, don't!" I cried into the wind, but the words were torn from my throat and lost into the chasm between us. She couldn't hear me, and unless I learned how to fly, I couldn't reach her.

Eli rushed towards her, snarling like a rabid dog. Armella's new-found power emanated through her and she shocked Eli with a blast that rocked the creature back to her knees. It wasn't enough. While Armella was taking a breath to recover, Eli launched herself and landed on top of Armella, crushing the girl to the ground. She bared her teeth like she was planning on ripping Armella's throat out.

I ran for the edge and jumped, praying that gravity here didn't follow the same rules it did in the living world. I landed with an impact that flung me forwards through two awkward summersaults into the gray beast, dislodging her from the girl. Eli landed on her face with me on her back.

Armella rolled over and reached for me, her hand and arm streaked red and blue with blood and sky. As our hands clasped, I felt her power pouring into me, an endless stream that bolstered my new-found destructive energy.

I centered my weight on Eli's upper back, trying to hold her down while I forced our new power into her. My cataclysmic reaction blended with Armella's own gift; the sky and sunshine, the pulse of the living world.

Eli pushed herself to her feet with a feral cry of rage. I clung to her back, wrapping my arms around her throat and gripping around her ribs with my knees. My energy faltered with the lost connection to Armella but she had given me more than she knew.

This wasn't just the power to release ghosts, it was more than that. I felt like I was connected to all of the energy in the universe.

From Eli's cries of agony, I knew I was hurting her but if I'd expected her to die, I was wrong. She dislodged me with the skill of a bucking horse, twisting out from under me and dropping me to the ground. She turned to step on me and I avoided the foot with a quick roll onto my knees, scrambling away like a frightened crab.

Armella pulled me to her, the two of us were safer together than we were apart. I knew we could injure Eli, but hurting her wouldn't be enough to save us.

Eli lunged towards us and I braced myself for another fight.

"We have one chance." Armella's breathy voice was filled with fierce determination as Eli's legs pumped towards us. Time seemed to stall, the beast moving in slow motion while I ran through our options. My nuclear core was useless but the sky had done something strange to me, storing some sort of energy throughout my body. I didn't know what it meant but the blue fire rolling through my veins was different than anything I'd felt before.

"Help me?" Armella implored, Eli almost upon us.

I took Armella's hand and hoped I understood what she needed me to do. When Eli launched for us, we released our power together, and I drew on that line to the universe, the cool blue energy that was so different from my own.

Eli tackled us, and the impact disrupted our attack. The group of us skidded backward, towards the edge. I felt teeth against my neck and instinctively hit her with another batch of blue energy before she could rip my throat out. Eli convulsed on top of us and I couldn't breathe, crushed under the beast's weight.

Fighting through our attack, Eli pushed herself up, planting one great hand on my chest to hold me down. Armella was pinned next to me with Eli's other hand on her chest. Armella stretched her fingertips out to meet mine.

Eli's breath came in ragged gasps that I hoped meant she was getting tired. The blue fire in me was depleting, nearly gone. The weight on my chest shifted and then the clawed hand was on my throat, the pressure cutting off my airflow.

Terror flowed through me with pure adrenaline and I fought, the seconds blurring to the point I could feel each beat of my heart. The world dwindled to two things: my deprived lungs, and the rapid thud of my panicked heart.

*I'm dying.* The certainty was there, and with it again a sense of serenity. My body still clawed for life, scratching at the hand against my throat, but my eyes closed. I didn't want Eli's ugly face to be the last thing I saw. The serenity of the stars waited for me and I focused on that memory, drew that feeling of peace to me. Armella's fingers twitched in mine and I thought she would enjoy the sound of the stars.

Lights flickered beyond my closed lids in a rapid staccato, and then my view transitioned to the night sky. The stars sang, so clear in their beauty and I reached out to them, touch their energy.

My body filled with hot white light and I thought I might explode. I released it, the only way I knew how, forcing it up into the beast above me.

I heard a distant squeal, and then Eli dissipated in a shower of sparks that rained down around us.

I collapsed against the hard earth, gasping for breath and hoping that my esophagus wasn't crushed. The sound of someone scrabbling across rocks reached my ears but I couldn't move.

"That was intense. Are you okay?" Armella loomed into my

field of vision. With her blue-tinged skin and shockingly dark eyes contrasting with her purple hair she looked like an ethereal and frightening creature.

"Intense." I started laughing, because it was easier than crying, and I hoped it would help mask my hysteria.

"Are you okay?" she reiterated.

"I think I'm still alive." It was a pleasant surprise. I pushed myself up on my elbows and tried to look Armella over. "How are you?"

"I think I'm all right. Except my arm."

"I'm hoping that's just here. You should be okay when we get back. Last time I got hurt here, the physical wounds didn't come back with me." Of course I'd never been hurt by one of the fallen before.

"Where are we?" She settled next to me, cradling her injured arm in her lap and reclaiming my hand with her good one. Knowing that your injury wasn't real didn't help when it hurt like hell.

"The ghosts say it's a space between life and death. I'm unsure how to explain it. We get to it through our minds. These aren't our real bodies. I just figured out how to get back myself. Maybe I can take you with me." I prayed it worked, because there weren't any spirits here to send us home.

I forced myself to my feet, ignoring how my body complained. I walked to the edge of the cavern and looked down into the dark nothing of the abyss.

"What do we do?" She peered over the edge with curiosity.

"We jump."

"You're joking." Her voice resonated with the sickening knowledge that I wasn't and I tried to sound braver than I felt.

"I wish I was. Look for the door, and when you see it, aim for it."

"Aim?" Her voice was shrill.

"Trust me. And hold my hand. I won't let go of you."

She offered me her hand in slow stages, like I was a feral dog who might bite. Our fingers intertwined, painfully tight. I stepped behind her, clasped my other arm around her, and stepped off the edge, taking her with me.

We fell, our screams wrapping together.

I entered my body with a disconcerting rush, and found a ghost inside me. This time I knew how to bypass its access to my neural receptors. The spook resisted, but this body was mine. I didn't give it a chance to fight me for control. My nuclear core was still there and I tapped my energy, releasing it with a quick pulse and then shivered as its essence melted through me. My body fell to the ground as I felt the ghost sliding out through my arms and torso, into the wet grass beneath me.

I calmed my breathing and then rolled over to find that Jed stood over me, sword drawn. His ragged breathing and sweat beaded face said he'd been using it. The air had the faint stench of the newly departed dead. His eyes were guarded as he saw me watching him and the sword blade hovered over me.

"It's me," I hurried to assure him. "Don't use that thing on me."

"Prove you are Anna."

*Shit.* "You snore so loud the whole bed shakes." Jed's eyes narrowed into slits but he stepped back and lowered the sword.

"Help me up. Where's Armella? Did she make it back? What happened with all the other spooks?"

Jed offered me his free hand. "I defeated them. Are you well?"

"I'll be fine." It was my automatic reply to having been nearly killed. The fact that I was soaked through to the bone and freezing cold wasn't worth mentioning since Jed was in the same state. "Where is everyone?"

"The priests fled when the dead attacked us, right as you left. Belial vanished but the girl is still there." He nodded to a point behind me in the snow. "I'm unsure of Ty's location. We should find him."

"You stayed to protect me."

"I tried to." He gave a fierce scowl. "One slipped past me but the rest are gone. I wasn't sure if I should . . ." He waggled his sword a little.

"Thank God you didn't." It would have sucked to have survived Eli only to wake up to find Jed's sword embedded in me, draining my life away.

"I did wait," he reminded me. I braced myself against his left side, since the sword was on his right. My neck hurt, so I'd either come back with the damage Eli had given me, or something had happened to my body while I was away.

"I don't know that we killed Eli."

"Since the fallen are not living beings, I don't know that they can die."

"Either way, I don't think she'll bother us again."

I thought I saw him blinking wet drops from his eyes, but it must have been sweat because all he said was, "Based on your return, I suspect not."

Armella looked like she was sleeping, but when I touched her flushed cheek with rain cooled fingertips, her eyes opened with a start. Her irises were a disconcerting midnight blue with flecks of white that looked like the stars.

"Your eyes have changed color," she informed me.

"So have yours." Biologically it wasn't possible, but the evidence was in the reflection of Armella's gaze. "How do you feel?"

"My arm hurts."

"I was afraid of that." I hadn't unzipped my jacket to check how swollen it was, but my throat felt like it had been crushed. I feared the bruises, like the eye color, had come back with me. That had never happened before. I assumed it was a testament to Eli's power. "Can I see it?"

I helped her extract her injured arm from her jacket, taking care not to jostle it any more than I had to. Her reaction to me touching it was enough to tell me it was broken.

"We'll get you to the emergency room. I'm sorry."

"This isn't your fault." She gave me a soft smile and patted my arm with her good hand. "You saved me there. That thing would have killed me."

"It was going to kill us both, and if you hadn't tapped into your power, I wouldn't have been able to stop it."

"Do you think I can do what you can now?"

"I don't know."

"I feel different."

"Different how?"

"Like something is on fire inside me."

"Maybe you can, then. That's kind of what mine feels like. Do you think you can stand up?"

We got her to her feet but keeping her balance and protecting her arm while stepping over downed logs proved difficult. Jed picked her up and then staggered, and set her on her feet again.

"Jed, you're exhausted." His body was still recuperating, and he'd been in a swordfight with a bunch of skeletons. "Come on, Armella.

Lean on me." I got on her good side and wrapped my arm around her to give her more stability.

We were halfway back to the church when my senses caught the radiant light of a living soul, clouded by a ghost, far enough off the trail I wouldn't otherwise have found them. I sat Armella on a log and went after them.

Ty was writhing on the forest floor in a mix of dead leaves and snow. I pushed the ghost out of him with a quick touch and his body convulsed twice in quick succession. I was able to protect his head from a nearby tree trunk. Ty didn't wake up.

I heard Jed and Armella behind me, but they stayed quiet as I ran nervous hands over Ty's scalp, checking for a head wound.

"I don't think he hit his head when he fell. He may just be unconscious because of the ghost." I heard myself talking, a reaction to how scared I felt with Ty down on the ground in front of me. There wasn't any way I could get him back to the church without Jed's help. "Walk Armella back and then have someone come back for us."

"I'm not leaving you." Jed's objection carried the sound of finality, like arguing would be futile.

"Jed, you can't carry him." Pointing out the obvious was sometimes necessary when dealing with a being that had the stubborn instincts of a mule.

"You come with us now and I'll come back for Ty." He tried to make it sound like a suggestion but I knew an order when I heard one. Jed wasn't the only one who could be stubborn.

"I'm not leaving him alone. Get Armella back and then send Blaise to help me." The young Italian ought to be strong enough to help me get Ty back to the church. "Ty may not have much time and Armella needs to get to a doctor, too." Broken arms were on the list of things I couldn't fix in a field.

Jed's glare said volumes about how little he liked this proposal, but there was no better option. He offered his arm to Armella and steered her towards the cemetery.

I leaned over Ty, trying to shelter him from the rain. His breathing was shallow but steady, and the pulse at his wrist thrummed with a healthy beat.

Jed was back with Blaise in less than ten minutes. Jed grabbed me by the shoulders, pulling me upright so he could stare into my eyes, and I thought he was making sure nothing else had taken me while he was gone.

"Can you walk?" He released his grip on me and I sagged before my legs remembered how to hold my own weight.

"About as well as you can. Blaise, can you help with Ty?"

Blaise evaluated the situation for a moment and then with Jed's help got Ty situated over his right shoulder in the fireman's position. Blaise started towards the cemetery in slow deliberate steps.

Jed wrapped his arm around my waist in a firm grip.

"I can walk, Jed. I'm fine," I protested.

"I can see that." He ignored me, pulling me forwards through the muck behind Blaise and Ty. If Ty were awake, his position would be uncomfortable, but he wasn't, and I didn't think it would cause any harm.

When we made our way into the cemetery, Matthew and Grayson were waiting for us.

"Anna." Grayson stopped in front of me, shaking his head like he had water in his ears that he couldn't get out. I reached out to touch him and felt the second soul inside of him. I stepped away from Jed and pulsed a small piece of fire into Grayson and then tried to catch him when he fell to his knees with a cry of pain. I fell with him, my knees sinking into the mud over someone's final resting place.

"Sorry. I know that hurts. Are you okay?"

"It doesn't look that bad when you do it to other people." Grayson rubbed his arm where I'd touched him. "Prayer may be the kinder method."

"I'm willing to concede that point. Matthew, can you help Blaise get Ty back? Jed and I will walk with Grayson."

Matthew turned his attention to Blaise with reluctance, helping him carry Ty back to the church hall. I followed with Grayson on one side of me and Jed on the other. Our arms were around each other so I didn't know which of us was holding the others up.

Ty groaned when I inserted the needle into his arm, hitting the vein and sliding the catheter in. The priests had laid him on a rectangular cafeteria table in the church hall so I could work on him.

"Welcome back. How are you feeling?" I taped the needle in place, pleased with myself.

"You suck at needlework." His words were a welcome whisper,

and I sank onto a chair next to him, satisfied that my job was done, for the time being. I'd been on my feet nonstop since Armella and I had battled Eli.

"You're lucky I hit the vein the first time around. I'm glad you're back with us. Feel okay?"

"Horrible. I hope you killed that bitch."

"I did," I assured him.

"How's everyone else?" He forced himself up on one elbow and surveyed the small group, taking note of the matching needle in Grayson's arm. "Oh man, she got you too. I'm sorry."

It was unclear whether Ty was talking about the ghost I'd banished from him or the fact that I'd stuck an IV needle in his arm.

"You two need lots of fluids and lots of steroids but I don't think either of you needs a visit to the ER." Armella was another matter. Getting her arm splinted was next on my list of things to do, but I needed to rest for a minute.

"Is it over, now?" Ty asked the question that I'd been wondering.

"Maybe. I think it is for now, anyway."

Eli and Adoni weren't the last bad ghosts out there, and whatever remained of the Council, they were divided. They'd just proven that they weren't willing to risk their existence for the living world.

"Where's Blaise?" I realized he'd disappeared while I'd been focused on the injured.

"He went to his car to get another blanket," Matthew explained from his spot next to Armella. He'd gotten her out of her wet coat and had a blanket wrapped around her shoulders.

Jed and I locked eyes as we heard the unmistakable roar of a car engine starting. "Oh shit. He's running." I crossed to the window and watched as a red sedan pulled forward, jumped over a curb, and out onto the street on the other side. He was gone from sight in an instant.

"I'll find him," I promised myself. I wouldn't be able to unless Blaise was dumb enough to stay in the area. Now that the imminent danger was done, he'd be gone, taking poor Father Lombardi with him.

# EPILOGUE

THE GARAGE DOOR OPENED and Ty walked in, setting a box on the floor along the wall of the dining area with a grunt that indicated how heavy it was.

"This is the last box from your office. You've gotta call Rita. She won't stop crying."

I looked out the upper windows and realized that several hours had passed by while I was focused on packing the contents of my life. It was twilight, but there must have been a storm moving in because the sky was dark gray. The blinds on the lower windows were drawn because we were still having a problem with reporters peeking in.

"I know she's upset. I'll call her," I agreed. Rita had delivered an earful to me after I'd told her I was selling my clinic to the local teaching hospital. "She'll be better off though, as a hospital employee. You will too, you know. You'll both have better benefits than I could ever give you, and they'll fix the building up and staff it the way it should be." I worried about my patients, but I couldn't take care of them now the way they deserved.

"I'm looking forward to the retirement plan, but it won't be the same. I don't like being the nurse for those kid doctors. They don't know what they're doing yet."

"I didn't either when I was their age," I reminded him. "They need your help. A nurse as good as you are can teach the baby doctors a lot about the real-world practice of medicine."

"Now you're just trying to flatter me," Ty grumbled with a grin that said he both knew I was telling the truth and liked it. "I'll help 'em the best I can." He settled cross-legged on the floor next to me in front of the pile of books I was boxing up.

"Your eyes are still freaking me out," Ty said. "I mean, the color's pretty. But strange."

"I know it is. I try to not think about it." My continued tendency to see sounds was as disturbing as the changed color of my eyes. The deep blue startled me every time I looked in a mirror, and I'd started avoiding them. It was easier not to be faced with how different I'd become.

In the same way, I didn't focus on my inevitable death, or allow myself to worry about the inferno inside me bursting into flames and consuming me. I ate a lot, but my weight was stable.

"Where are Jed and his . . . I mean, Tobias' mom?" Ty changed the subject and I thought he wouldn't bring up my eye color again now that he knew it bothered me, too.

"Karin's leaving this afternoon. He took her to the airport. She's on a 4 p.m. to Atlanta, and then heading on to Switzerland. He was going to wait until her flight left, so he should be getting home soon."

"I forgot she was going home today." He peered at me with interest. "How was it having her here?"

I sighed, weighing my words about one of the subjects I'd struggled with over the last few months, before deciding to share it with him.

"Look, it's awful. She thinks he's her son, but he's not."

"She's got to know he's different."

"She does. We even talked about it. The doctors there told her the personality change is related to the terrible head injury he sustained." It was true that anyone with a brain injury of that magnitude would see personality changes if they were lucky enough to survive it. That fact didn't make it any easier to deal with someone who had known, and loved the person whose body Jed inhabited.

"It's kind of creepy," Ty admitted. "You know I like Jed, but the fact that he's using this guy's body is still pretty weird."

"I know it is. I rationalize it because I'm in love with him, and because Tobias was gone long before Jed took over his body."

"I don't begrudge Jed a body that was brain dead, I'm just saying it's strange. Anyway, I'm glad you're finally getting some, even if it is with some guy who's been dead for a hell of a long time." Ty winked at me. "At least he chose a nice bod to steal. Tell me that isn't enjoyable in the sack."

I choked back a laugh. "I'm not talking to you about my sex life."

"Why aren't the hot dead kings ever gay?" Ty mused.

"I'm sure there are some, but you are in a relationship with a wonderful man and we're not having this conversation." I stood, went to the fridge, and surveyed the meager contents. "Do you want a beer?"

"I thought you'd never offer." He took the bottle I handed him and took a drink, taking in the myriad of boxes lining the walls. "Are you sure you want to do this?"

I was and wasn't sure. "I don't think I have a choice. With all the publicity, I don't think I can stay here." For the two weeks we'd been in the city, I'd had news vans parked outside, and the curious and sick kept finding their way to me, hoping I could heal them. Random ghosts had been coming by and I didn't think it was safe, for me or anyone else. Jed had taken to opening the front door with his sword in hand. It was only a matter of time before someone got hurt. And then there was the clinic, and what the community needed.

"The clinic can't keep limping along without a full-time physician," I reminded him, "and I can't afford to keep it going and pay the mortgage here when I'm not working."

"How long can you manage at the farm without working, though?" Ty slid into the seat next to me. "I mean, it's none of my business, but if you need money . . ."

"That's very kind of you, but I'm fine, I promise. One of the benefits of not having much of a social life is that I've been able to pay off my med school loans and save some money."

"I'll stop worrying about you, then." His inflection said otherwise.

"Besides . . ." I hesitated, reluctant to make Ty mad. "I have a job. I start next week."

"What? Where? Why didn't you tell me?" He peppered me with questions, offended that I'd been hiding this information from him.

"I didn't know how to tell you. It's in town by the farm. Dr. Green runs the family practice office there and he's been trying to get me to join him for ages so he can spend more time fishing and playing with his grandkids."

"So this is permanent." Ty sounded like he'd just discovered a worm in his salad. "You're really leaving."

"I've sold the condo." I didn't think he needed to be reminded of that, but if that didn't suggest permanence I didn't know what would. "I don't know what's going to happen. I talked to the emergency department at Unionville Regional and they say they're still seeing 'virus' cases every day."

"Why aren't we seeing the ghosts here?"

"It's strange there aren't more." The lack of them made me uneasy. I'd been in the city for two weeks, walked the streets between my condo and the clinic with my extra senses wide open, looking for ghosts, and I'd only found a few. I'd caught one walking down the street. It was as surprised to see me as I was it, so I didn't think it had been looking for me. The others were brought to my clinic by their relatives, under some duress. They were the few cases of people looking for a miracle cure that I'd been able to help.

I'd met with a dozen other patients who figured out where I was and hoped I could cure their ailments. Ghost possession I could help. There still wasn't much I could do for problems related to degenerative diseases, Alzheimer's, and paralysis.

"It's like fallout. All those ghosts were lured here by Eli and Adonijah."

"And the Council," Ty added.

"Where do you think the ones went from that first night at the farm that I didn't release?" These were the things that had me tossing in my bed at night, unable to sleep.

"I couldn't see anything other than the crashed helicopter and a bunch of flying snow since I don't have your superpowers."

I wrinkled my nose at him. "Well, there were a lot of them. Thousands."

"And now they're just wandering around bothering people and doing who knows what."

"Pretty much. Most of the virus cases seem to be up that way. If I'm there, then I can keep helping some people that no one else can cure."

"What about you and Jed?" I gave him a questioning look and he continued. "You're just going to shack up with him? Is this love? Is this the guy you want to spend the rest of your life with?"

It would be easy to say yes but this was Ty and I always told Ty the truth.

"I didn't plan on falling in love with a ghost, but I can't imagine my life without him now."

Then again, what had I planned on? I hoped life would return to something that resembled normal, but I didn't know if it ever would. How normal could it be with a three-thousand-year-old king living with me?

The biggest problem wasn't all the people who were possessed by ghosts who were too weak to control them. I worried about how many there were that were strong enough to control their host.

How many of those thousands had taken over a body, gotten in a car or on a plane, and disappeared? What was their plan now that Adonijah and Eli were gone? How many of them were living their new lives and tormenting the poor hosts they'd overpowered?

One thing was clear to me—destroying Eli had done nothing to rid the world of evil. It was out there just as it had been before the ghosts came after me. Ty broke through my thoughts, startling me.

"I still have trouble comprehending that we live in a time where ghosts are trying to take control of living people."

"Me too, and I knew the ghosts existed before all this."

"I knew that too, because you told me you could see them." Ty had been one of two people I'd trusted that secret with until I met Jed and all hell, literally it seemed, broke loose.

I was responsible for the deaths of three people. Two were inadvertent casualties of a helicopter crash in my field, caught in the crossfire of a ghost war that landed on my doorstep. The third one I'd murdered. The last one didn't bother me anymore, not as much as it probably should.

The back door opened again, bringing me back from the dark abyss of that knowledge.

"Hey, chica," Chaz's voice boomed as he entered, followed by Jed's heavy steps. "We pulled in at the same time, which was fortunate because there's another news van parked across the street. I didn't want to be caught on camera ringing your doorbell."

I resisted the urge to peek through the blinds. "It must be a slow news week, because they've been there every day, off and on. I keep thinking they'll come up with some real news to report on and leave me alone."

"They figured out their miracle doctor is in town, so it's news."

"Shut up," I growled. "I hope you brought food and didn't just come over to heckle."

Chaz set a large grocery sack on the counter. "Panang curry?"

"Oh, yes please. You're forgiven. Heckle away."

Jed brushed his fingers across my cheek and tucked a stray strand of hair behind my ear.

"Did Karin get out okay?"

"Her flight was on time." He nodded, drifting to the fridge behind Chaz and extracting a bottle of beer. "She likes you."

"She's nice." She was lovely, but I hoped she didn't come visit often. The situation was too awkward.

We ate on paper plates with plastic forks since I'd already packed the kitchen, while we hashed out plans for my move the next day.

~

The afternoon sun was so relentless that it was hard to imagine winter had ever been here, or would ever come again. I pulled another weed out of the ground and tossed it onto the small pile at my side. My small farmhouse garden was producing, but the early June heat was starting to take a toll on the greens. Kale and lettuce wilted in equal measure, while dandelions, stray grass, and thistle thrived in the heat. The tomatoes were dripping with small green globes, and fragile squash blossoms opened up towards the sun.

The air vibrated with the sound of a car engine and the light shifted with the waves of noise. I shook my head to dispel it. The gate was in, so no one came down the road anymore that shouldn't have access.

I grabbed another weed and tugged as a shadow fell across me. Jed was shirtless, sweat in a sheen across his well-tanned chest. There was no way I looked as good. The heat made my cheeks go patchy red, and the humidity had my hair puffed out in an uncontrollable mass of frizz. His dark eyes suggested he wasn't put off by my appearance. For a moment I forgot to breathe under the intensity of his gaze.

"Carrie is here."

"I wonder what she made this time?" Peeling off my gardening gloves, I stood and wiped the dirt from my knees.

Jed's eyebrows furrowed together. "When she has the baby, she may quit cooking for us."

"That's a possibility." I leaned forward, allowing myself the liberty of a quick kiss, because I could. "Then you'll be stuck with my cooking." His pause said that Carrie's cooking was infinitely preferable to mine.

"I may not be as good as Carrie is, but I can cook!" I protested, throwing my garden gloves at him. They struck him on the arm and fell to the ground, harmless.

Carrie came around the side of the house, a yellow cotton dress that looked more comfortable than pajamas draped to her knees. Three days past her official due date, her walk was more of a waddle, her belly so full with baby that acquaintances had started speculating she might be having twins. She'd refused a second ultrasound, but accepted my reassurance that she carried one extra soul, not two.

"I thought you two might need some fresh bread," she called across the space between us.

I eyed the final head of lettuce I'd been trying to nurse through the first heat of summer. "We could have BLTs for dinner tonight."

"Perfect!" Carrie beamed, adding a little more sunshine to the bright day. Then her visage darkened, changing so fast that I looked up to see if a cloud had obscured the sun. "I've got a favor to ask you."

"How can I help?" I crossed towards her and met her outside the garden gate. We walked together into the shade of a towering oak. The air cooled ten degrees, drying the sweat from my skin and making me feel chilled.

"My friends that own the dairy called. There's something weird going on in their barn. One of their farm hands has been acting strange, and things keep moving around that shouldn't. Their cows are so upset they've quit giving milk."

"I can go check it out." It had been a few days since I'd banished a ghost and the fire banked inside me felt ready for release. It had become a power I needed to use, instead of one that I could, if I needed it. I didn't let myself think about what that might mean, and I didn't ask Jed about it. I didn't want to know.

"That's the closest one we've had in a while," Jed speculated, reaching for the sword that wasn't, for once, at the ready.

"You don't think a member of the Council is hassling cows, do you?" I was teasing him, but the question was a valid one. I hadn't heard from the Council since they'd abandoned me in the devil's den, but they were still out there. Someday I'd go looking for them.

"I do not presume to predict what the Council will do. I'm no longer in their confidence." Jed stood upright, his back to the sun so I had to put a hand over my head to block the glare while I looked up at him. I didn't point out that the true Council hadn't ever told him their secrets. "Let me take care of this ghost," he suggested.

I had a brief vision of him swirling through the cowshed, sword swinging.

"I'm afraid you'd wind up hurting one of the cows," I countered, instead of pointing out that we still didn't know if his sword could hurt one of the fallen.

"We'll take Armella, then. It would be good for her training," Jed offered, stiffly. I knew he was offended. I didn't know if it was because he thought the cows were an acceptable casualty or that I didn't trust him with it.

"Armella hasn't released more than a few ghosts." With her unpracticed skill, we might lose more cows than we would with Jed and his sword. "I'll take care of it. Things were starting to get a little boring anyway."

"You frighten me a little sometimes." Carrie laughed as she said it, but wrapped her hands around her belly like she needed to protect her unborn child from me.

I took a deep breath, centering myself on the heated core inside me which was the root of my power and the key to my darkness.

"I scare myself, too." I looked down at my dirty hands. "Let me go get cleaned up, and then we'll go find your dairy haunt." Find it, and kill it.

# THE END

# ACKNOWLEDGEMENTS

**M**Y HEARTFELT THANKS to everyone who helped *When They Come Alive* make the transition from the initial *very* rough draft to publication. The assistance and guidance of editors Abigail Hodges, Christabel Barry, and Atthis Arts' own Emily Bell is invaluable and much appreciated. Friend and author Clare Meyers generously did her own round of editing and offered insight on ecumenical matters. And thanks to Marybeth Flanagan for providing the final proofread.

Dr. Turner, who again spent hour upon hour helping me with medical scenarios—In many ways, Dr. Anna Roberts is more your character than she is mine. Thank you to Deacon Helen Mountford, for your advice as a lawyer and on the church, and Matthew Johnson for offering your own perspective, and friendship. Your expertise was much needed. Hilary—the only person I know who can make me laugh until I cry—I'm very lucky to have you as my sister and my friend. Thank you for painstakingly proofreading the final draft of each novel.

Greg—you have my gratitude and love for your unwavering encouragement over the last thirteen years – for my writing, letting us adopt our latest rescue, and my dreams of moving to a warmer climate. M—thank you for understanding that when I say "I'm writing", it means you have to be a little quieter while you play video games. You're an amazing young man, and I love you.

For the fans of Anna's Nightmares—who have written kind reviews and emailed me notes of support, I appreciate you more than you know. I keep writing for you (and because the thoughts in my head won't let me stop).

And finally, to our canine friend Gus—whose courage and heart after losing a leg to cancer remain an inspiration to everyone who knew him.

# ABOUT THE AUTHOR

**SARAH FLEMING MOUNTFORD** lives in the Midwest with her family, two rescue dogs, and her inheritance—a cat. When she isn't traveling, Sarah is a runner, a cyclist and the family chef.